INVISIBLE YORK

Aden Simpson

Copyright

Author Note

I once spent a week in Manhattan in the summer of 2014. To this day it remains one of the best weeks of my life; simultaneously experiencing the novelty of a bustling new city and marrying this with nostalgia for a place I'd known only in movies and books. Later that same year, I came up with the idea for this book, but delayed writing as I'd just finished my first similarly-toned novel and wanted to write something lighter.

The intervening years have revealed another side to the United States. I wrote most of this manuscript from 2020–2021, while in and out of lockdown, watching from afar a place I once looked up to descend into lunacy. I have tried to reflect this in my work, and though this book takes a cynical view, I still hope to return one day.

Disclaimer

In places where you may ask how exactly I knew what I knew, and did what I did, then you must understand I make this confession under duress, and while I admit to exercising questionable judgement and an occasional penchant for Machiavellian mischief, I know what I saw and what I decided to see. As Radakovic says: "Breathe in, breathe out, all space is yours."

INTRODUCTION

They used to call it by many names...

The Big Apple
The Five Boroughs
Empire City
New Amsterdam
Metropolis
The Capital of the World
New York, New York (the town so nice, they named it twice)
The City That Never Sleeps
NYC
The Melting Pot
The Modern Gomorrah
Or plain old New York.

I just used to call it home.

Eyesight. The scientists never stopped trying to figure out this one particular thing about us. Even when everyone else had accepted it and moved on, distracted by speculation of further superpowers we were supposedly poised to gain, those dedicated scientists would spend the rest of their lives trying to understand how we saw. A marvel unto itself, a feat of magic in a sea of science gone horribly wrong. Everything else was explainable, they reasoned, even if no cure was imminent. No matter how many hours they clocked or how many theories they explored, they could never wrap their heads around the concept of invisible corneas refracting light, invisible optic nerves sending their stimuli to invisible brains, invisible brains unscrambling the resultant images by means of invisible circuitry, all for the benefit of invisible minds.

Truth was, I saw many things that fateful summer. Things I wouldn't wish on anyone. They always wanted to know *how* we saw, but really, they should have asked *what* we saw.

Was that too much? Too sweepingly grandiose? I'll start with myself then. Much less impressive.

I had dark eyes. Dark skin too. A balding head with specks of grey receding further backward. Firm muscles from a daily row session enjoyed in silence. On the surface, a rewarding job that gave me purpose. I had a warm smile, according to my half-sister, but that was because she brought it out in me. Burnout aside, I had a good life, even if sometimes I didn't fully appreciate it. And then there was the blastwave.

People experienced it differently. Some said they heard the sound first, others heard nothing at all. They felt their bodies shake before it was all torn away in an instant. I was anticipating the first bite of my Reuben on the sidewalk when the blastwave passed through me, robbing me of sight, sound, touch, all the senses that anchor you to this world, in that moment they simply ceased to be. If I think hard about it, maybe the sense of taste remained, the recollection of blood in my mouth. Maybe it was the first thing that returned after however long we were all knocked out for. The taste was metallic. Unnatural. Alien. And that's all I could hold on to, for what seemed the longest time.

The blastwave went through buildings, but it did not destroy them. The blastwave surged through the subways, yet they did not collapse. It passed through cars, glass, concrete, all the walls modernity puts up as barriers. We didn't even call it a blastwave until four days later. That's what the first reports concluded, the vague terminology of experts who weren't there, and we went along with it for lack of a better alternative. Everything was just an enormous pile of existential confusion as we tried to reconnect with the world. I guess it didn't really matter what you called it. If it got to you, then that was that. You became like me. You once had eyes, ears, a nose and a mouth, limbs, a torso, all the hallmarks of homo sapiens, and now...

Let's not get into the theories just yet. I'm waiting for Radakovic. Let him set the record straight. I'm in the 'localised energy wave' camp though, not the 'meticulously timed bombs in the subway' gas theorem, precisely because it is too impressive. Radakovic may have been a total genius, a modern prophet, but even he couldn't orchestrate that...

Two things folks always wanted to know in the early days. Number one: Where you were when it happened.

3

Number two: how you first noticed you were no longer there at all. It was the hands for most people; scrambling around after coming back to consciousness, clawing at the ground, your body, the confusion of an empty street that couldn't possibly have been empty, the confusion of not seeing any hands in the space where your hands used to be. And when you went to rub the grit of bitumen from your hands you'd force a blink. Then another, mind reeling in utter confusion.

All the stories went along the same lines, no matter how many times I heard them, and believe me, I came to hear them a lot. In those early days they said we'd eventually be able to function as a part of society, to reintegrate, adjust to our 'new normal,' at some nebulous point in the future never clearly defined. But there wasn't going to be any rosy outcome like that for us. No Hollywood ending. Those early days, we were caught in a loop of the past; trying to keep our memories alive so that when we looked at our empty reflections we could see someone, something, in our mind's eye at least. I was never one for hogging the mirror before, but times change. People too.

These are the stories of the brave people who lived in a city of ghosts.

And I was one of them.

Still am.

4

DAY OF

A quiet morning. One of those mornings that start slow and drags, opening up into a nothing sort of day, another Tuesday you're ready to be done with as soon as it's begun. I took a cold shower that morning, a desperate attempt at invigorating myself into some semblance of vitality. Our case wasn't going to budge today, I already knew it. Feng would not be reckless enough to run an errand of evil right out in the open, we weren't going to have some crucial piece of evidence magically gifted to us; no, this Tuesday would be another day of waiting, the kind of day the espionage movies and training videos uniformly neglect to mention.

I had my usual slices of PB&J on toast, the spreads laid thin as a token concession to my health. And then I was out into the world, West 23rd already bustling in all directions. I caught the A train heading downtown to Fed Plaza for an overdue briefing that would doubtless disclose little in the way of actual progress. Sanders, my understudy with all the makings of a future SAC, had been stubbornly resistant in nabbing Feng on a lesser charge, wanting, not unreasonably, to call a human trafficker to account for the crime of being a human trafficker. Feng had some irritatingly efficient cleaners for his paper trail and alibis likewise came easy, lies rolling off well-rehearsed tongues.

He was elusive, well-connected. We had suspected he was responsible for the smuggling of over three hundred hapless Chinese and Taiwanese nationals, with an estimated two-thirds of those being sold into sex slavery while the more fortunate remainder were forced to take part in his various criminal endeavours, of which the most harmless included illegal betting rings and green card fraud. But he paid off the right people, moved in circles we could barely fathom, and the chances of taking him in seemed more remote as the months and years dragged on.

Looking back, I reflect on my indifference to the spectacle of the morning rush, a tradition we accepted as inevitable but still inwardly groaned our way through, each and every day. A near-universal disconnect. Eyes glued to phones, or aimlessly glancing in every direction but at each other. Only brief, intermittent eye contact for courtesy's sake could be afforded. Ever stare at a stranger in New York and come off the better? Odds against. So I wasn't taking in the people I was travelling along with in the A cattle train, let alone pondering the vast expanses of the universe. It was a Tuesday morning and I was doing my Sudoku, trying to ignore the bodies pressing against mine on either side, uncomfortably warm, seeking a fleeting moment of respite in this halogen-drenched drudgery.

My line of work was more interesting than the average nine to five, and yet of late I'd found my passion waning. A flatness had come over me, like a post-orgasm malaise. Somewhere along the way I'd lost the thrill of honing in on the bad guys on those rare occasions we actually made a move. Now, despite my innate aversion to paperwork, I was content to drift from fieldwork into a full-time desk job if the opportunity arose. Sanders' pairing with myself was detrimental to both of us. I didn't want some energetic go-getter with a can-do attitude continually going against the grain, looking for the next big bust, running on the heady jet fuel of idealism. That 'can do' wave had passed me by years ago.

Sanders had been saddled with yours truly, I knew that, though he was polite enough not to let his disappointment show. Sure, on first impressions, you see a black guy with a trim(ish) figure, suit and badge and you assume a former point guard in college with inherent leadership skills and an assured sense of self. Fine to assume, that's what Sanders did at first. But look a little deeper. You can only push so much before everything becomes mechanical, and you get comfortable in the grooves your individual cogs have been calibrated to. And unfortunately for Sanders he did not get the athletically trim point guard with effortless street cred and countless war stories from the mire of human trafficking. He got the 41 year old cynical paper trail chaser, a shadow of his former glory, a lonely man without so much as a toe in the dating pool. Driftwood from a once grand vessel.

Funny that, first impressions. So much simpler back then.

Sanders must have irked a few superiors before they sent him down my way from Providence. A speed bump to modulate his brash trailblazing tendencies? At the tender age of thirty-two he was the youngest Special Agent in our

Child Exploitation and Human Trafficking Task Force, a name which, whilst apt, did not lend itself to easy acronyms. He was already in the office by the time of my tardy arrival, formulating an angle on an associate of Feng's who'd had a bad run at the cards. There was suspicion the man had slid headlong into full scale desperation, always a possibility when one insists on losing not inconsiderable sums to an inveterate psychopath known to extract payment by any means necessary. Plenty of legal casinos around, but I guess that wasn't as exciting. His solution, not a brilliant one, but befitting the mindset of his industry, was to invest what little he had left into the drug trade to recoup his losses and avoid having his legs, among other appendages, fed to farm animals. An opportunity for our cumbersomely named department to co-invest in his misfortune seemed to have arisen.

This was presented to myself and two others, detective Underhill and the other one whose name I could never remember, and I assented to the general concept despite the extra work it would no doubt entail. We then spent further time brainstorming exactly how to turn Feng's luckless associate. Numerous options were trudged out, all tried-and-true methods of cornering prey, as I waited, grunting noncommittally at regular intervals, biding my time for the real prize, a sandwich from Eugene's a couple of blocks over on Franklin St. His thick-cut Reuben gave Katz's a run for its money any day of the week, so this really wasn't as unprofessional as it sounds. Plus food was about the only biological driver I was capable of satiating these days.

No doubt it was a productive morning from Sanders' crushingly idealistic perspective. I played along as best as I was able, and here we find ourselves at the point in the story where I've headed out for a well-deserved lunch break and the world has come to be irrevocably changed forever.

Eugene's Reuben. Corned beef on rye, extra swiss, sauerkraut and homemade Russian dressing. My non-canonical addition was a dash of barbeque sauce, which Eugene was happy to accommodate: simple, but mouth-wateringly effective. An everyday ritual, combated by the lonely 45 in the gym after work. Row, row, row your bloat...

I usually waited until I was back in the office before gorging alone at my desk, but this day my famished stomach suggested we start the party early, right on the sidewalk outside of Eugene's. Clear as a bell, etched into eternity: I'm looking at the sandwich, my hands, the ones I've regarded countless times, even studied in overt detail a few times in college when I was high, those selfsame hands gripping that daily midday reminder that all was not lost. And then bam! A single moment ricocheting through time, and all was, in fact, lost.

It felt like an earthquake, yet the earth did not move—we did. A roaring tsunami that came and went in an instant, leaving no one in its vicinity unscathed. How exactly does an explosion create a blastwave that harms no buildings, lamp posts, traffic lights or trees—only creatures with heartbeats? I'd love to tell you how, and so would many well-paid scientists, some affected by our curious affliction and others merely curious.

First, we lost our balance, then our consciousness, then by the time we came to we'd lost ourselves. Radakovic had taken an eraser to our outlines and gone to work like a demented cartoonist, rubbing out all trace of outward appearance, discarding our forms forever with an alchemy that might never be fully comprehended.

Average time for reemergence stood at no more than ten minutes, but as in daily life I proved to be an early riser. I awoke to a wailing car alarm and the cracks of cement on the footpath. It was when I went to pick myself up that I, like so many others noticed the hands that raised me were simply missing. I slowly brought myself to my knees, mind reeling, and gazed at the space where my hands should have been, turning them over and over, palms up, palms down. Together. Apart. But alas, no hands.

Before the inspection of the body continued, a set of floating animated clothes wielding a baseball bat silenced the car making that racket. The man had clearly come to accept our new predicament with admirable aplomb. It was logical. The sound was annoying, and processing these kinds of life-altering occurrences is always better done in peace. I say a man, because that's what the clothes and their outline suggested, but who knows if this person lasted the summer in such attire? It wouldn't be long before 'the Itch' had become a medically recognised side effect and 'going native' the rebellious norm. Kudos to him for dealing with that noise, even if it was ultimately in vain, as for the next ten hours the screaming sirens of every emergency service available would echo throughout the walkups of

Harlem, the penthouses of the Upper East, the skyscrapers of downtown and the billboard vortex of Times Square.

I pulled my phone out and reversed the camera. No dark eyes. No balding head. Just the dated yellow signage of 'Eugene's' peering at me from the space above my collar, the space where my head used to be. Naturally, this was concerning. To make matters worse, my sandwich had also been tarnished; an unfortunate bout of contact with the sidewalk had rendered it completely unfit for consumption. I felt something wet dripping from my head. I wiped my chin and brought my fingers up to my eyes. As I couldn't see my fingers, let alone what was on them, I had difficulty confirming if it was my blood from a head wound, or my tears from the state of my sandwich.

You can imagine how enlightening doctor's visits would be from then on.

My immediate diagnosis was that I was, plainly speaking, invisible. (A long-standing position in law enforcement meant I was finely attuned to analysing the available evidence.)

Invisible or not, I was still hungry and my sandwich was ruined. So I returned to Eugene's. The would-be lunchtime clientele of his poky 'hole in the wall' remained strewn all over the ground, a sea of clothes without bodies. I double checked my phone for the time. It had been around six minutes now, by my hazy count. Finally, a handful stirred from their Radakovic-induced repose, rolling about and gasping in shock as the unthinkable reality began sinking in.

Knowing what I know now, if they had asked, I'd have

told them to go back to sleep. Delay the inevitable horror. Eugene was in a panic in his bathroom behind the kitchen. I could hear him ranting hysterically.

I slid over the counter like I'd done it many times before, and, after briefly admiring the kitchen and the view from the other side, I knocked on the bathroom door.

"Eugene?"

He opened the door a crack.

"Leonard? My face..."

"I know."

"My face... my arms and legs... my body... they're gone. All just.... disappeared."

"And a damn shame, because that smile was the reason I came here (it wasn't). But let's not get ahead of ourselves and assume this is a permanent state of play."

Eugene slowly cracked the door open. A set of shoes, pants, underwear and a shirt with the logo Eugene's embroidered on the breast covered the floor.

This was to be my first encounter with what you would call 'going native,' not that Eugene's symptoms fit the profile they would later establish and disseminate to a bewildered public.

"You gon' find out what's going on?"

"Course I will, Eugene. We're going to get answers."

"Then what are you doing here?"

"In order to perform at optimal levels, first I need to quell my appetite. I'd like to buy another Rueben."

"What happened to the one I sold you?"

"An unfortunate casualty to the mayhem outside."

There was silence for a moment. Hard to tell exactly what Eugene was thinking, given the lack of facial cues, but I was confident logic would win out. Such a thing doesn't tend to dissipate instantly, and thankfully my instincts were correct.

"You're not supposed to be on this side of the counter."

* * *

The first scientific experiment conducted post transformation: the journey of digestion, visible or not? Thankfully, all were spared the gruesome details behind the curtain, food vanishing once consumed. If this had not been the case, I shudder to think how long your appetite for us would have lasted.

FBI RESPONSE

Getting back into the office was tricky to say the least, badge and ID not quite cutting it while the recently-installed facial recognition software found little in the way of faces to scan. Eventually my Group Supervisor Halifax vouched for me over the phone and I joined an office-wide crisis meeting up on our floor on the 23rd. I'm told we lost the atrium thanks to a squabble between Homeland and our ADIC, the head honcho, as to whom should lead the coordination effort.

The head honcho stood on a hastily erected podium. I recognised the voice, as Halifax had mine. There were maybe four hundred floating suits crowded in among the desks.

I missed the first portion of the speech, but later found out it went something like this:

The National Guard has been called into Brooklyn and New Jersey. The exact range of the areas affected is still being established, but it's looking like most of Manhattan and parts of South Brooklyn absorbed the brunt of the anomaly—we're still trying to ascertain how it spread, and what in the hell caused it. Is it contagious? We don't know. But we are going to quarantine the island as a precautionary measure.

Manhattan. Ground Zero. Again.

Our immediate tasks were divided into assessing damage, establishing the extent of the blast zone, and coordinating the quarantine. Constructing what would become our future prison. Sanders found me in the tumult, recognising me either by my wristwatch or the Russian dressing stains on my lapel, and asked for my immediate impressions. His wife and their newborn were in Queens, unaffected.

"You'll see them again soon enough. For now, let's just focus on the task at hand. The quicker we get this quarantine set up, the quicker we can get out of here." At least he had a wife and child to go home to whenever this insanity all blew over.

"Yeah, I guess you're right. I mean Jesus Christ, Leonard—we're invisible! It's like being trapped in some bizarre nightmare."

In hindsight, there was quite a lot at stake in this exchange. Though he was chummy enough with me for the sake of maintaining appearances and a tolerable equanimity, Sanders had never given my opinion much weight, because I was exactly the kind of agent he detested. At the time, I thought he sought my counsel simply because he was scared. Fair enough. But by day's end I had unwittingly confirmed his second-worst fear. That by standing by his post, something an unassuming drone like myself would have done, he was equally doomed.

A handful who were somehow prescient enough to realise the quarantine net would become permanent found their exit to Hoboken by swimming across the Hudson. Phillip

Chauncey from Corporate Fraud was one such intrepid individual. It had helped that he was captain of the swim team in his heyday, and that he'd kept up the practice at his local aquatic centre, a place I doubt he'd be welcome now.

At one stage in the aftermath of the blastwave I walked past someone who had a chrome dot hovering in the area where their head should have been. My confusion was eventually dispelled by an update on the TV that night. Radakovic's homebrewed potion only affected living organic matter, leaving fillings, braces, hip replacements and artificial limbs off the list. While the majority of these implements remained hidden behind our unseen skin, the flash of a toothy grin exposed what lay beneath.

All told Chauncey had four fillings, and to escape detection when he reached Hoboken, he had his wife pull out all four tell-tale teeth with a pair of pliers. This would later prove a fairly common theme when the Itch hit and going native became the vogue, but as far as I know, Chauncey was one of the earliest adopters of such drastic means. As I said before, an intrepid individual.

How late were we expected to remain at work that day? How were we supposed to work at all, given the circumstances? When it had been a regular Tuesday, only a handful of hours earlier, I'd been thinking of ducking out no later than 5:30pm, but what was expected of us now? Human Trafficking had been assigned quarantine coordination northbound into the Bronx, assisting the 32nd Precinct. Though the majority decided to stay put, either shell-shocked into inertia or too busy placing panic-stricken calls to family members to worry about antiquated notions like insubordination, Sanders and I put our hands up to head over there. By that I mean we raised our sleeves above our heads, like amputated mannequins offering a salute.

"Thank you, gentlemen," offered Halifax, chest heaving with palpable relief. Take care out there. Represent the team with pride."

"We got this, sir," replied Sanders. The fucking suck up.

"I knew I could count on you, Sanders. Er, you too, Walcott."

We promptly departed, exchanging the befuddled commotion of the field office for that of the streets outside.

Sanders wanted to gauge how just far north had been affected. He had relatives in Yonkers, so I was told.

For me, it was about checking in on Sasha. Aside from a single profanity-and punctuation-laden text message received shortly after the blast ("L, what the actual fuck?!?! I can't see myself anymore!! WTF is this!!! some new terror attack?? Are you ok??? what the fucking fuck?!?" etc) I'd had no other contact from her before the cell service went down citywide. No chance to reply. The landline at the Rec Centre was also down, though whether that was due to the widespread pandemonium or simply a casualty of the centre's perpetual lack of funds was anyone's guess.

That's where she'd be. Her shift wouldn't have started yet, but as soon as she could orient herself I knew she'd head straight there, to check on and if need be console the ragtag charges she referred to affectionately as her kids, or sometimes as 'the brats', depending on their level of misbehaviour.

Sanders and I didn't discuss the best mode of transport, or which lines were likeliest to still be operating. We just walked, as if this were the best way to clear our heads. Nevermind the three hour ETA.

Sirens blared, people screamed, a post-apocalyptic soundtrack of unbridled despair, but the cacophony grew somehow more muted with each passing block, the first signs of a burgeoning disconnect between our absent bodies and the outside world. I remember the distinct lack of coordination in walking those first few hours, when you thought too much about the fact you caught your hand strangely missing as it failed to swing by in your periphery. The headless reflection in the store windows matching me stride for stride inspired dread, disorientation, something akin to seasickness. I made it as far as the Flatiron District before I dropped to my knees and violently retched in the gutter.

I felt something come out of me, heard it hit the ground, but saw nothing. Invisible vomit. The only thing familiar about the experience was the burning in my throat and the acid taste in my mouth. My stomach heaved a few more times, then the churning began to subside.

Suddenly I felt a weight on my shoulder. A hand.

"It's OK, Leonard. It'll all be OK. Somehow."

"Yeah," was all I could say in response. "Yeah." I knelt there a few more seconds, took a couple of deep breaths to a backdrop of car horns and breaking glass, then Sanders helped me to my feet. A rare if somewhat unorthodox moment of tenderness between us.

We pressed on.

The source of the broken glass became apparent as we neared the intersection of East 21st and Third. The windows of the Valley Bank comprised a jagged gaping hole, out of which eventually emerged a black garbage bag, presumably filled with whatever petty cash the tellers had not already appropriated for themselves. Said floating bag then bobbed along the street at a considerable pace, yet another surreal sight to behold, then rounded a corner and was gone. We did not give chase, even the stalwart Sanders realising there was plenty else to worry about.

"Clever of them to take their clothes off," was all he said.

The looting had started in earnest.

Some had abandoned their cars in the middle of the road. A crashed fire truck had, ironically, caught fire, and was burning unattended outside the Public Library, completely blocking off Fifth Avenue. Most cross streets were equally impassable, banked up with vehicles and crowds of wandering invisibles, another reason we'd left on foot as opposed to taking a fleet car. Some were so desperate to flee, either not knowing or caring that the National Guard was already in the process of setting up roadblocks, they simply drove onto the sidewalk in their haste to get out of the city.

After another hour dodging would-be absconders and other assorted insanity, we finally arrived at our destination. My dogs were well and truly barking.

"My dogs are well and truly barking," I informed Sanders. "On the way back, we're commandeering a couple of mopeds."

"Agreed," he said, as we flashed our badges and had a uniform beckon us in.

★★★

The 32nd Precinct was, not unlike our field office, a madhouse of near-hysteria. Sanders did most of the talking, or rather shouting, competing with endlessly ringing phones and the resultant mantras conveyed by panic-stricken officers to an equally terrified public: "We don't know the exact cause. Please, just stay home. Don't go into the streets. I told you—we don't know." No sooner had they slammed the phone down before it immediately rang again, and the whole refrain was repeated. Good to know the phones were back up.

Sanders gave little indication as to the FBI's overall plan of action above the NYPD. The precinct's captain (only identifiable via his badge) spoke of multiple armed robberies and the 'prospect' of wide-spread looting, correctly assuming that the citizens would continue the long human tradition of naked opportunism in the face of a crisis.

"Naked is the exact right word, given some of what I've seen today, and the looting is more than just a prospect. You're a little behind the curve there, Cap."

"Who the fuck is this asshole?" blustered the captain.

"This is Special Agent Walcott, and he's one of the best agents in the entire Bureau!" Sanders shot back. A boldfaced lie, of course, but no one else present knew that.

I was really starting to warm to him. "We've been sent here to liaise with you in getting this section of the city under quarantine. Have you actually set foot outside this building in the past few hours? It's complete pandemonium out there."

"Well... yes. I'd gathered. I knew it was bad." From the way his sleeves were moving I could tell he was scratching insistently at his arms. "Sorry for my tone, Agent Walcott."

"Special Agent," I corrected him.

"Special Agent. We've just been... this fucking uniform. My wife must've used a new kind of detergent. Sorry. We've been absolutely snowed under. Sixty thousand people are served by this precinct, and they all want to know what we're doing to help. They're calling, coming down in person, crowds of them barging their way in, banging on the windows. We had to pepper spray the lot of them, cordon off the entrance and threaten to shoot anyone who came back. I haven't had a lot of time to personally roam the streets.

In between bouts of scratching himself, he addressed the nearby throng of faceless uniforms.

"Where's Molina?"

"Right here, sir," replied the uniform to his immediate left.

"Ah. Could you go and get these fellas some water, and a couple of chairs? Actually, let's move this into the briefing room. I can barely hear myself think in all this ruckus. We'll have a proper debrief in there. Share what we know. Which in our case, is one-tenth of fuck all. Jesus Christ! Is anyone else's uniform irritating the hell out of their skin, or is it just me?"

"Well, now that you mention it," replied another of the officers hovering around the Captain's desk. I noticed one or two more rubbing away at their necks.

"We did get pretty liberal with the pepper spray. Anyway. Duchene, are you still in here?"

"Yeah, I'm here."

"Go check if we've had any further briefings come through from the National Guard. Then call the colonel and see if he's got anything else for us. Anything at all would be useful at this point. I don't care how pissed off he gets. Just keep calling him."

The uniform known as Duchene briskly departed.

"This way," said the captain, rising from his desk. As we followed him down the corridor, he shared what little he had. Of course we didn't tell him it was more than the two of us knew combined. That would have been unbecoming.

"Right, so I know we've already closed off the Macombs Dam bridge and the 145th street bridge. That was at least an hour ago. No way to get to the Bronx on our end. Presumably you already heard about the tunnels being blocked, given that's your neck of the woods."

"Oh, absolutely we did," I replied, gratefully taking a swig from the bottle of water that had just been handed to me. Fiji. Classy.

"Right, well, I know they were waiting on concrete bollards from the Army to finish barricading the Brooklyn and Williamsburg Bridges. That's your part of town too,

22

you'd know better than me. Just in here."

We filed in to the briefing room and I slumped down in the nearest chair, posture and decorum be damned. Sanders sat next to me, maintaining his straight-backed military mien, and I almost started to dislike him again. The rest of the spaces gradually filled. One of the PO's dropped a manila folder onto the table in front of the Captain and he rifled through it.

"So basically, I'm told the entire island should be sealed by midnight, if not before. Appears to be... what did they call it? Oh yeah, here it is. An entirely local phenomena of unknown origin. Specific to Manhattan. Other boroughs unaffected."

I heard Sanders breathe a sigh of relief, doubtless thinking of his parents or whoever he had up in Yonkers. "Thank God," he said.

"Well, just pray to that God of yours that the reports are correct. 79th in Brooklyn was reporting cases earlier, still waiting to hear back whether they were locals or people who came across after the bomb went off. As far as the cause of this... event, or whatever you wanna call it? Nothing. Crickets. No one seems to know the first thing about it. There was a blast, we all fell on our asses, and when we got up again we were like this. Don't know who or what caused the explosion, or whether it even was an explosion in the strictest sense. Entirely unprecedented in human history, I heard them say on CBS. No shit!"

He took a presentation pointer from the lecturn, lifted up his shirt and began rubbing at his stomach with it.

"Ooh, that's better. Apologies all, but I am fucking itchy. It's like being covered in poison ivy. Right. That's all I've got for now. We should have more once the latest briefings come through from the Guard. Got a couple of liaisons at the Times, but they haven't provided much. The other precincts have been in touch, not that they're faring any better than us. Seems mostly true about this being isolated to Manhattan, from what I gather, but I can't say 100%, fellas. I've also got a contact in the army, a colonel. He might have something more for us soon too. OK? Your turn."

"You go," I said to Sanders.

* * *

From a theoretical standpoint, of course, there were a few things we could help with. Minor things like coordinating traffic, delegating responsibilities, encouraging people to remain calm and not to riot and pillage. Sending regular reports of the situation back to headquarters ('Everyone still invisible. Cause still to be determined'). But neither Sanders nor myself felt much like doing grunt work, and I was getting the sense we weren't the only ones. Turning invisible without explanation or warning will have that effect on you, I've discovered. Quite a few of the uniformed officers present at the Precinct had simply abandoned their posts and walked out over the course of the evening. It was time for us to do likewise.

We shared a glance—at least I think we did—that implied

we both understood our work for the day, what little of it had actually been achieved, was done. No one was getting any less invisible by us sitting around watching the Captain attack his skin with whatever implements happened to be at hand.

When we stepped outside I told Sanders I needed to go see Sasha and he was free to sort his own affairs out. My Chelsea digs were offered if he needed a place to crash, a moment of supreme generosity on my part, but he advised that wouldn't be necessary. He had some thinking to do, he said.

We parted ways and that was that, for the time being.

SASHA

Sasha Owens was born nine years after me, six years after I was adopted by Barb. Our birth mom's tale was beset by the routine trappings of addiction: a junkie single mother whose longest bouts of sobriety were spurned by both myself and Sasha. Our mother kept Sasha for longer than I, a fact I remained jealous of, despite the grim reality of what it entailed.

When Sasha was fourteen, she reached out to me, and eventually Barb adopted her too once our birth mother returned to her old ways.

I'd always respected the way Sasha could take a hit, grit her teeth, and find unconventional ways to get even. She often seemed to take what one could safely categorise as the high road, before the petty streak we both shared shone through with a vengeance.

Case in point: the broken jar of pickles and the resultant blaming of Sasha Owens. I'd known her for a year at this stage and, having never had a sister but seeing all that niggling shit siblings did to one another in the films, I thought it a good chance to make up for lost time when I accidentally broke a jar of pickles while Sasha and I prepared dinner for Barb.

Barb came in, everything in the kitchen at full boil, and I went on the offensive, blaming Sasha. While there was no proof and Barb was her usual "aw shucks not to worry" forgiving self, Sasha was about to complain but then saw me grinning, like it was all some grand joke. And maybe it was because we were getting along so well that she swallowed her anger and apologised for her clumsiness. Lunch was good, if somewhat burnt, the culinary arts not exactly running in the family. Over three months later I asked Sasha if she could make me a sandwich and she said sure. She returned from the kitchen with a sweet smile and handed me two plain slices of bread, with most of a jar of Vlasic pickles wedged between them. Wearing a grin, I swallowed both my pride and the 'sandwich' in silence.

Then there was the other approach she took, like when one guy in her senior year tried to force himself on her during a night spent drinking in Central Park. First she smacked him with a rock. Then, with her trademark Dr. Marten boots, went to town on the knee she'd noticed giving him grief on the basketball court. He never did end up getting that athletic scholarship. With this in mind, I considered myself lucky to have got off as lightly as I did for my own (albeit far less serious) transgression.

The Greens Athletic Rec Centre in Hell's Kitchen saved Sasha, much as it saved the attendees who frequented its chaotic halls. An indoor court designated for hoops and soccer comprised the dusty beating heart of the centre, while the rooftop held table tennis and Tai Chi for the few seniors brave enough to climb the tight spiral stairs on a Saturday morning. A little haven away from the bustle below.

The first words from Sasha when I moseyed on into the main hall:

"Well, least the kids are having fun with it."

She recognised me from my over the top stiff frame, rigid gait and air of professional order in chaos; a character I played from time to time when the situation called for it. I'd taken this cue from the sleek cool of my favourite actor, Denzel Washington and it had served me well over the years, be it intimidating perps or prowling bars in my twenties. Evidently no one else representing any form of authority had attempted to come to their rescue. She was happy to see me, I think. She was always somewhat hard to read, even when she had a face.

"Parents on their way to pick most of them up, bit of gridlock though, what with... well, you know."

A flurry of little clothes without limbs or faces swirled past like a tornado, laughter still light, all innocent and unharried, despite the oddness all around.

"I'm trying to stay strong for them. Not much use if I fall apart. They were crying for the first hour, but they've adapted. I think they're actually embracing the novelty of it."

I think she stared at me, wondering if we would be able to do the same, though it was equally possible she was looking at the wall or the floor.

"There's every chance it's reversible," I finally offered, before putting up my spare room to show solidarity. Sanders wouldn't be taking me up on my tokenistic offer anyway.

"Sounds like a plan. But we may need to take Yolanda.

Haven't heard from her mother yet, as usual, and she said her Dad was in Red Hook today. If that's the case, he won't be getting back in anytime soon." Sasha's place, like Yolanda's, was also in Brooklyn.

I agreed, and we got to work wrangling the kids. Varying ages, some short, some tall, others sort of in between as far as their heights went, each comprised of about 12 megatons of restless energy. A few of them knew me and called me by nicknames I chose to interpret as affectionate. Uncle Tom, Special Agent Nigga etc. Unfortunately I could no longer tell which of the children were black, so it's possible some of the few white kids used the occasion to drop a few opportunistic n-bombs. (A peculiar take, given our current circumstances had neutralised the racial divide, but I wasn't in the mood for debating the finer points with these youths.) The arrival of older siblings, parents and guardians heralded a chain reaction of crying from adult to child alike, the simple comfort of familiar faces severed from their reach. Eventually all the kids peeled off, All except Yolanda.

We walked back to my place in Chelsea, as if I hadn't walked enough for today. As we did so we passed by many in a state of numb, stumbling shock. Not a single soul in Manhattan spared from the affliction. Even without eyes they knew we were staring, not solely out of paranoia, at least not just yet, but more out of a blend of fascination and shock. Amidst this thick neurological smoothie it is not surprising that the mind took some time to catch up with reality.

Anyone who had found refuge for the day, be it in their office or a friend's apartment or the nearest McDonald's/Starbucks, tried to lose themselves in their phones, scrolling for updates as to where their bodies had gone and why their lives had been so rudely upended.

We did the same once I'd set up the bed for Sasha and Yolanda in the spare.

Barb left me everything when she passed. She never had kids of her own; her late husband Freddie was a wonderful example of a gentleman, but he wielded an arsenal consisting entirely of blanks. He went early in my childhood, not that this derailed Barb's determination to raise me. The show must go on, it is what it is, all the clichéd idioms one espouses in the face of dire luck. I changed little with the apartment I'd inherited from her. Kept the piles of leather-bound books on botany. The array of early jazz records and the old oak-cased gramophone too. It felt inappropriate to remove her history, the traces of her earthly existence. About the only newish thing was the flat screen. We sunk into the couch and immersed ourselves in the various competing forms of digital crisis coverage.

"You gonna show up at work tomorrow?" asked Sasha.

"Poor choice of words. But yeah, I guess so."

"Good. I'm gonna keep the Rec Centre open. Got the keys, just need them to keep the power on. Kids still need a safe space to run around in. Poor little fuckers."

I nodded in agreement, then remembered (after an awkward silence) that she probably didn't see that. "We'll keep the cogs turning. Hold on to some kind of normality. I just nodded, by the way."

"Got anything in the fridge?"

We had passed several grocers on the way here, yet declined to indulge in the frenzy. I was regretting my decision to cancel Fresh Direct. Their pricing didn't seem so unreasonable now.

Not to fear. Uber Eats was still a company, surely? People still needed to eat, right? Certain basic facts hadn't changed. So we ordered a pie from the local dominoes. If anyone was still slinging dough, it had to be that thrifty enterprise.

And so it was.

The delivery guy was more skittish than usual, which was understandable, but we were awed that society, at its most important level, was still functioning.

'Good luck with the whole invisibility thing,' I told him, settling on a sensible tip that took the impending societal collapse into account. "You too..." he muttered with anxious hope. See, we were all in this together.

Post-dinner, we returned to our immersion in reports of 'the situation', as we were calling it here at the Walcott home, while Yolanda busied herself with preoccupied, unenthused colouring in of a rainbow variant of the daisy.

Where to begin with the wider ripples of the situation?

Speculation as to the cause? Unconfirmed for another three days. Right now the pundits had their money on a government project accident on the scale of Chernobyl, charges that resulted in a swift denial from our Commander in Chief, springing to action with the suspicious sort of swiftness that makes one look even more guilty. The finger was then pointed at an array of our innumerable enemies, both domestic and international.

The financial impact once trading resumed? Sell, sell, sell. The financial green heartbeat teetering toward a decidedly irreversible shade of red. That defiant bull with the bronze balls suffering the same fate as the rest of us, all bravado having evaporated.

Or how about one of their own reporters, a faceless apparition in a pantsuit, victim of a naturally applied greenscreen, trying to remain upbeat and desperately remind the rest of the Nightly News team of her ongoing value and humanity. Despite the reporter's best efforts, her (non-invisible) co-hosts poked and prodded in dehumanising fashion, a whisper of things to come.

"We've spoken to a leading scientist, who has said that it is impossible for a translucent eyeball to refract light, thereby negating the possibility of your being able to see anything at all."

"Well, I can see," she said flatly.

"That's amazing," the news anchors nodded in wonder, "and what do you feel right now?"

It was then that their curiosity downgraded from semi-professional empathy to something more akin to spectators gawking at the zoo.

"Do you think we could zoom in on your eyes? Or rather, the space where your eyes should be? I just want to make sure—Zak, can we zoom in there please—oh wow, that's amazing... There's really nothing there at all, is there. How utterly extraordinary."

To finish, they cut to the break with a photo of the reporter in happier, more visible, times.

As the news broadcasts continued to prove more depressing than informative, and the day had been rather long and irreparably life-altering, Sasha announced she was going to go get ready for bed and take Yolanda with her.

"Don't think tomorrow is going to feel any less long," she declared.

"Maybe we'll all wake up to find the symptoms have cleared overnight," I offered somewhat wanly.

I sensed Sasha staring at me with that usual look I knew so well, the one which traversed the middle ground between 'oh really?' and 'are you a fucking moron?'

"And what, pray tell, do you base that on?"

"Just hope, I guess." I added an appeal to authority. "Call it a professional hunch."

"Mm'hmm. Good to know the powers that be are really pulling out all the stops on this one." My appeal to authority had not had the desired effect. Perhaps next time I would try making my voice sound a little deeper, more like I knew what the fuck I was talking about. People respect people with deep voices, I've found.

Looking to further subdue the neurons firing relentlessly inside my brain, I flicked through the channels some more, for the first time properly realising that hand-eyed coordination wasn't coming so easily now that I couldn't actually see my fingers. At times I felt like a stroke victim, re-learning the most basic of necessities, until I reached

ESPN. At least the Knicks had been spared. Playing the Bucks away, down 3-1 in the series. Much to my chagrin, however, the Milwaukee commentators were swept up in the strange plight of New York, while the Knicks themselves also appeared distracted, leaking buckets every which way. Good to know some things never change. The players on the bench even appeared to be checking their phones every so often, hoping like the rest of us for some clarity.

On the street below me, a siren shrieked past, its beam momentarily staining the walls red, and I sighed. At what point does all of it—the sirens, the whirring lights, the panic—all of it—just call it a day? I drove for five straight hours after 9/11 to reach Barb from the academy in Quantico. To help. To do my part. But though there was madness then too, and chaos, and fear, there appeared some measure of respite to counteract the nightmare. An identifiable enemy. A response to offer. A galvanising sense of solidarity, patriotism, of wanting to protect what we all on some level stood for. This was different. This wasn't picking through rubble in search of survivors, sifting through a scene of wanton destruction to determine who could and couldn't be saved. This time our bodies were Ground Zero.

Deep within this reflective mindset, I heard a loud knock on my door, startling me out of my reverie. Sasha, still unable to drift off into the currently more tangible realm of dreams, rose from the spare bed and went to fetch the baseball bat. I stood by the door and asked, in an appropriately deep voice, for the unsummoned visitor to state their name and purpose.

Sanders' voice, the last I expected to hear, breached the timbers of the door.

"We're going after Feng tomorrow morning. 0700. You in?"

FENG

I needn't have bothered with an alarm, for as you know, we were not the only creatures who suffered the same fate. Two flights up in 12B lived a little yapper whose confusion of her master's predicament would not abate. This became the common cry of all our furry friends across the Island, and so a solution was sought. The volume and complexity had to be muted. Countless animal lovers from across the world scorned us for the cold relinquishment of our pets to the authorities, off to the government farm, where your lab coats gathered crucial data from cooperative subjects before their termination.

Forgive us, we were not yet the evolved beings Radakovic taught us to be.

We were still as primitive as you.

Living in a dog-eat-dog world.

The Feng hit provided an excellent opportunity to refocus the mind. I wasn't going to question how the intel pertaining to his whereabouts had been confirmed, or by whom. Nor did I know how Sanders had been able to wrangle an entire tactical response team for this last-minute operation. Nobody outside our department had spent countless painstaking hours following up leads on Feng and sitting in boardrooms reporting the resultant steady lack of progress, so the fact that Sanders had convinced an entirely different department to go after this small fry in a pond of pure pandemonium spoke volumes about his rising profile within the Bureau. This same charisma and magnetism would eventually assist him in forming his own militia to oppose your occupation, but I'm getting ahead of myself.

That morning in the shower was also the first time I experienced the wonders of going full native. There was a brief moment the night before, when changing into a fresh pair of pyjamas I'd felt an uncharacteristic thrill, but that morning, removing said pyjamas and feeling the water wash over my body generated a rush of liberation I could only cite as something akin to a sense of budding enlightenment. Imagine your body growing progressively lighter, being absorbed into the air all around it, a feeling of simultaneously being air and lighter than air. Then came the spreading of soap suds across my body as I reacquainted myself with the contours of reality, a blissful smile plastered across my face. I'd experienced nothing quite like it.

Putting on clothes after that felt like returning to prison and requesting the shackles. They often hypothesised about the true cause of the urge to 'go native'—was it merely psychosomatic? A chemical side effect somehow occasioned by the constituents of Radakovic's transformative concoction? In any event, the end result was the same: a pathological intolerance to clothing, and the compulsive desire to shed them at all costs.

This overpowering urge eventually became known as the Itch. A progressive affliction common to all who dwelt within these new invisible bodies, it drew scepticism from the skins as a convenient excuse for indulging in our most deviant form.

At first, symptoms were manageable enough: general restlessness, an impossible to verify impression of being covered in extensive rashes, a vague yet increasingly insistent sense of claustrophobia. But once it truly hit, it came on with a vengeance. The best description I can give is a feeling like thousands of spiders burrowing into your skin whenever it felt the weight of clothing, any clothing at all. Type of material was irrelevant, all fabrics were equally oppressive, the priciest cashmere grated against the dermis like it was woven out of stinging nettles. The relentless pin-pricking eventually drove you insane, breathing became ever more difficult, until finally in a fit of rage and discomfort you abandoned propriety entirely, flinging whatever clothes you had on into a messy heap and glaring at it, chest heaving, intoxicated with utter relief, the feeling of having overcome something hateful, of having vanquished an oppressive foe...

Personally? My bodily sensations were not so dramatic. I felt it more up here, between the ears... a subtle gnawing temptation that was still somewhat nebulous. Despite the curiousness of my experience in the shower, I still hadn't put two and two together. How could I? There was no precedent for any of this. The thought of going native, of being naked full time, simply hadn't occurred to me. Yet.

Still clothed, I met Sanders a couple of blocks away from Chinatown, on Broome Street. Feng official residence was in Midtown, but Sanders held firm to his intel that Feng was currently holed up in one of his smaller processing centres, tucked behind a fishmonger, accessed via an adjacent alleyway. Sanders speculated that, cut off from his usual place of work in Brooklyn, the processing centre in Chinatown was his most logical hideout for the time being, not least because that was where they likely had sufficient weapons stored in the event of a siege. It promised to be an interesting morning.

There were nine of us in total: Sanders, myself, and Lieutenant Kowalski's A-team; seven of the craziest bastards God ever shovelled guts into. Kowalski himself was absent, Sanders assuming the Lieutenant's role with his usual panache. The entire crew were decked from head to toe in tactical gear, their black helmets and goggles giving them the appearance of particularly malevolent aliens. They were twitchy, veritably itching for action, although that could have been a side effect of all that tactical gear on newly invisible, sensitive skin—the Itch in its infancy, slowly taking hold. Someone handed me a tactical vest. The Fifth Precinct was already setting up a perimeter, Sanders claimed, though the conspicuous lack of comms on the radio suggested otherwise.

The van pumped its brakes outside the fishmonger, the storefront entrance closed off by metal roller shutters. Sanders and the others hopped out, the call made to enter through the door in the alleyway. I was told to remain in the street, covering the front of the premises in case Feng tried to slip by us that way. It was at this stage I realised uneasily that I hadn't actually seen a warrant, but what with all the adrenaline pulsing through these cowboys' veins, the bone-shaking speed of the van ride over and Sanders' grim air of detached determination, there hadn't been an opportunity to query the mundane matter of legalities.

"Wait, where's the Fifth Precinct? What about the perimeter?"

"They must be running late," called Sanders as he and his crew ran towards the alley, which did little to quell my rising sense that something wasn't quite right. "Don't worry Leonard. We got this. Success through readiness!"

I heard the telltale thud of the door knocker in the alleyway. I drew my gun and waited, pacing, beside the van. It was times like these that I wished I was a smoker. Soon there was muffled shouting and gunfire from inside. Lots of gunfire.

I'd never been in a proper gunfight before. For whatever reason, call it a peculiarity of fate, resistance in the raids I'd helped coordinate usually tended to take the more civilised form of panicked flight.

As though on cue, a window on the second floor rumbled open, and an escapee wearing a grey singlet and purple underwear crabbed his way out onto the red corrugated shading of the storefront before losing his balance and tumbling to the pavement with an almighty whack. Thus began the screaming, our suspect clutching at the ankle he had just shattered. Though the streets remained blessedly empty, I sensed reflectionless others in the surrounding buildings were now gazing out their windows, our recent affliction lending itself nicely to most forms of voyeurism.

Raising my gun, I slowly approached the tangled mass of invisible limbs writhing away on the sidewalk.

I reached out with one hand to ascertain whether he had a weapon stashed in his underwear. My hand was swatted away, and the man hissed something at me in his native tongue. I assumed it wasn't anything too polite.

"Are you Feng?" I asked, with a tinge of hope. It would bode well for my next employee review if I could single-handedly bring down a criminal mastermind, even if gravity had done most of the work. "Feng?" It was going to be hard to positively ID any of these perps if they refused to answer questions honestly.

"Fuck you," hissed the man in a heavy Chinese accent. It turned out he spoke English after all.

"And here I thought we were going to be friends," I replied.

I ordered him to roll onto his stomach so I could cuff him, but he just erupted in another tidal wave of bilingual vitriol, so I kicked him in the ribs. Quite hard. I don't generally approve of violence in such cases, but I was sick of having criminals not listen to me.

Closer inspection revealed he was too thin to be Feng. Sighing, I knelt down and eventually managed to get the handcuffs on. I'd like to say it was my first time cuffing a man naked from the waist down, but this was New York.

Then the same window our perp had tumbled from was rattled open once more, as a body-armour laden set of clothes dove from it onto the corrugated shading before deftly dismounting onto the pavement beside us with all the grace of an Olympic gymnast.

"That's how you should've done it," I informed our half-naked captive. "But we all live and learn."

"Call a fucking ambulance," was all he hissed in reply.

The rest of it happened even quicker than the stuntman-esque leap, Sanders firing without warning into the suspect, hole after hole appearing in the grey singlet as the body beneath it shook and then, with a final groan, grew still.

A warm mist graced my pleats and my exposed hand. The city would soon enough be awash in rivers of blood and unbridled violence, but my sensibilities to such things hadn't yet been deadened. Later that day I would shower and, despite that feeling of budding enlightenment returning, I desperately scrubbed at my hands and shins, certain I'd missed a spot.

"What the—Why would you do that?" I asked, once the whipcrack of gunfire had ceased echoing in our brains. "The fuck were you thinking?"

This question seemed to surprise him, though he had surely considered the possibility that I would react to the cold-blooded execution of an unarmed suspect, even one embroiled in the vile world of human trafficking, with some level of discomfort.

"What, you're going to get all weepy over a dead Snakehead? They're scum. Besides, we killed everyone else inside. He would've felt left out if we'd taken him in and booked him. Let him join his friends in hell."

My mind reeled and I had that faraway feeling, like his

words were coming at me through a tunnel. I wondered momentarily if this new renegade Sanders was an imposter.

"But... how are we going to write this up? How the fuck are we going to explain any of this?"

From the slight pause before Sanders replied, and the odd tone in his voice when he did, it dawned on me that this entire raid had been off the books. The Fifth Precinct wasn't coming. Nothing had been sanctioned. This entire thing had been a clandestine op. A setup. Shit. So much for my next employee review.

"Leonard, buddy, you're looking at this all wrong."

The rest of his answer was something to the effect that there was simply no time to process criminals of this ilk through to conviction in these new and extremely trying circumstances. By 'new circumstances' I took it he meant 'opportunity to indulge in wanton madness and bloodlust.' I was regretting offering him my spare room even more strongly than before, and more than a little glad he had declined.

"We could have got some good intel out of him!" I protested meekly, "Led us to Feng, if you hadn't found him in there," I looked down at the body. "There is technically still such a thing as due process."

"Look at you, breaking out the legalese! I had no idea you were such a bleeding heart traditionalist. It's a brand new day, Leonard. New rules. The boys are doing a thorough sweep. All the evidence will be in there, Feng included."

His nonchalance was frightening. Chasing this ghoul for two and a half years and not the slightest hint of satisfaction in his voice once the job was done—in dramatic, extra-judicial fashion, no less.

Stunned, all I could manage was a mumbled "congrats" to which Sanders responded with an equally inauthentic "couldn't have done it without your help."

I couldn't tell if he was staring at me, seeing right through my posturing as easily as he could see through my skin, and so we stood in awkward silence until the rest of the hit squad emerged from the alleyway.

With professional gusto, the men all filed past us and into the van. I noted a suspicious absence of anything resembling paperwork or files. Sanders then informed me they had more stops to make.

"Who's going to clean this up?" I asked, frozen to the spot, fixated neighbours doubtless watching unseen from every vantage.

"We're not finished, Leonard. Joining us?"

It was important at this stage to not provoke Sanders, to tread carefully, lest I be reclassified from a trusted accomplice to a loose end to be tied up.

"Uh... no. I think I'll stay here. Do one last sweep. See if I can turn up anything interesting," I said, trying to sound pally and light hearted. "Debrief whoever shows up on this arrest gone wrong. Get them off the scent. The work of the Dominicans, say."

Sanders put a hand on my shoulder, and I jumped slightly.

"I know I can trust you. Stay safe out there, partner. Be smart. It's going to be a strange new world." He climbed into the van, closing the doors behind him. I heard a few celebratory whoops from inside as they peeled off. Nothing like wanton bloodshed to instil a sense of camaraderie.

The Lieutenant from the Fifth arrived shortly thereafter, a floating uniform with no hands, atop of which floated a cap without a face. My initial attempt to parse this affair off as a shootout between rival traffickers fell apart immediately; whichever concerned citizen who had alerted the Fifth in the first place had swiftly retracted their caution after spotting the SWAT van. "Oh, don't worry about it—you're already here."

Pivoting to a more truthful recollection of events, I explained what happened and his annoyance at having never been informed by the FBI was eventually just shrugged off. Literally, I saw him just shrug. "Ah well, fuck it. They were evil cocksuckers, they had it coming, I guess."

I decided not to piss anyone off in this new world.

As in the case of the pizza delivery man the night before, we weren't entirely sure if the coroner would arrive, but arrive he did, taking photos of bullet holes in walls and intermittently tripping over bodies.

As the FBI liaison, sole witness and partial participant of the shootout it fell upon me to submit a report to the Fifth and confirm the FBI's skin in the game (of which we obviously had none anymore). Given the circumstances, I was doing a fairly decent job of making the operation appear official, despite the glaring lack of a warrant or the fact none of the other participants had stuck around (by the playbook, two absolute musts), until my phone buzzed and a 'calm' Halifax requested my presence at headquarters.

The Lieutenant, less interested in the scene before him and more intrigued by potential FBI intel on the wider shenanigans deconstructing our bodies, offered to give me a ride. How could I possibly refuse?

The FBI were prepared today. Reception had laminated name badges. Unfortunately, the wave of invisibility had also infected this once proud and respected organisation with a notable case of absenteeism, and the bulk remained unclaimed.

HALIFAX

The Child Exploitation and Human Trafficking Taskforce had twelve agents covering Manhattan. Including myself, only three were in attendance. Group Supervisor Gerrard Halifax was a nice enough guy. Halifax had been running Human Trafficking since before I finished high school. A hero on 9/11, as well as on numerous other dates not emblazoned in the cultural memory. He'd always been acutely conscious of his receding hairline, so I thought this turn of events may have brought him the faintest of silver linings.

Janet Hosking was the other party. When I told her in confidence about Sanders' unauthorised hit, and how he and his merry band of psychopaths had gone racing off on another mission, she swore she'd break his neck if he went after her target, David Henríquez. Janet had slept at headquarters and apologised for the rumpled state of her clothes, but as my own were spattered with the unseen blood of a murdered people smuggler, I felt I was in no position to judge.

"At least I don't have to waste time doing my hair and makeup," she chuckled.

The paltry attendance displeased Halifax, most of all with the absence of Nate Sanders, the apple of his eye, the shining light for all other departments to marvel at with envy. I objected to this admittedly dismal turnout being described as a full-blown abandoning of the ship, protesting that as it was still only eight thirty in the morning, surely the rest would arrive in their own time.

Halifax grunted with his usual surliness. "We need all hands on deck now! It's not like they got any sleep last night? Did you?"

I did not mention that thanks to a fortuitous combination of owning an apartment in the city, having no family apart from Sasha, nor any fretful lovers to comfort, I had slept like a baby. Sanders' bloody breakfast run had not been relayed properly to HQ yet, my assurances to the lieutenant on the ride over that I'd be in touch shortly with the appropriate warrants, buying me some time. And though I knew it would be pertinent to get on the front foot and bring Halifax up to speed with Sanders' rogue outing, I failed to utter a single word of confession when he asked if I'd heard anything from his protégé.

A general office-wide meeting was held in a repeat performance of yesterday. As we awaited the Assistant Director, we exchanged chatter with the other departments. Topics were confined to the potential restructuring of roles and responsibilities and a general lack of oversight as to what exactly the hell was going on. Oh, and for the less inhibited at 9.00am, the otherworldly experience of parting with one's clothes for the first time and regarding our new selves in full.

Numbers were noticeably thinner this day than on the former, but the ADIC proceeded with gusto nonetheless. A rousing speech on the merits of patriotism and the need for law enforcement officers to stick to their posts, and to not lose their heads no matter the circumstances.

"Some of us, at least, are still proud Americans," the Assistant Director concluded. Right on cue, an image flickered to life on the screen behind him, and we were introduced, via tele link, to our new Czar, the short-haired, rosy-cheeked General Phillip Bracken.

His smile was business-like; polite, controlled, but with the smallest hint of violence. At this difficult time, it helped to see a smile, any smile, that suggested some concern for our plight. Faces are like that. Reassuring. You don't really miss them until they vanish suddenly one Tuesday.

Publicly celebrated for eradicating ISIS in Northern Iraq and swiftly condemned thereafter for his calculated abandonment of our Kurdish allies, post eradication, the general was the obvious choice for the Commander in Chief to turn to in managing this developing humanitarian crisis, recognising the position required someone with a certain measure of flexibility, but who also had the bearing and fortitude to ensure orders were carried out.

"Don't worry. We're going to get the bastards who did this. In the meantime, just hang tight. Reassure the public, maintain order, and go about your business as best as you can. I know this situation is all kinds of terrible. I don't understand it any better than you. But help is on the way."

Gen. Bracken broke down our priorities into three, easy-to-digest focal points. A third of the branch would be dedicated to investigating the cause and culprits of this unmitigated disaster. The other two thirds would support the entry of the National Guard that was currently undergoing rapid deployment to help support the police in their bid to maintain law and order now that the city was officially sealed. A major component of this process, Bracken suggested, would be ensuring that Manhattan's citizens complied with all quarantine regulations and the usual rule of law, so that their fellow Americans outside the quarantine zone could be assured of their own safety.

I nodded my head in agreement, saw right away where the man was coming from. Our existence disturbed the rest of the country, and rightly so; maybe this would change, maybe it wouldn't, but for now we were an unknown quantity, a literal swarm of bogeymen and women. I got it, no hard feelings. We still didn't know the cause of this bizarre affliction, how long it would last, or whether it was transmissible. If they started baying for our blood and hunting us down that would be perfectly understandable, if a little difficult to enact.

For now, apparently, we were to be the eyes and ears on the ground. Although it wasn't implicitly stated, we were not simply the FBI anymore. We would be granted extra-judicial discretion and powers; the new Gestapo, perhaps, but surely for the good of all Americans.

General Bracken's closer was a carrot-dangle of the highest order. Commitment to the cause of crisis management would not be forgotten; on the contrary it would be rewarded handsomely. Yeah, sure.

"To quote the inscription on the Washington Square

Arch, this event is in the hands of God. But we can do our part too. Good luck."

Returning to our desks to await reassignment to one of Bracken's aforementioned priorities, the hours passed with little achieved. This was becoming something of a theme. To be fair though, it wasn't entirely our fault. Be the eyes and ears on the ground. What the fuck did that even mean? I wasn't going back out there, not unless it was to buy a sandwich. There were vigilante groups just roaming the streets, for God's sake! I should know. I'd inadvertently been part of one not two hours before. Besides, there was no sign yet of the National Guard.

Sanders didn't show up and Halifax grew increasingly distracted, pecking away at the keyboard in his office in that absentminded way he had when he was browsing antique furniture on eBay, lost in thought. We all had our methods of coping.

Janet expressed a fear that our department was going to be directed into quarantine control at the ports and docks (the surly bastards down at harbour patrol were even more tiresome to deal with than the NYPD). She preferred to be among the ranks of those chosen to pursue the terrorists that had done this to us, finding it more noble and vengeance-fulfilling than whatever the hell we were doing, which at that moment was still mostly nothing. My own thoughts were more pragmatic, and I found myself unable to escape the burning question of whether Eugene's Deli would be open for lunch and whether it would be unseemly to go there on my morning break, which I was hoping to take sooner rather than later. There was also the not-inconsequential matter of informing Halifax about his golden boy going full-blown Colonel Kurtz on us.

Then we received a company-wide HR email advising that someone had slipped on an invisible shit in the men's bathroom on the fourth floor, and that brought some welcome levity to the morning's proceedings. It also raised the question of exactly why someone had decided to take a dump in the middle of the floor, as opposed to doing it in the toilet like the rest of us. End-of-the-world stress manifesting itself in a case of the fuck-its, or merely a puerile prank occasioned by the otherworldly weirdness we all found ourselves in? Whatever the motivation, I inwardly saluted the boldness of the anonymous floor-shitter.

Subsequent orders from Hallifax for the day were to finalise reports on all current cases so that we could indefinitely put them on the back burner, and stand by to receive our new assignment by close of business at the latest. While Janet furiously typed away and made numerous harried calls, I rehearsed my statement regarding Feng, in which he had presumably gone into hiding in Chinatown until this pesky matter of being invisible was resolved. Or some hopefully plausible bullshit along those lines. Why not? Weirder things had happened than a people smuggler under heavy surveillance taking a bit of a breather. Thankfully, rehearsing a look of wide-eyed innocence was not a requirement anymore. I just hoped that Lieutenant from the 5th kept his goddamn trap shut, and in all the chaos forget about the fact I hadn't yet made a report on the killings and had no intention of doing so. Despite the likelihood of being caught in my lie I actually enjoyed writing out my fantasy scenario, perhaps because it helped ease my conscience on a subconscious level, or possibly because it was some time since I'd done any actual work. In any event I worked straight through my morning break, surprising myself, and dropped it on Halifax's desk with feigned casualness just before lunchtime.

"I worked through my morning break to produce that, sir. I just thought you should know." The unspoken subtext was that I would take an extended lunch break to compensate.

He accepted the paper, but didn't read it. "Walcott, what do you think the odds are of Feng leaving Manhattan?"

"Well, sir, I mentioned it as a distinct possibility in my report, but for what it's worth I think he may keep a low profile in Chinatown for a while. Wait and see how things play out."

He exhaled, and a stale Marlboro-tinged stench permeated the confines of his office. There was a packet on his desk. Stress relievers, he called them. "If it were up to me, we'd go out there now and execute a warrant for his arrest. What do you think about that?"

"Uh, well, I think that's got some merit to it, of course, sir. But then again, perhaps we have bigger fish to fry?"

"We're the fish now, O—ah goddamn! I mean what are we doing just waiting here for official reassignment? What in the hell are we doing? Right now, out there in the chaos, Feng must be running rampant! You've seen the news; the crowds at the tunnels, the ports, I'll bet he's already there, probing for weak links, setting up routes! A guy like that doesn't just rest on his laurels. He's a slippery, snaky beast."

It was clear that sleeping at work had not given my boss neither the requisite time nor comfort to recharge and collect his thoughts.

"Nothing's changed, sir. We're still going to be catching bad guys. We just need to catch our breath a moment, is all. Figure out the best plan of attack."

Halifax exhaled again. "OK, we'll wait for an official reassignment from the ADIC. But in the meantime can you see about getting an arrest warrant for Feng? One for each of his last known locations. Use those extra-judicial powers the general mentioned. Twist a few arms if you have to."

"Certainly. I'll look into it after lunch."

I could tell Halifax was somewhat incredulous at this, imagining his brows furrowing, nostrils flaring and eyes glaring. But what could he do? It was 12.45pm and I needed a Reuben. We couldn't all survive on a diet of Marlboro Reds and espressos.

Janet intercepted me on my way out and suggested a grocery run, something I'd been putting off, given all the unbridled looting and carnage. Besides, I was planning on eating nothing but Reubens and Dominos until this whole shitstorm blew over.

"Come on! Let's try and get what we can, before the shelves are completely stripped bare."

I reluctantly agreed. After all, Sasha and Yolanda might not share my dietary philosophy. We set off for the Walgreens on Third, a few blocks in the opposite direction to Eugene's deli.

An average-sized mob was in the process of stripping this particular grocer clean as we arrived. I imagined the fights over tinned food and toilet paper had been protracted and vicious; survival of the fittest out here, and we were only on Day two. Janet and I shared a look of hesitation (again, assumed) before we sighed and piled in with the rest of them. The cans of beans and tuna and other essentials one would place high on a doomsday prepper list had already been cleaned out, so we were left to pick through the few discarded perishables left to rot in the produce section. As I questioned the wisdom of stocking up on a handful of flaccid green beans and one well-bruised pear, I was tapped on the shoulder by a concerned citizen. Her voice was soft, mousy, bespeaking of a liberal arts major with a sketchpad few had seen and even fewer would care to.

"Excuse me, but are you the police?"

Those fucking name tags! I'd forgotten to take it off.

Janet appeared beside me, having grabbed an assortment of miscellaneous items, cooking utensils and gossip mags and so forth, more because she could than out of any inherent survival value.

Before I could deflect further annoying questions and make a dash for Eugene's, Janet had engaged with the impudent young woman, who immediately thrust a sleeve in the direction of the counter and noted indignantly that not only were people not paying for items but that equally no one was trying to stop them.

Yes, it's called looting, you stupid bitch. It's what people do in times of lawlessness and panic.

We dutifully glanced over at the frantic mob, hopelessly out-numbered and, at least in my case, largely indifferent. Over by the entrance, a man and a woman were having a heated argument over a roast chicken. From the way their empty clothes were angrily gesticulating, things were about to turn ugly. It was then the concerned do-gooder with the mousy voice allayed our fears that she wanted us to somehow subdue the mob and return all pilfered goods to the shelves whence they came. Instead, she shared her deep suspicion that the shopkeeper had been beaten to death and was still lying on the floor behind the counter.

"There's an awful lot of mess behind there and I touched something I couldn't see. But it felt like a body. And it was stiff."

Janet and I looked at one another, or specifically we both gazed into the empty space that contained each other's faces. Her usual can-do attitude had seemingly been replaced by something much more familiar to my sensibilities, namely a willingness to shirk one's duty. Initial emotional responses may include feelings of discomfort, but thankfully this dissipates into relief as one feels the burden of tiresome responsibilities lifting. This dawning realisation would doubtless keep her up that night, questioning whether her own personality and its attendant morals would simply up and leave too.

"We'll take care of it."

Peeking over the counter, I observed someone had violently wrenched the till from the register, the drawer gaping and the cash long gone. After jumping over the divider, I stomped until my shoe connected with an unseen object. I knelt down and my fingers soon found toes, then a bare foot. I did not care to confirm the rest.

We stood there a while as what little remained in the store was ransacked. In our silence we came to a mutual agreement that the rules had changed and society had shifted well beyond the usual notions of propriety and restraint. So until we were formally allocated to our new roles, it was easy to argue we were merely caretakers, bystanders to the decimation of the social contract. Janet called the local PD and I placed a five for my groceries in the till as a symbolic gesture, an empty (if nobly intended) act of gravitas.

I stopped by Eugene's on the way back to the office to find his little hole in the wall deli, my second home, all locked up. Peering through the window I glimpsed a dishevelled gust of wind sweeping the floors with lacklustre looseness. Eugene was naked again.

I banged on the door and said "Eugene! It's Leonard, your favourite customer! The one who's single-handedly putting your kids through college! Open up, man!" Pleas to that effect. Eugene shuffled over and unlatched the door. We traded stories for a bit and I did my best to cheer him up, thoughtfully trying to distract him with a mechanical task he could focus on, namely the prompt making of my sandwich. It was hard to tell whether he saw through my subterfuge, but in the end I got myself the Reuben. It appeared to lack the care and love he normally put into its preparation, and so it was that I mourned another small part of my world irreparably altered.

I spent the rest of the afternoon obtaining a warrant for

the arrest of a criminal whom I knew to be well and truly reformed.

***

After six, Sasha returned to my place with Yolanda once again in tow. A sad little ghost girl in a yellow dress. My heart went out to her.

"Aw, you miss your parents, huh, sweetheart?"

"Course she does, you idiot," replied Sasha in her stead. "She's seven. How would you feel?"

"I don't know, do I? Jesus! I'm just trying to console her."

"Well, you're doing a terrible job."

Once we eventually finished bickering, and I could establish that Yolanda's father was still trapped in Brooklyn (but thankfully not affected) and the mother flying in from Chicago, we compared spoils from our respective grocery runs. She'd gone with Yolanda and a few other kids to their plot in the community garden, and the old lady running the place was nice enough to give each of the kids a bushel of carrots to take home. This nice old woman would eventually be brutally raped and murdered, and the community garden itself plundered, defaced beyond recognition, then torched, but for now this is the feel-good part of the story.

For the second night in a row we waited in anticipation for the delivery man. Dominos pizza could and frequently did taste like oily rubber, but their delivery people certainly were tenacious.

School had been 'temporarily' shut down for Sasha's

charges. For those families stranded in Manhattan, dragging their kids around seeking shelter presented a unique challenge. Organising such accommodation was a priority of the National Guard, but they were yet to arrive themselves, so a smooth process seemed unlikely. For those separated from their children, each waking moment offered unending anguish. Sasha organised a video call with Yolanda's parents and copious tears were shed by all parties. The parents offered money and relentless gratitude for Sasha and myself, trying to alleviate their guilt at not being there for their little ballerina, to which we politely declined.

I told Sasha about the poor turnout at headquarters. She expressed a similar concern about whether the kids would keep turning up to the Rec Centre. In times of political or social instability, funding for local YMCAs traditionally went from 'uncertain' to 'non-existent'. We discussed the emergency alert text the government had sent to everyone in Manhattan, advising of the imminent arrival of the National Guard to restore order and organise food and shelter. Sasha had overheard a few cops on a street corner speculating as to where the Guard would set up shop; according to her eavesdropping one of these units would likely be stationed at James Earl High, just around the corner from the Rec Centre. I said I'd look into it after I received my new orders and the outcome of Halifax discovering I'd been lying about Feng.

Was it going to get better before it got worse? Only Radakovic knew the answer to that.

On the TV were multiple replays of the National Guard rolling in across the Brooklyn Bridge and Chinook helicopter drops in Central Park. A home delivered pizza was looking less likely by the minute. Sasha speculated via text with her colleague Devon whether troops would station at the high school nearby. Devon, layabout that he was, did not reply, likely because he was getting on the drink. Several of the National Guard troops wore clunky thermal vision goggles, of a style unknown to me, though they were soon to become a requisite accessory in the tracking and monitoring of America's most freakish. Television presenters eagerly pounced on a new public health directive handed down by the mayor, endorsed by General Bracken, the Joint Chiefs of Staff and the president, that all individuals currently suffering from the emerging ailment known as TBS (Translucent Body Syndrome) be required to wear clothes at all times, with fines for first time nudists and potential jail time for repeat offenders.

Within days of this public service announcement, corporate America bravely sprung into action, Nike coming to the rescue with a marketing campaign promoting their new skinwear range, to make you feel *you* again. The Itch and its tenacious persistence was yet to become common knowledge, but how were the marketing team at Nike supposed to predict this debilitating impact on their ROI?

With our department yet to be repurposed to one of Bracken's three focal points, there was more time to pursue the spurious warrant for Feng, and to Halifax's relief we were granted it.

Two agents from our team, Pradesh and Oxley, had shown up this morning to assess the FBI's handle on the situation, but they quickly dispersed by lunchtime and were not seen again. I certainly wasn't going to complain. The fewer sets of prying eyes snooping into my business the better. Their unexplained absence was nothing out of the ordinary, with abandoning of posts by this point reaching epidemic proportions.

Remaining personnel were informed of and equipped for a dawn raid scheduled to take place the following morning. The location? Feng's Chinatown hideout. I spent the first hour after the announcement wondering how I'd explain the empty crime scene, which no doubt by now had been taped off and subject to a thorough forensic examination by the Fifth Precinct (assuming that department was still functional). But truthfully, my panic abated quicker than usual, any guilt superseded by the curious, exhilarating lightness I had been feeling at intermittent intervals ever since the blastwave struck.

I sat at my desk and wondered if others were feeling this way too, the same all-pervasive levity flooding the innermost core of their being. Janet's fear of developing my lackadaisical demeanour had frightened her initially, but now it seemed she'd be transforming whether she wanted to or not. We all would. Radakovic's potion was seeping into every cell of our bodies, changing us, making us new. The feeling was one of all earthly cares abating. Who gave two shits about Feng, about how they'd managed to wrangle a warrant, about anything? If I continued to feel this good they could lock me up in Guantanamo Bay until the end of time for all I cared.

Shall I skip to the part where Halifax realises Feng has already been slain and I'm hauled in to his office to explain myself? It has a happy outcome, so I'm untroubled enough by the telling of it.

So we rolled up again, much the same as before, only this time with less psychopathic personnel and a bona fide warrant in tow. Halifax, on one of his rare appearances outside his office, oversaw the operation.

For the hell of it, I stood in the same spot as I had the day before. Under normal circumstances, the local PD would have been notified of our intention to execute a warrant and alerted us to any pertinent developments, say for instance a previous blood-soaked raid on the same premises a day prior, but these were not normal circumstances. Since the whole island of Manhattan, from the barnacle-clad docks of South Port to the Dominican enclaves of Washington Heights, had become overwhelmed by the 'TBS' plague, departmental wires were either crossed or completely non-existent, partly because of the chaos, but also the peculiar, internal withdrawal currently progressing in all those afflicted. It seemed fairly safe to assume the memo had not been shared, much to my temporary relief.

Considering all the crime scene tape, bullet holes in the walls, the arresting officers finding no need for their breacher as the door was already off its hinges, and a local asking why we had returned with all the guns, maybe it was a blessing I couldn't see Halifax's veins pumping pure molten rage up his neck, past a jaw clenched so tight that a crowbar and pliers would not suffice to separate it.

"Looks like someone beat us to it, sir. A turf war between rival traffickers? The Dominicans maybe. Or the Bully Gang looking to expand its scale of operations?"

"Perhaps..." His seething tone did not bode well for me.

And so, the resultant dressing down back at HQ. Halifax made a few calls and finally discovered from the Fifth Precinct that I'd provided a statement at the scene of the previous raid. Should have given a false name, or even thrown Sanders under the bus. Or could I have just said I was Sanders? Probably. The possibilities for identity theft were endless now.

Halifax knew I wasn't one to take such initiative unaided and grilled me as to my accomplices. He quickly deduced Sanders was the ringleader, and since I didn't bother to deny it, he promptly established this as a fact. I distinctly remember during this lengthy dressing down I felt my mind detach from my body and float like a feather above the swearing and spittle, the sensation of the odd droplet hitting my face not dissimilar to the blood spatter of the day before. Drifting ever upward and away, finally coming to rest in some elevated space where I didn't work for the FBI, where mundane concepts such as work and tedium no longer existed, and my mind could simply be absorbed into the air and let the wind take me wherever it felt. I waited until the end to tender my inevitable resignation with some small measure of dignity (of course afterwards I would take an invisible shit on the floor) but even this contingency was denied to me.

Halifax had finished his energetic explosion and was

looking out almost wistfully at all those empty desks, spare pairs of hands being found urgently wanting. My resignation, it emerged, was not to be.

"You're being promoted," he choked, the words tumbling from a throat hoarse with disbelief, the absurd reality doubtless chafing at his innards, prodding away like the cold fingers of a doctor asking him patronising questions about his packet a day habit, and at his age no less.

You could've knocked me down with a feather, until I realised we were all being promoted. A reward for loyalty, apparently, amidst our ever-thinning ranks. The principal perks were tarted-up job descriptions and 'extra' salary (the actual benefits of which were too early to surmise, though it seemed churlish under the circumstances to demand to know how much extra), both ploys to instil the belief that allegiance to the restructuring program (read: nascent regime change) being undertaken by General Bracken would somehow reap freedom (of an unspecified type) in the future. Given that I had just evaded a possible lengthy jail sentence, I thought it best to swallow my reservations and accept this new turn of events with equanimity.

Halifax then summoned Janet, and she was also debriefed on these developments. I hoped she would ask how much the pay rise was going to be, but she didn't.

A top priority was reconnecting with former employees and offering them reemployment, or, failing that, to ascertain their present location and monitor their movements.

"I don't mind offering them their old jobs back, but I refuse to run surveillance on my colleagues," I informed

Halifax. "I can't in good conscience do it."

"You'll do it, or I'll have you arrested for treason."

"Yes, sir," I said. I don't think what I'd done was technically treason, but Halifax was evidently still pretty miffed I'd lied repeatedly to his face.

Halifax also tasked us with investigating and documenting any efforts to smuggle individuals out of the quarantine zone, which was expected to become a thriving enterprise in coming weeks. Undercover infiltration of any of these spawning operations was deemed highly meritorious. Before Halifax dismissed us, he reiterated what he believed should be our first priority: Get Sanders.

MACCREADY

Captain Macklin MacCready of the National Guard had a rip-roaring laugh that boomed harder than the bass at a thumping, sweaty nightclub, punctuated by occasional rapid-fire cackles not dissimilar to those of a maniacal hyena, high on the hunt. Not that Mac was a hunter by nature, he was in fact no doubt a helper, one of the many thousands of well-intentioned souls who tried to help in those early days. He was the friendly face of Bravo Company, stationed at James Earl High right by Sasha's Rec Centre. His strawberry blond hair and soft blue eyes put you at ease, in spite of the rest of him being built like an Irish refrigerator; large, and full of Guinness. Cheerful, big on meet and greets. Even in those early days, when the verdict was still out on whether we were contagious, MacCready was thrusting his hands awkwardly into every pair he could locate, a veritable frenzy of friendliness. Over the top? A little. Genuine? Absolutely. Appreciated? Very much so.

He didn't wear thermal goggles like the bulk of his subordinates—many of whom by tour's end suffered nightmares wherein hordes of orange heat signature blobs surrounded them, encroaching, suffocating them slowly. MacCready would look you in the space where your eye should have been with his own and give you a look that let you know he was hoping for the best. Even on his final day he still wasn't peering through the cold mechanical binoculars of thermal discrimination. I really liked MacCready. Shame what happened to him.

Sasha first encountered MacCready at a community meeting he held in the middle of an intersection between James Earl High and the Rec Centre. I don't recall exactly when the traffic subsided, but at some point, when the chaos reached its apex, people seemed to give it up, largely obeying the order that vehicular travel should be the purview of those in authority with places to be. Perhaps they tired of all the blockades, confusing road signage and intimidating checkpoints staffed with soldiers and cops. Better to walk and feel unencumbered.

MacCready spoke to the crowd about the purpose of the National Guard's presence (restoration of law and order) the reasoning behind their being stationed inside the school (functional convenience) and what it meant for the children (stunted education, to his dismay). This was all temporary, he reiterated, until they could set up a more permanent base of operations, ideally in Central Park, yet the rise of sandbags overtaking retailers suggested greater permanence. MacCready finished his address and started speaking one on one with concerned citizens. The other soldiers kept the maximum distance from the crowd they were charged with controlling, wary of both questions and contagion, if their face masks and surgical gloves were anything to go by.

Those who spoke with MacCready stared deep into his

eyes and got away with it too, fascinated by his features, as though they were revering ancient artefacts or seeing the Mona Lisa up close for the first time.

"He seemed nice; genuine, at least," Sasha remarked later that evening. Yolanda's crying had worsened, she was missing her mom and dad; not even the pizza (same delivery guy as the last two nights, I think) settled her. Even some of the other kids who did have homes to go to had asked to stay with Sasha for the night, to give their parents some space to drink away their loud emotions without fear of becoming a target for their ire. Phone reception was down at the time. Perhaps the NSA was upgrading its technology to better surveil a population of potential dissidents? Whatever the cause, I didn't receive Sasha's request and she had to turn the kids away.

"You wouldn't usually ask for permission," I said.

Her body language left no doubt. She needed her own break. The kids could come over tomorrow, maybe. Or she would stay at the Rec Centre, just for a little while.

***

Finding Sanders proved easier than expected: Once the phone service had resumed, I called his cell and he answered it. He agreed to take a break from whatever clandestine operation he was currently overseeing to meet up with me. It was fine sleuthing on my part and I resolved to use this method in future cases, assuming any of us actually had a future. There being no real need for any covert meeting spot due to us both being invisible, we sat on a park bench during my lunch break, outside the GreenMile Church, the one with the golden spire signalling heaven and the statue of Jesus looking lithe and strong, a gilded Hebraic Adonis. Just a couple sets of clothes catching up. I revealed to Sanders he was a person of interest due to his involvement in the Chinatown massacre. By 'involvement' I meant 'masterminding the entire bloodbath,' but I was trying to keep him on side.

"Finding you is now my number one priority," I informed him.

"Well, I'm found. What next?"

"Halifax wants you back on the team. I think he misses having his star operative around. I get the impression he's even willing to let Chinatown slide. The Bureau's become surprisingly lenient. It's refreshing, actually."

"I'm not coming back."

I shrugged. "Suit yourself. I tried my best."

"Good. So that's that?"

"I guess so. What do you intend to do with yourself?"

Sanders remained quiet.

"Fair enough. Let me know if you need any intel." Why did I offer this, future investigators and historians may ask. Why had I not brought backup and cuffs to our little lunch date? Simple. We were all in the same leaking boat, no sense in making enemies in close quarters. Who knew the power brokers that would emerge from the wreckage of this new shaped reality?

This offer appeared to please him very much. He put his

hand on my shoulder. "We'll be in touch."

The 'we' Sanders referred to was, even then, a fairly unsubtle nod to the private militia he was amassing.

I wandered over to the church to gauge what the faithful made of this whole mess. The pews appeared full to overflowing, the priest at the pulpit a frantic frock of inspired mania. We were being punished, was the long and short of it. God had grown tired of our vanity and our incessant squabbling over skin colour and status and so, as in the case of Job, reduced us to nothing. This was some real Sodom and Gomorrah shit (I'm paraphrasing). No more haughty self interest. Instead of the blind leading the blind, it was the invisible leading the invisible. We could only be made whole again with an unrelenting barrage of Hail Marys, confessions and, of course, donations. So more or less the same message they'd been preaching for millennia, tried and true.

Hear, hear! Amen! came the boisterous reply from the congregation.

If it ain't broke...

I listened on for a while longer, half-heartedly searching for any signs of dissidence worth noting, but this congregation appeared harmless enough, at least for the time being...

As I left, another headless man of the cloth came barrelling out of the vestibule, claiming the priest at the pulpit was an imposter, a wild man off the street. The man in the pulpit threw these claims right back at him, and the crowd bubbled in further excitement at the spectacle and drama of it all.

As with the dead cashier at the supermarket, I decided it was best not to get involved. I left telling myself that sanity would eventually prevail.

***

That afternoon we finally found our Bin Laden. Turned out it wasn't God, just another man who thought he was. Some mad scientist, the precise whereabouts of whom were still unknown. Nevertheless, it was a good day. We had identified the source of the blast.

Dr Emile Radakovic.

RADAKOVIC

The office was abuzz with rumours posing as facts and gossip clothing itself as privileged information, the entire lot jacketed in plenty of hearsay, all of which had approximately equal weight under the circumstances. Meaning no one knew quite what to believe.

An emigre by way of Yugoslavia before its collapse, the doctor had resettled in Massachusetts, where he lived and worked for over 22 years, until three years ago when he moved to New York.

His resumé was nothing special, so we were told to work from a theory of foreign agent and fill in the blanks from there. We were given purpose again and our modest taskforce finally felt like an approximation of its old self, absences notwithstanding. You no doubt know his story well, but I don't mind repeating it here: Radakovic had been experimenting in the field of human camouflage for over thirteen years. Top secret military stuff. His diligent research and eventual obsession were attributed to various things—former colleagues insist he was a bit of a pervert whose initial motivation was simply the desire to watch others fornicate from an unseen vantage, but this has since been discredited and expunged from the Movement's history of our beneficent leader.

Despite all those years working alongside Radakovic in the lab, these same colleagues insisted their capabilities were nowhere close to whatever had caused the current catastrophe affecting upwards of four million people. Whatever breakthroughs Radakovic had made, he had left his research partners out of the loop. He was known for taking various chemical compounds home from the lab and testing them on himself in his leisure time. One of these impromptu experiments turned his hair bright green; another had blinded him for the better part of a week; yet another left him almost dead (he ingested a synthesis of strychnine he'd extracted from corn husks and banana skins). Whether he was a genius or a madman seemed open to dispute. Then, around three years ago, he abruptly announced he was quitting his work to move to New York, to live in an apartment he'd inherited. His colleagues were surprised but ultimately wished him well, possibly glad to see the last of him. They'd had no contact with him since.

This obscure origin story didn't explain the mysterious 'blastwave' that had irremediably affected so many millions of souls, and in doing so changed the course of history.

Historians never agree on anything, and most of them weren't present when it happened. Do you want to get into it here? Personally, I like the 'novel chemical element setting off a thermal chain' theory. That's more or less how it felt when I was knocked to the ground: a localised big bang radiating outwards, pulsating through me like heat from a furnace, setting my molecules alight, inducing the radical cellular change that would leave scientists worldwide in a perpetual state of befuddlement. All at once, a new and entirely speculative element entered into existence, Radakovium, atomic number unassigned, electron configuration undetermined. All that was observable was the effect, the uncanny spatial violation, the transgression of physics that turned all known natural laws on their head. No mechanism heretofore known could have achieved all this, and in a single instant, no less. These are all just theories though. Radakovic was never one to share his secrets on our origin. Only on our destiny.

Compare this to the lone wolf theory, the painstaking endeavour of the first invisible man who, over the course of a mere three years, rigged every street corner, ventilation system of every office block and subway with his special recipe of gas, and completed this exhaustive mission undetected? I'll give points to any analysis which duly credits the genius and determination of our saviour and the unprecedented scenario he engendered, but this is a bit much, surely?

Here it is. Radakovic vaporised himself in the blast, and by the time his Promethean potion had evaporated, his particles had passed through our own. We had ingested him, and in a sense, become him. Simple as that.

I texted Sanders with such details as I was able to surmise. He thanked me for my scant updates, advising he too was keeping abreast of developments and, somewhat more cryptically, that "every little piece of the puzzle has meaning." You're doing a good job, Leonard, read one reply. Keep going. Unfamiliar feelings of importance and usefulness swelled in me. Sanders was highly regarded in many departments of the Bureau, not just in our little corner of Human Trafficking. It was only smart to keep on his good side. There would be further opportunities to prove my worth in whatever clandestine enterprise he was running.

Before I could complete the transition to self-appointed double agent, there was another general meeting led by HR and flanked by department heads, most of whom, ironically, lacked heads. They wanted to address the falling dress standards. We represented the federal government, and part of that honour involved presenting ourselves in a professional manner at all times. At no stage should we be showing up to work in just a T-shirt and shorts. Flip-flops were absolutely forbidden. No exceptions. "This is different to the heatwave last year and rest assured we will blast the air conditioning if current trends continue." Meeting adjourned.

It's funny now, the naivety of it all. The Itch was yet to permeate the collective consciousness, though glimpses rose to the surface; every shower and changing of clothes; the briefest caress of naked air on naked skin instantly calling into question the necessity of pants...

***

Sasha and I shared updates after Yolanda went to bed that evening. No other children had joined us yet, Sasha guiltily sending them away. "The army is going to deliver food," said Sasha. "Rations of some sort. On account of all the looting."

"Who told you that?"

"Mac came into the Centre today, was going around to houses, businesses; well, the few that are still open anyhow."

I thought of old Eugene at the deli and mourned for the untimely demise of my daily Reuben. The last one he'd made me hadn't even been that good. That was the real tragedy of it all. Perhaps Sanders' people could rough him up a bit until he got his recipe back on track?

I hungrily considered the prospect, until my train of thought was broken.

"But they said they're going to organise permits for fast food joints, and find a way for them to remain open. With the National Guard on duty at every outlet to maintain order," said Sasha, snapping me back to reality.

Thank God for the Will of the People.

***

News soon went quiet on the Radakovic front in terms of concrete facts, so instead we allowed our imaginations to run wild. We withdrew into the safe bosom of technology in our cubicles, going around in circles looking for clues, answers, cures. It was natural to want to retreat during this adjustment phase, it being one of the main signs of depression. We don't need bodies, people told themselves, we'll live vicariously through the internet, news feeds, television, till this whole thing gets cleared up; by such methods have we been sustained before. Some found comfort knowing Hollywood was in preliminary talks to adapt their struggles for the big screen, immortalising them in both thought-provoking and occasionally mindless ways, as was Tinseltown's wont. That wasn't even taking into consideration what the rest of the mainlanders, the skins, thought of the situation, of us. They were outside the bubble looking in, and boy were they afraid. Message boards lit up with confusion and conditional sympathy, but the discussion would rapidly dissolve into speculation as to the best means of 'taking care' of 'the problem.' Many even suggested following the example of the History Channel's favourite dictator. Sasha would have done just that (the retreating into a fantasy world part—not advocating for another Holocaust) if she didn't have her kids to take care of. More and more were turning up now that school was 'temporarily' suspended.

Devon, her colleague at the Rec Centre, struggled under the weight of it all and kept inferring he wanted to cut loose. Sasha begged him to stay, and he did for the rest of his shift, but then neglected to show up for an entire week.

That's when Sasha asked MacCready for assistance. Whether in the interests of PR or just because he was a good guy, Mac sent over two of his most child-friendly and non-terrifying soldiers to help out with the basketball and some light ad hoc home learning.

When Devon returned without so much as acknowledging his absence, Sasha punched him flush in the face and had to be restrained by Mac's men. The rest of that day she cried.

A few of the older kids worked together to mend the rift between Sasha and Devon. They guided the little ones in crafting a macaroni peace card with doves, their wings made of bow tie pasta. A sweet gesture, if technically in violation of rationing protocol. To his credit, Devon stayed, despite the cold air of Sasha's presence any time she gave him orders. When her trademark pettiness necessitated a second card decorated with uncooked pasta, this time Sasha helped out with the words: Don't you ever leave again, or else...

They fashioned the ellipsis out of gnocchi. I thought that was a nice touch.

***

One day during those first few weeks Janet reported that most, if not all, of the target suspects in her ongoing investigations had disappeared under suspicious circumstances. We'd also forgotten it was her birthday.

"Technically, we've all disappeared," I offered helpfully, though this did not help. She was already cursing the clandestine forces that had taken care of business without her. Halifax was quick to point the finger at Sanders and his rogue posse, complaining that we hadn't done enough to track him down. I hadn't informed either of them of our little rendezvous by the church, so telling them now felt ill-timed.

"He's running around like Colonel Kurtz out there. As if things aren't chaotic enough as it is!" Halifax barked.

Unwilling to openly defend Sanders, I conceded we

could spend the day checking out the reported hotspots of Janet's targets, and when Janet mentioned an address within walking distance, I noted that Carmen's Cakes and Pastries, her favourite, was right around there. Could stop in after we take a look. This cheered Janet, only to set her up for more misery, as we soon discovered that Carmen's had been set alight during a small-scale riot along Mulberry Street. What remained was the charred skeleton of a store in which a half-mad woman, presumably Carmen, was busily trading what little undamaged stock she had left in exchange for medical supplies and marijuana, if you had any.

Janet appropriated a muffin with an authoritative badge-flash and ate half before simply dropping the rest on the ground like a petulant child. This was a woman who in her free time, led initiatives to clean up local parks, and whose desk was habitually neat almost to a fault. The drop in her standards inwardly appalled me, but as it was her birthday, and only a few weeks ago I had literally stepped over the corpse of a murdered cashier without saying or doing anything, I decided to let it slide.

I tried to arrest this dip in mood, telling Janet we'd get lucky with her cases, but she told me to shut it. Don't say anything till we get there. How unfortunate that Janet's birthday had clearly coincided with her time of the month.

My vague assurances not having the desired effect, I then busied myself for the next several minutes trying to figure out the difference between a muffin and a cupcake. I should have asked the half-mad Carmen when I had the chance, but she seemed preoccupied, sitting there amid the smouldering ruins of her lost livelihood, shedding invisible tears, her shoulders heaving up and down in torment.

Never mind, I would just google it later.

FACT CHECK: Muffins differ from Cupcakes in the ingredient and mixing process, with cupcake batter beaten significantly longer to create a consistent fluffy inside, while Muffins are sparsely beaten to make for a densely baked good. The amount of butter and sugar is higher in Cupcakes. Cupcakes tend to have frosting, while muffins often already have a variety of additions eg. dried fruit, chocolate, to complement the taste.

Tattered police tape surrounded the second of Janet's potential hotspots, a rug store in the Upper East Side whose shutters were now riddled with bullet holes.

Enquiries with a local in Middle Eastern garb sat smoking on a nearby stoop confirmed our suspicions.

"Six men wearing SWAT uniform came rushing out of van, into store. I hear lot of screaming, then shooting—rah rah rah" —he mimed the gunfire for us in heavily accented English. "When they finish, they leave in a big rush. Just like that."

"Rah-rah-rah," I repeated, as I pretend-jotted in my notebook. "'Just. Like. That.' Got it."

I apologised to Janet that we came all the way up here for bad news and suggested we should have tried calling the local PD first.

This prompted a tirade from Janet, which, given it was her birthday and she was obviously in a bit of a mood, I felt compelled to take without comment.

"So, what, they can identify the bodies? Check the DNA? See—SEE if they can identify dental records? Are they going to spray paint the teeth? See if they can find a match? ... What fucking use is any of it anymore?"

She went on some more, then broke into a sob. "I mean, there was so much I wanted to do... so much left... I wanted to get married. Have kids... Climb fucking Mt Kilimanjaro! This isn't fixing itself, Leonard. They can't even cure damn cold sores!"

"You can still do those things, maybe, and some people, the blind for instance, will never see their kids," I offered for perspective.

This antidote proving ineffectual, Janet gave a wail and plopped down onto the ground in the middle of the street, ready and willing to be roadkill for the few cars (mostly military) that still had places to be.

Thinking about Janet's future made me also consider my own. There was no Mrs. Walcott. My skirt-chasing years were long behind me, and comparatively few had been chased in retrospect. None had stuck around for all that long. One even suggested I was too close with my half-sister, intimating that it weirded her out. Somewhere along the line my interest in the fairer sex had waned, and I hadn't bothered going about getting it back.

But now that it was supposedly the end of the road, I was angry at the world for taking away what I had given up so easily.

I considered trying it on with Janet, thinking perhaps

it could cheer both of us up. It had been a while since I'd propositioned someone, so I paused momentarily before finally deciding this may not be received well either. Janet might think I was only making my move now that our blemishes were safely hidden from view; a partial truth. So the sex in the middle of the road did not proceed, likely for the best.

Dwindling libido or no, the fact I was willing to consider fucking Janet in the middle of a public street in broad daylight was probably a sign my dry spell required urgent attention. Given the apocalyptic fever currently gripping the city, not to mention the prevailing air of moral relativism, there was bound to be an orgy or two taking place somewhere. I resolved to investigate the matter further.

As we made our way back to the office, we encountered a woman dancing in the middle of Union Square. All we could make out of her was her necklace and the gold bangles on her wrists, shimmering in the sunlight as she twisted and gyrated.

"Try it!" she called to the few onlookers. "It feels fantastic. I'm free!"

Her discarded clothes formed a rough circle around her performance space. She was humming and singing softly to herself as she moved, lost in private reverie. "I never felt anything like this before," she kept saying. "Never, never, never."

She gave a little pirouette, then yelped with unbridled glee.

"Are you finding clothes a little... uncomfortable these days?" I enquired of Janet, not taking my eyes off the spectral dancer.

"Now that you mention it..." she replied, absentmindedly scratching at the skin under her collar.

HEDONISM

Your typical sex dungeons and brothels in this brave new world did not spawn out of the blue, though a few did emerge later on when the Movement and its followers sprung up like flowers ready to pollinate. They were more organised than that, being built from legitimate sadomasochistic businesses that paid their taxes and already had the infrastructure in place for ambient hedonism. Working in Human Trafficking meant our department was familiar with these haunts. Some of the longer-standing agents were even required to go undercover as Johns from time to time, a role that historically had not suffered from a shortage of volunteers.

At any rate, even though dealing with these places and this industry in a professional capacity was arguably what blunted my primal urges in the first place, I thought it best to reenter the realm of sexual exploration carefully and under the guidance of professionals. My destination that night was a lovely little establishment in Soho. I felt no shame in walking in but was shocked to find the waiting room filled with men with only their pants on, and one guy who had dispensed with pants entirely in favour of a polka-dot neckerchief. The nice lady at the counter said they were fully booked for the rest of the week.

"What can I say? It's been a game changer. A revolution

84

of feeling, sounds, touch—the complete loss of inhibitions. People simply don't know where they begin or end anymore. It's all so new, and endlessly titillating."

"Logistically though, isn't it a nightmare, figuring out what goes where?" I asked her, surprised I was engaging in philosophical discourse with the receptionist of a brothel.

"That's part of the fun," said one of the waiting topless clientele, his deep voice lending a resonant wisdom to his perversion—he was clearly an old hand at these sorts of things.

I put my name down for the following week but had already half-resigned to cancel, the scene in the waiting room causing discomfort to glide down to my stomach rather than blood to my member.

Leaving, I decided that maybe I needed to alter my levels of sobriety before attending further to my nascent sexual awakening. I entered the first drinking establishment I passed, a tropical-themed upstairs joint tucked away at the top of a narrow stairway, pumping out thumping beats.

I hadn't been to places like these in almost a decade, especially not on a weekday afternoon. When I finally ascended to the sunless den and its doof doof music I was greeted almost instantly with offers of ecstasy and cocaine by the voice of some rambunctious entrepreneur. How encouraging. For the first time in a long time, I didn't look like a tired, lonely office grunt with greying hair and a bald patch. I was a blank slate, nameless, ageless, identity-less, to these people. Stripped of baggage, no longer saddled with the cloying air of stale desperation, I could be anything I wanted to be, do things I wouldn't normally dream of doing.

I accepted the young entrepreneur's ecstasy pill and went to the bar for a beer, the line busy with chatter, and the bar staff seemingly heavily inebriated themselves. When I was eventually able to order a pilsener, I washed down the ecstasy tablet before finding a seat to watch the youth celebrate the end of life as they knew it. Bits of clothes grinded up against one another, kept on only for the sake of finding one's bearings, to better suck on the supple neck of their counterpart. I nodded my head in time to the music, and actually felt like a part of it.

When the drugs kicked in and the DJ mixed it up with some early De La Soul I subbed in from the sidelines. I promptly bumped into Tiffany, a short thing with a big booty. She was a senior at NYU, studying finance, originally from Philly.

"Excuse me!" I shouted over the music, in the direction of her earrings. "I didn't mean to bump into you."

"Are you black?" she asked me.

"Do I sound black?"

"Yes. And older." I was mildly deflated. So much for turning over a new leaf on the dating front. I thought the jig was up.

"I like black guys," she said, taking me by the hand, "especially if they're older. That just means you have experience."

She led me over to a sofa in the corner and believe it or not we began copulating right then and there, protection and prying eyes be damned.

What did it feel like to touch an invisible, you may ask.

The Guard skins swore holy sensations, hairs raising on the back of necks. Repatriation Day, I know the relatives gushed at the feel. Hot commodity of experience in the outside world. *I touched one of them. What did it feel like, Reggie? Like nothing else.* They played it up, let it spin grander and grander.

Felt pretty normal when we touched one another, ghost to ghost. Surprise, but an understanding. Acceptance. A truce with the strangeness of it all.

Afterward, she showed me pictures of herself, all done up with dark flowing hair and these rosy cheeks, as if to inform me of what I'd just enjoyed. I feigned the appropriate measure of interest, finding it weird that I didn't actually care what she looked like, just that her skin felt soft and her vagina was wet and it was good to connect with someone, no matter how odd the circumstances. Weren't you supposed to care what a person looked like? Whether they had a hooked nose or weirdly spaced eyes or a monobrow? I no longer did.

Tiffany then appeared to dip into some kind of depressive lull as she scrolled further back through her old posts. She began to sob quietly, so I did the gentlemanly thing and put a reassuring post-coital arm around her. Tiffany poured out all her deepest fears and anxieties, much like Janet had done earlier whilst lying in the middle of the street. She was so young, where was she to go from here? What kind of future was even possible? She'd been applying for internships all over the place. Now what? What was going to happen to the financial hub that was New York? Would Manhattan itself eventually be destroyed? Would the army bomb us to smithereens, douse us with nerve gas, wipe us off the face of the map out of their fear of becoming infected? What kind of life was she looking at, the aspirations inked on her 5-year plan curling under the flames of uncertainty, her hopes and visions extinguished?

With MDMA massaging my brain, I did my best to allay her fears.

"Your life isn't over, you're still doing new things—for instance, I'm pretty sure you haven't done that before."

"Oh, no," she demurred. "I've fucked plenty of guys I just met. You're not even the first guy tonight."

I couldn't hear her properly over the music, so I just nodded.

"That's right. Look, don't feel bad—it was my first time having sex with someone I couldn't see too, but I'm just saying it's not over yet. I work at the FBI! And we're figuring it out RIGHT NOW and this isn't some accident— it's all part of some grand design. Maybe even the start of something new and wonderful that we can't see the beauty of just yet. Don't give up hope. This all happened for a reason, I'm telling you!"

"You really think so?"

I awkwardly leaned in and eventually found her lips. "I know so."

I'm a great liar.

***

The average National Guard member has a height of 5'8", an age of 29, a decent chance of having been deployed to either Iraq or Afghanistan, and works a full-time civilian job. The 'One weekend a month, two weeks a year' slogan was finally starting to contain a kernel of truth after that ugly extended jaunt in the Middle East, then everything went pear-shaped again, thanks to an elusive Slavic genius. Nothing could have prepared them for the miasma of soul-crushing PTSD that would follow, cross-pollinated with the inescapable paranoia of being surrounded by voices whose precise location they could never quite pinpoint, not to mention the nightmares of thermal heat blobs running maniacally in their direction.

The battalion of VA psychologists attending to the Guard Soldiers after they were done babysitting us found the word to best describe their sullen, thousand-yard stares was, funnily enough, the same term the Guard used for us: ghosts.

MacCready and his men were eating dinner in the cafeteria of James Earl High. Their jovial banter stopped abruptly when they noticed I'd entered—still high on MDMA, no less.

MacCready was at the head of the table, positioned like the school principal. He was suitably welcoming, as ever, and apologised for the overt tension in the air. Most of those eating in the converted mess hall paused what they were doing to observe, to see what this apparition wanted, their forks suspended in mid-air. The hostility was palpable.

"Maybe we should speak in my office instead."

"Sorry about that. I'm trying to get them to be more friendly," he said, as soon as the door closed. "But they have their doubts. Some of them won't even leave the barracks without their goggles."

"This is a school, MacCready." I reminded him.

"Yes," he deferred, "of course."

"And you're supporting American citizens..."

He shook his head ruefully. "I know. You're right. Drink?" he offered.

I stayed perfectly still. One of the many techniques we invisibles would learn to employ in order to unsettle the skins. To make some attempt to correct the power imbalance inherent in the circumstances thrust upon us. An empty suit of clothes, staring, scaring.

"We have water, tea, coffee, whisky?" he fired off into the silence.

"We don't require the intake of fluids anymore," I pronounced ominously. "Our skin absorbs all the nutrients we need directly from the air."

"Oh, is that so?" he asked with genuine interest, and I watched his eyes, ears, cheeks and lips try to conceal a sense of naivety and mistrust, not wanting to be taken for a fool.

"Nah. Just something I read in Newsweek."

MacCready's shoulders relaxed, and he sought some water to better stomach the dryness in the air. I meanwhile pulled up a chair and made my feet comfy on top of his desk.

After taking a big gulp, MacCready spoke again. "This is far from ideal, for any of us. I can only imagine what people in your predic—I mean, situation, are going through. But let me assure, we're working hard on pushing integration, debunking some of those rumours you allude to, countering certain... myths that may have arisen."

I made a little pyramid out of my fingers, and rested it on my pursed lips. Not that he could see the gesture, but it still made me feel pensive, wise. "I totally understand. I appreciate the work you're doing, and the way you're going about it. That's actually why I stopped by. I wanted to thank you and your men for helping out Sasha and the kids over at the Rec Centre. They speak highly of you and your people."

MacCready's eyes lit up at the mention of Sasha. "Oh, so you're Sasha's brother! Leonard, with the FBI. Of course! Sasha is really lovely. Gutsy. Truly inspiring what she's doing, keeping it all together for the sake of those youngsters. Just the kind of person we need to ensure our community doesn't completely implode. Keeping the kids engaged and out of trouble has been quite the challenge, I gather. Children are difficult enough to look after when you can actually see them."

I laughed at his little joke, even though it wasn't as funny as my one about us no longer requiring fluids to live.

"And the teenagers, that's a whole other story," he continued. "There's been a lot of trouble in the parks. Skirmishes, robberies. Organised fight clubs too, if you can believe it. Some where they paint themselves up beforehand, and fight completely native."

"Truly barbaric," I remarked, staying outwardly calm, even as a sudden urge to undress took hold. His mention of going native had stirred something in me. I shifted uncomfortably in my seat.

"No, no, that's not what I'm saying," he backpedalled. "It's understandable; kids that age pushing boundaries, even boundaries we didn't even know existed. They're just being young, letting off steam, angst. We try to keep that in mind."

I barely registered what he said. The pins and needles pricked all along me. If I didn't get my shirt and trousers off soon I would start screaming like a banshee. I had to wrap this up and remain professional. It was critical that, here of all places, in the lion's den, I exuded the confidence befitting a resourceful, powerful FBI agent.

"Well, I'm grateful for your time Captain, and I'm sorry to have interrupted your dinner. One last thing I wanted to add—I'd like to help, in any way I can. We have resources at the FBI that I can put at your disposal, and I personally have experience infiltrating and conducting surveillance on various... groups, and gangs... and..."

I leapt out of my chair like it was on fire, startling poor MacCready.

"...I trust you will reciprocate such attentiveness when it comes to ensuring the safety of Sasha and the little rapscallions at the Greens Athletic."

"Of course!" MacCready nodded profusely. "We're here to help, and I'm personally grateful for your offer."

The Itch subsiding as quick as it came, I felt calm enough to offer a parting compliment. "You're definitely one of the good guys, Macklin. Say, did you know you look like that actor, Brendan Gleeson? The Irish one. Younger, of course.

"Yes," he said. "I get that. The accent puts people off

though." He chuckled nervously.

"What did you look like?" he returned the courtesy, unsure if he was causing offence, sweating on the tense of 'did'.

I cracked a grin a mile wide. "I looked like Denzel fucking Washington."

Cool, calm and professional.

> FACT CHECK: Leonard Walcott, pre-transformation, did not resemble Denzel Washington, pre-transformation.

MORA

I didn't finish telling you what happened with Tiffany. We exchanged numbers after our couch tryst, at her insistence, no less. She was operating under the assumption I had important departmental connections, inside lines on food and supplies not available to the general public, an assumption I admit I helped to foster via a series of vague half-truths. My luck with women had improved considerably now that they couldn't tell what I looked like. Just as I was thinking this new world wasn't all bad, some fellow reveller, emboldened by the heady liquor of anonymity (as well as by actual liquor), took the occasion to relieve himself in the corner not two feet from where we were seated. Kind of a mood-killer.

The unmistakable aroma of piss flooded our nostrils with all the subtlety of ammonia salts; the overbearing fragrance of societal implosion. Stinging. Inescapable. A chorus of boos and ewww's and "that's nasty" erupted from those nearby. The culprit just laughed shamelessly, shaking himself dry. Who could foretell that such occurrences would soon become the norm?

This proved too much for Tiffany. She promised she would call.

You know what they used to say. Those wild rumours that ghosts produce extra odour to make up for the fact

94

that they can't be seen. And that they deliberately abstain from showering in order to locate each other via their heightened olfactory prowess. The human equivalent of decorated airport sniffer dogs.

Reports from skins, civil through to military, declared we did in fact smell. And of course we did—we were still human after all. It was spring and we were blooming. But you can't tell me the loosening work ethic from 'New York's Strongest', the overworked garbage men and women, played no part in proceedings. Once the collections came less and less and the streets overflowed with wrappers, plastic bags, cans and stale muffins, we blended right into the environment. Got more than used to the scent.

I used to have a whole cabinet dedicated to avoiding my natural odour, but as the steadfast Radakovic would note: We are all the smells now, we are the wood of the timber finish, the tar of the pavement, the mustard on dollar hot dogs, the air of absence and where the wind blows, our stench is not that of the individual, but of the collective. A whole city, melting into one. The more Manhattan stunk like the downtrodden and desperate, the more it became ours, not theirs. Our big Island with its own personal musk. Perfect for moving around unnoticed, unsmelt.

* * *

If you thought the pre-Radakovic government had a hard-on for surveillance and invasion of privacy, the intrinsic peculiarities of our new lifestyle eventually proved an NSA wet dream. Funding proceeded with a blank cheque, new legislation passed without protest, and before long they had drones, phone taps, bugs, double and triple agents, continuous cyber monitoring—all the tools of the trade installed and upgraded and dedicated entirely to us. They would be damned if communication between potential dissidents could occur outside the bounds of their digital panopticon, their omnipresent surveillance apparatus.

They didn't trust us one bit, and weren't shy about letting us know it.

But one thing they and other members of the ruling autocracy seemed to miss was a small pamphlet stapled to the Community noticeboard of a cleaned out Walgreens in The East Village. I happened to walk past one afternoon, whether as a matter of fate or out of simple chance I couldn't say. A grainy black and white leaflet, barely the size of an envelope, inviting interested citizens to meet at a yoga studio to discuss how to become invisible. A joke of some kind, surely? Had we not already achieved that state which the leaflet was touting?

This is the part you've been waiting for. The solution to my current predicament—our predicament, I mean. We were all in this together, after all. A glimmer of hope that hinted at salvation, found in a yoga studio above a phone repair shop on St Marks Place.

I showed up just before the time specified on the pamphlet. A queue was already forming on the staircase, which led to a bright green door. After several minutes, the green door opened from the inside by hands unseen, and we filed in, a ragtag assortment of curiosity seekers from all walks of life.

Rows of plastic chairs faced a mirrored wall. We each took a seat, and before long the modest-sized studio was full. A few wore gym gear, and several had brought yoga mats, evidently assuming we would be taking a class. Most present were, like myself, dressed in smart casual, scratching and making awkward attempts at small talk. It felt more like an AA meeting than anything else. No one seemed quite sure what to expect.

There were around fifteen of us at this first gathering. Once all the seats were filled, the door was closed, again by hands unseen, then the gentle patter of footsteps indicated this same presence positioning itself in front of the wall of mirrors.

This was Mora. She took a purple shawl off a nearby table and draped it around her shoulders, so we could at least have a focal point for the duration of the talk. At the appropriate moment, the shawl, like whatever clothes we happened to be wearing, would be cast adrift.

"Greetings, friends," she said, "and thank you for being here."

She spoke slowly and deliberately, with a calming authority. Her melodious intonations rippled out into the room; the gentle, life-changing waves easing their way into our collective consciousness. I was enamoured from the moment I heard her. My tryst with the finance student had awakened something long-dormant in me, but it was more than just that. Once she spoke, there was a sort of clarity to the madness around us. Behind her tone, there was purpose.

Her name was Mora Kelly. A yoga instructor in her mid-thirties who, like many of us, grieved for the loss of the body and the life that once was. And in the darkness and despair of these days, she asked herself the same question we all did. Why? Why had this happened? But unlike the rest of us, she actually found the answer.

Here's the monologue, as best as I recall it:

I was in the middle of getting divorced.

We had lived in Queens. When our skin dissolved, I was alone in my studio. This studio. No more than six blocks from Radakovic's apartment.

This was my home for the next few days, as I pondered, worried, cried, prayed like the rest of you. When the last of my food ran out, I went hungry. This is before they started handing out rations. Classes were cancelled, as you might imagine. And then, the first of the month came. Didn't matter what had transpired, the landlord came for his rent. I didn't have any money, didn't have much of anything at that point. He told me what he wanted. I threatened to call the police, or a lawyer, but he just laughed. Said he'd put me out on the street if I didn't comply. There was no one to call, no one could help me. Finally, in utter desperation... I gave in. Got on my knees like he ordered. It was sleazy, degrading. Disgusting. I shut off my thoughts, and my mind went somewhere else. I didn't want to be there and most of me wasn't. Funny enough, of all possible moments, that's when it hit me. There was a reason for this invisibility, a will behind it. A purpose. And the only way to know it, find it, was to surrender entirely to the reality of it. What was the use of undergoing such a radical transformation of the body, if the mind and soul did not follow?

The landlord finally buckled his pants up and left, and I got to work. Explored this notion further as I tried to get the taste out of my mouth and showered in that small bathroom just over there. And what I found when I focused on this particular thought, was that I felt stripped back, naked, the way we all felt our first shower after the event.

I stopped struggling... let go of my control freak's hold on reality... surrendered completely to an understanding higher than mine... doors began to open in the inner world... I didn't attempt comprehension... and so it came it to me: a sublime state of peace and intuition that had eluded me forever, its fingertips caressing my soul... and once it arrived, it stayed for good. I learned how to hold on to it by letting go.

At this stage most of those present, including myself, shuffled slightly in our chairs or leaned forward with a twinge of recognition.

That's when I broke through all the pain and fear of this world, and truly became something else. Connected. To everything, and nothing at all.

I wanted to start out small, just share the technique with friends, like-minded seekers, make sure I wasn't crazy, as if what we've all experienced these past weeks could make us anything but... I can describe it to you. But I'd rather show you...

99

It emerged there were two requisite steps to achieving this enlightened state, this inner sanctum of total acceptance, that made one feel incomprehensibly as light as air itself. This, according to the calmest one in the room, was how a person truly disappeared. She had everyone move the chairs to one side and stand. The shedding of clothes was highly encouraged (a handful of those attending had already pre-empted her on this point).

Step one: Become so small in size, weight, thought, that you felt no larger than the size of a molecule, your entire consciousness shrinking, until finally it was so minute it could balance on the head of a pin. Then go smaller. Hold it there.

Step two: expand back up again, unfurling like a leisurely big bang. Release. Become so large in size, weight, thought, that you slowly expanded in all directions and became one with the universe around you.

Close your eyes. hold your breath. Be as still as possible. Feel yourself shrinking, the universe filling into the space that once held you. Release. Count backwards from 20. I want you to think of yourself changing, vanishing, and being OK with it. Let it take you wherever you need to go. Now, open your eyes.

I made it as far as the count of six. I remember smirking as I closed my eyes. Smug. Certain that nothing untoward or otherworldly would occur.

As my consciousness expanded, I was no longer in the studio. I was at home some thirty or more years ago, lying on the carpet with my hands running along a checkers board spilled of its pieces. A warm autumn day from long ago. I couldn't tell you who chose this moment, nor its significance, only that I recall the peace of the memory as one that had crept up on me and clearly left an impression.

My atoms inhabited every nook and cranny of that memory. An out of body experience, taking place in a long-forgotten corner of the universe.

Blink.

I am back in the studio. I am light as air. No sound. I am space.

There's no time to look around. I only have time to realise I have become everything else. Saturated within the moment.

Blink.

Finished.

Deep breaths. The sound of everyone returning from their own form of astral flight. We exist once more. Soon enough there is laughter, peal upon peal of gleeful, ringing laughter. Healing.

That was the beginning of a brief, intoxicating interlude of my life where I actually believed in something. It didn't last, but it sure was something else.

We had many questions.

She answered them, candidly, to the best of her ability. She didn't have all the answers yet. But one thing she was adamant about was that it be referred to simply as 'the Method'. The Method was a way of holding on, and simultaneously letting go. This experience, she concluded, was the true gift of Radakovic.

I waited patiently. When no one was looking, I tried it again. The entire universe shrinking down into one little particle, before voila...

There I was, back on the carpet thirty years prior, inspecting the surreal components of this dream, squeezing a red checker piece between my fingers, proving its solid state until I was satisfied.

I opened my eyes once more, to find my soul encapsulating the room like an out-of-body experience while the conversations with Mora continued apace. I was unsure how long I stayed this way, ten, twenty seconds perhaps—but I was certain it was longer than the first, and became excited by the promise of further tangible improvement.

Re-entry to the mundane world of form was jarring in its disappointment. Mora was wrapping up pleasantries by the front door, seeing her thankful guests out, and I the returned astronaut learning to accept gravity again. When I got her alone, I enumerated my earthly credentials in a torrent of uncontrolled desperate gratitude. I'm with the FBI. I can be this and that and this to you. If you need anything, I will be at your complete service.

Mora already knew what she wanted. Information on Radakovic. If there was a key to truly unlocking the deeper meaning of all this, he'd surely be the one to hold it. We were his creations, after all, and the Method which Mora had chanced upon was the culmination of his life's work. I promised to provide her with copies of our files by the next day. I also took the time to warn against her spreading knowledge of this newfound shortcut to enlightenment too widely.

"You will definitely, definitely, attract unwanted attention from the authorities over all this, and I can't guarantee they'll be as enamoured with you and the Method as I am."

She appeared unperturbed. In her mind, the more people saw the unbridled truth, and the more people experienced that spiritual fever fit, that delirious rush of holiness, the more they'd accept their lot and come to understand precisely what there was to be gained by it.

That kind of freedom was catching.

THE MOVEMENT

What happened next was that I told a lot of lies. Little lies in order to deflect; big lies in order to mould.

To lay the foundations of a brave new world. A world full of hope.

What was my primary motivation for all this deceit? Always the question they ask. You're no doubt wondering yourself. Had I become an idealist, a staunch believer in the new cause? Had I fallen desperately in love with Mora, like so many of her other acolytes? Or was I simply trying to weave myself into the grand scheme of the cosmos?

No matter the motivation, my intention was never to cause harm.

The cycle went like this. Every few days Mora summoned me to her yoga studio for private counsel. There, after an intimate celebration of the Method, I would provide information about Radakovic; some factual, some speculative, and some downright fanciful, and together we would sift through it, looking for kernels of useful truth. She would often ask questions, technical ones. Like how Radakovic funnelled the presumed gaseous agent over so widespread an area with no dilution in its potency, why it had been unable to pass the waters of the Hudson and Harlem Rivers, how it had permeated every crevice and corridor and duct and airway of Manhattan before dissipating just as enigmatically. I rehashed the prevailing news reports and added a bit of flavour to lend the appearance of an inside scoop. Radakovic was not alone, according to these early reports; he had a team, a ragtag bunch of apostles who helped dispense the mystery gas across the city. They'd been planning this for years; we even found one of their passports in a drain next to one of the alleged dispersal points.

And then when the big blast theory came into prominence, that of the loner Radakovic setting off his mystery bomb with its single point of origin and supernaturally selective spread of devastation, gone were my twelve apostles, the 'Invisible Twelve' as the media had dubbed them. Their stories discarded wholly and without question, never to be mentioned again.

When Mora asked why he had not left a plan, detailed instructions on how to reach this elusive nirvana, or other as yet undiscovered abilities, I told her most of his notes were eradicated by the explosion at his apartment—an accident, as it happened, an unintended alchemical by-product which forced his grand plan to be enacted in somewhat slapdash fashion—but that we were currently piecing together what little remained.

She asked if I could retrieve for her a fragment, a memento, from the scene; a relic to revere. Of course, I said, wondering how advanced Sasha's kids were at arts and crafts.

Following these top secret, partly improvised debriefings

from myself, Mora would fill in her growing audience, by then appearing for scheduled sessions every second day. Enlightenment could technically be achieved anywhere, but they enjoyed rehearsing it with Mora, and with each other. There was an in-group sensibility present in these spiritual awakenings, a feeling of close-knit togetherness, that counteracted the strangeness and hostility of the world outside. This was how I got to know the rest of Mora's inner circle and quickly joined its deliberations as a trusted source of Radakovic wisdoms from my role as a government insider. There was Peter and Yvonne, tenured academic professors of NYU in history and psychology respectively, and regulars of Mora's studio. Mora deferred to them first and foremost. Then Douglas, Wendy, Parvin, Bella, Lorne, Vasquez, Gomez, Ryoku—Doug and Wendy already friends with Mora, the others simply hooked by that first session.

We had an electric time together uncovering this beautiful new world. Oh, how I miss those days.

When word of the group spread, the NSA, CIA and various international alphabet agencies (as well as a handful of unfortunate foreign spies caught in the quarantine) promptly hastened to infiltrate our space. Government agents quickly flocked to these impromptu meetings, undercovers infiltrating the burgeoning meditation groups (or as they termed them, 'fermenting dissident terror cells'). These intruders listened to Mora's tales of Radakovic, and her philosophical speculations as to the nature of our shared affliction. So, when it came time to undress and join in the wonder of the Method, it felt rude not to partake.

An unfortunate casualty of this renewed vigour in the hunt for Radakovic and his co-conspirators was Sasha's hope for the reunion of her charges with their legal guardians. While myths persisted of sexual transmission when skins coupled with invisibles, the CDC officially deemed the affliction non-contagious by the end of the first month since the Transformation. No one was suggesting an immediate dismantling of the quarantine, but the substantial protests made by residents cut off from their homes and loved ones were gaining traction in the media, and even the mayor conceded a formal process of repatriation was unavoidable.

But the frenzy engendered by the confusion surrounding the source of the outbreak, and the resultant alarm inspired by headlines regarding the rogue Russian scientist and his disciples, quickly put paid to any talk of lifting the quarantine.

Sasha was devastated, and I knew better than to tell her who had helped plant those imaginative fables swirling around Manhattan's terrorist-turned-saviour. I'll admit now I had gotten a little carried away with my role of myth-maker.

"How much longer can I do this?" Sasha grinded her axe. "How long can we live like this? I don't want to become some fucking rooftop soybean farmer or a surrogate mother to forty struggling kids."

"You can do it for as long as it takes. Those kids need you, Sash."

"And you need to catch this asshole, so those kids can see their parents again."

"I promise I will. We're close. You just need to hang in there."

I am not a sociopath. I just did what I had to do. You don't know Sasha like I do. And in the next part of our story, you cannot deny the good that came of my tales—what hope they gave, for the brief moment my version of reality was true.

The MLM-like growth of the Movement was simple. Mora instructed the 'inner circle' all ten of us, to be fruitful and multiply. The technique of obtaining this secret bliss, the transcendence of all earthly cares, was now ours to share with an unbelieving world. Mora tasked us with teaching the Method en masse to others, in the few spaces still free from government surveillance. At my urging, we stuck with 'word of mouth' to shield our identities and build loyalty through the personal gratification of being on the inside of a well-kept secret. You do not talk about fight club, so they say.

I heard of one class being organised in the lunchroom of the Target on Union Square; another in the basement of a bar where men used to bare-knuckle box. Churches, synagogues and mosques were the last places to fall, but fall they did. I recused myself from leading any sort of group lessons, to maintain a low profile as I was still technically working for the FBI, but I happily offered Feng's former hideout above the fishmonger as a suitable teaching space, once I checked it was secure.

Each class drew in swathes of curious invisibles, those who had heard or read about the gift from their friends, practised it unaided at home, in their showers, in their beds and heads. There came an excitement in the aftermath of discovery that had to be shared, discussed, the many wonders of the Method expounded in rapturous tones of adoration. Nudity was encouraged at these gatherings, with clothing recommended only because it aided in the logistics of reaching one's designated meeting.

The prominence of the Method increased concurrently with growing acknowledgement of the Itch, which sceptical skins continued to decry as a convenient excuse for us to remain in various states of undress. The Itch, Mora had me confirm, was far from being a sin, and was in fact nothing less than a direct sign from Radakovic we were moving away from outdated puritanical notions around bodily awareness, towards a New Age of self-acceptance and love.

Naturally, it was prudent for the outside world to blame the Itch on the Method, timelines of discovery be damned.

It was a problem of ideology. If the government was trying to restore control with vast allocations of taxpayer resources, then it wouldn't do for the populace to instead be following some mystical renegade in a new and subversive spiritual movement. Once the wider media outlets reported on these meetups, and on the implications of the Method itself, pity turned to anger. *How dare these ungrateful citizens flaunt this new way of life! I always knew they couldn't be trusted! Freeloaders! Degenerates!* Conservative pundits suggested the Method was actually a gateway to the demonic, socialist realm, a deliberate rejection of the godly staples of church and capitalism.

To help ensure their integrity, undercover government agents were asked to make a formal pledge of allegiance each morning following their briefing, and comms were distributed, penned by General Bracken himself, about the need to avert the Method, as if they would grow blind in its wake and forget they were foremost patriots. Salary packages increased once again, to remind us of the power of the greenback and the American way. They strongly encouraged undercover agents not to actually try the Method, but rather use their imagination as to exactly what it might involve. Puff, but don't inhale.

The undercover cop who attended my class at Feng's bullet-riddled hideout sought me out quickly. I picked him straight away, noticing the uncomfortable rigidness in the way he unbuttoned his shirt and dropped his pants. Much more stiffly than a typical first timer. After class, I told him I was operating under a multiplicity of guises: infiltration, assessing potential smuggling networks in and out of the Island. I also told him to actually try the Method, just once, so he wouldn't stick out like the biggest narc in history.

His eyes widened. "Just once?"

"Just once."

He was reluctant at first, his daily pledge of allegiance having been uttered a mere two hours prior, though ultimately he was swayed by the fact I was a senior agent, and that clearly the Method hadn't yet done me any visible harm.

Afterwards, I told the class leader, Lorne, to monitor him, but I needn't have bothered; that pledge of allegiance soon became mere lip service, his true sense of being and purpose finding their ultimate expression via the forbidden fruit of the Method.

The Movement. That's what they called our gatherings. Stroke of genius, calling it that. Where were we going exactly? Where did we exist when we practised the Method, when we were under its thrall? What did we come back as? What changes did it effect in the blood, and in the mind? The Method was showing the way, moving us in directions the rest of the world wasn't altogether sure we should be heading.

The Movement gained followers from all walks of life on the Island. Former CEOs, hobos, celebrities, Republicans, Democrats, all found solace in its unvarnished revelation of the Method. We'd invented a new wheel that only we could see. And yet, despite widespread popularity and the whispers of their names on the tip of everyone's tongues, neither Mora nor her inner circle spoke publicly, or revealed themselves in the media; for it so happened that Radakovic himself extolled the virtues of silent, mysterious leadership (with the added-value of those still working their government job maintaining their anonymity). Whether she'd taken my specific advice of keeping herself hidden for safety reasons, I cannot say, but am glad precautions were being taken.

Halifax, for his part, remained doggedly focused on hunting Sanders. He had the option of a relative's loft, as well as quarters offered by the National Guard, but I'm certain he never made use of them. Janet believed our superior was mostly living in his office. Janet believed correctly. It allowed him to endlessly monitor the situation with relentless paranoia. Great for keeping the mind focused on the task at hand: Sanders, the elusive star pupil who'd broken the spirit of his proud leader. With all this buzz and chatter about the Movement and its potential ties to Radakovic I'd fed back to the department, there was a good chance of Sanders being corrupted, Halifax reminded us. Of turning to the dark side.

Janet suggested Halifax take the weekend off. At the very least a longer lunch down at the convoys of food trucks lining the street, a mishmash of soldiers handing out MREs and bread.

"What day is it?" he asked.

"It's Tuesday."

"Well, it's not the weekend then, is it?"

"No. But you didn't take the last one."

"See! That's what I mean. It doesn't matter what day it is. They're all the same."

Janet gave up. Halifax's descent into madness wasn't her responsibility, nor was it her job to remind him to shower. Her job, much like mine, was to provide daily updates on Sanders' presumed whereabouts, a personal assignment that may well have benefited from a cost-benefit analysis of the assigner's current mental condition.

The other place where our routine and duties converged: down at the Chelsea Piers, which had swiftly returned to its roots as a port, and even converted the driving range into a miniature container yard (to the uproar of all keen golfers on the Island). Day and night, an endless stream of commercial vessels, importing permitted luxuries for the wealthy, under the watchful eyes of the CBP. Here we tasked ourselves with identifying and closing any potential escape routes into the free and rapidly deteriorating landscape of the rest of the country. Janet became fond of the Hudson breeze as she assessed the processes and procedures of this new supply channel, the inspection of paperwork in a new location seeming to really do it for her.

But of course, no one was escaping anymore. The only Movement we needed was right here.

Janet's idea of killing two birds with one stone was to report that neither Sanders nor his potential new higher power, Radakovic, had left the Island. This would ease our manic boss's obsession whilst simultaneously adhering to her preferred duty of monitoring people smuggling routes. She had noted, with disdain, the growing presence of representatives of the wealthy and famous getting awfully chummy with the CBP as they received their bosses fancy imports. "These rich elites praise the Movement, yet still need their designer wear," she complained to me. "Next thing you know, they'll probably ask the CBP to let them take their yachts out for a damn cruise! No quarantine for thee."

Unlike Janet, I didn't bother with the piers, taking a lead from my other life and fabricating my reports with growing confidence. They were also late too. But every so often I whetted Halifax's insatiable need to hone in on Sanders, and duly peppered my reports with potential sightings. Suspect spotted at a Bed, Bath and Beyond in Kips Bay;

photo of hovering hat highly inconclusive. And so on. When I felt it was safe to do so, I also shared knowledge on the Movement's expanding understanding of the Radakovian reality which we were all now living in.

Finally, Mayor O'Reilly publicly ordered a sit down with the true leaders of the Movement to discuss its intentions. Officials from bordering states, keen to win a few votes and capitalise on a sinking ship, were chomping at the bit, threatening the removal of food trucks in light of our perceived abandonment of traditional values and alleged insurrectionist tendencies. More well-intentioned folk suggested creating a giant urban farm in Central Park as a self-sufficient sustainable food source, though the logistics of revitalising the soil of the Great Lawn made it an easy one for the 'too hard basket'.

But it all boiled down to a one-way list of demands under siege.

The inner circle trembled at the prospect of such a meeting, a publicised sit down with seasoned political operatives who could sell us a pup. In my humble opinion, none in the group, not even the radiant Mora, would hold up under the scrutiny. So when the inner circle sought my advice, I recommended avoiding such a confrontation, or at the very least, looking into legal representation. A lengthy discussion ensued on which firm would be willing to bear the responsibility, pro bono, no less.

But Mora, sparkling with inspiration, declared that all we were going to do was agree to the meeting; Radakovic would handle the rest.

***

A growing crowd had amassed on the steps of City Hall, bubbling at the possibility of glimpsing their secretive leaders. Yet with Mora & co a no show, Mayor O'Reilly fronted the media scrum, ready to harness the disappointment of the crowd and spin this no-show as pure cowardice. "Oh, I was just as excited as you were to meet them..." he smugly began—only for a pack of activist lawyers to rise up from the crowd and defend the Movement.

Just as Mora had prophesized!

These brave lawyers, clothed in government-issue Nike skins bearing graffitied slogans of protest and eager to earn the good graces of Mora, asserted that there would be no further meetings if the food supply was cut off. What kind of self-respecting administration would put this ploy on the table as a legitimate bargaining chip? The devotees asked. What kind indeed.

The crowd of hundreds roared in support and the officials present knew that they'd gone too far. The food would continue to be distributed for now, and the Movement able to continue for the time being without their leader so much as making an appearance at the negotiation table. Not that we needed their permission. The Movement would continue, whether they liked it or not.

***

The food thing. Which one? What I did or what your people did?

The invisible diet? I had no choice in how that spiralled. Not my fault whatsoever. Mora was a yoga teacher, it wasn't as if she could advocate greasy double cheeseburgers. The leader I was cultivating required a healthy lifestyle in line with the oneness and spirituality of the Method. Ascension depended on it. Personally, I wanted nothing more than for Radakovic to exalt Eugene's Rueben sandwiches and guarantee their ongoing existence, but I had to be realistic. And to top it all off I was on deadline. Questions of health exploded online in a world where feeling good naked had become top priority. Mora confided that those in the inner circle had pressed her. Five hundred words of divine fatherly advice.

See. My hands were tied.

So, much like my joke to MacCready about our no longer requiring the earthly proteins and nutrients of meat and three veg, I discovered that Radakovic had also envisioned a similar future, one in which those who practised the Method did away with the primitive need to stuff their mouths for sustenance. I took my inspiration from the many sects of breatharianism, which claim that one can survive almost indefinitely without water and food by simply absorbing energy from the sun and the atmosphere; photosynthesis for humans. Within the ranks of those practising the Method it felt like we were expanding, absorbing, so I figured many could easily make the leap.

At first, I feared I'd gone too far and the inability to

literally survive, Method or not, would sow doubt in my sources. I need not have worried, as many took it to heart. Some, like the famous food blogger Kylie Oberon, claimed it was the only way to truly ascend, and so began a fad diet that left quite a few dead, including poor Kylie herself.

I can assure you all efforts were made by myself to rectify these unforeseeable consequences. I uncovered further evidence that, although fasting might assist in the feeling of the Method, it didn't hurt to ingest a meal now and then. Talk of starving oneself for spiritual gain soon withered, and I breathed a sigh of relief knowing that most believers had moved on from this kooky tangent, now treating it as more of a generic metaphor for keeping mindful of one's consumption of healthy food. I didn't know about the government cheese at the time and the resurgence it would cause in Radakovic's breatharian ways.

FACT CHECK: Kylie Oberon's death sparked the reassessment of the invisible diet. No evidence exists of Radakovic's 'correction'. Radakovic, as replicated in Mora's notes, offers only this:

> *Lightness within is determined by intake without.*
> *Feast on naught but the breath of the world.*
> *It is all you will need.*

DEATH SQUADS

I spent a few hours a day helping Sasha with the kids at the Rec Centre. Keeping them occupied, and helping expel their anxieties. MacCready popped in every so often to check on things and talk security intel with me. Sometimes, when he wasn't trying his darndest to hover around Sasha, these intel disclosures took on a more relaxed tone, shared over refreshments as we reclined on deck chairs atop the roof. Ah, the good old days.

One day while Sasha was busy putting out a small blaze those damn little firebugs had started in the games room, MacCready came to me in need of mediation. One of the invisible cops from the local precinct had allegedly pantsed a Guardsman, after a game of goodwill pickup got out of hand. In response, the Guardsman threatened to take away the offender's food access as punishment, echoing the common catch-cry doing the rounds on the internet. Needless to say, the cop was livid, believing his standing was somehow above that of the common ghost—did the soldier not bear witness to his gun and badge? (This was an attitude that became endemic in the NYPD as they struggled more than most to accept their translucent circumstances and diminished authority.) Fists were thrown and a few soldiers popped shots off into the air.

MacCready assured me the soldier in question had been reprimanded, though he quietly confided, with those gentle eyes that did not match his imposing figure, that he felt he had lost the respect of some in his unit.

I wasn't sure what he wanted me to do about it, but I knew why he asked. It wasn't merely that the FBI outranked local PD. It was because I was one of them. A ghost. So I went over to the station and talked to the prick's Captain.

Despite his assurances they had reprimanded the officer for his little prank, I sensed the Captain was giving me the fuckaround. Hey, I didn't want to do my job properly either, amidst all this uncertainty and widespread mistrust between skins and ghosts, but Sasha was a big fan of MacCready, and I had previously intimated that I looked like Denzel Washington, so there was a certain standard to uphold.

I allowed an icy silence to fill the room before I conducted my dressing down. I noted to the Captain the growing spread of the Movement, infiltrating all facets of life— police departments included. It was counterproductive to allow such pointless antagonising of the Guard soldiers, who were selflessly volunteering their time and risking their safety, and it was in the interest of all ghosts, and the wider populace, to keep the peace. The Captain, Briggins, brushed it all off, but I assured him, "You think the situation is bad now, don't forget that things can always get worse."

"Ha! You mean like your death squads?" he muttered under his breath, which caused me to lean forward in my chair and demand he repeat what he'd just said.

No, I did not mean like my death squads. I wasn't aware at the time of any such death squads, especially ones supposedly at my disposal. But if I was to draw any lessons from recent hyperbole, it was best to remind myself this was a new me, a reinvigorated, Denzel Washington-like version that didn't stand for any nonsense. So I told him straight, one call from me and they'd come like thieves in the night, hack off his tongue, ensuring any future discussions on his part would be conducted with a notepad and pen.

The Captain concurred. "Animals! So it's true. I didn't want to believe it. Never thought they'd go against their own kind. Never in a million years."

"What can I say? These are unprecedented times. We can, and we will."

With that, I effected a melodramatic exit. Now if only I knew what the fuck he was talking about. Death squads? Roving bands of invisible assassins? I needed to find Sanders. If anyone knew about such matters, it was him.

★★★

MacCready said he owed me one. It felt good to flex my authority, to know I hadn't completely lost the ability to affirm my place in the chain of command. Mac didn't seem to know about the death squads either. But he would soon enough.

★★★

Take a walk down any street on the Island, and you'd witness folk waltzing about leisurely. The food, tasty or not, was free, the queues orderly, the weather getting better. An American summer in Central Park felt like a fine idea. People were outside, undressed, sometimes in circles like a quad of college burners stretched out in budding sunshine.

They chatted and shared videos of a recent incident where a large collective practicing the Method had undressed in Sheep Meadow. This particular act of communal disrobement must have crossed the numerical threshold for acceptable nudity, for military intervention did occur. Guard soldiers surrounded the practitioners and quietly extracted their clothes. Not one member of the party offered any protest, each having momentarily left the planet, and when these intergalactic travellers returned gradually to bodily awareness they appeared less than phased about their newfound circumstances. They were sternly informed their confiscated clothing would only be returned on the condition they wear it. The offer did not find any takers.

To the outside world, we were looked upon as plague victims; sentient, bipedal disease vectors, bearers of a new and supremely terrifying contaminant. Regular CDC proclamations to the contrary did little to quell the fears of the non-affected. Our skin was said to flake as easily as one peels a banana, and the resultant shedding held to radiate our mysterious sickness of nothingness. Most members of the army and National Guard not already doing so regularly took to wearing masks in public, despite the fact not a single case of ghost to skin infection was recorded. Facts took a backseat to fear in this increasingly paranoid new world.

Following the breakdown of attempted talks with the Movement's inner circle to discuss our voluntary dissolution, General Bracken was moved to take a 'fresh' approach. At his urging, Congress passed another round of emergency funding to ensure the country could mobilise against this rogue state in the most expensive manner possible. Military expenditure instantly quadrupled. Optronics and surveillance factories rekindled Detroit's ailing industrial sector. The national economy, largely stagnant since its matchless, once-bristling numbers exchange of money farmers on Wall Street had become a literal ghost town, boomed into action, the nation eager to band together in an old-fashioned struggle between Good and Evil. I was a little dismayed by how many of our number merely continued on in their daily dalliance with altered states of consciousness, blithely oblivious to the coming storm. The enlightening and oft-reiterated wisdoms of Radakovic were something I took pride in, having composed the majority of them myself, but they would not fare so well in the face of the impending onslaught. Bit by bit, hour by hour, soundbite by hateful soundbite, the corporate and state mouthpieces raged in unison, aggressively indoctrinating the masses into the required state of abhorrence towards their newfound common enemy.

Welfare cheats. Vagabonds. Shiftless navel-gazing airheads. Lazy, unwashed layabouts. Rioters, looters, lolling about in scandalous states of undress. Good for nothings, capable of violent uprising at a moment's notice. It's Them Or Us, screamed the headlines. Perverts, possessed of a hive mind capable of unfathomable depths of sneakery. In a nation of do-ers, these do-nothings were heathens, reflective of those celebrities famous for simply being famous. "Why should the rest of the country even try to appease this ghost minority? The time for appeasement is over," posted John Birmingham, VP of an Indiana autoplant reliant on federal subsidies in order to stay afloat. Veronica Haslett of Kentucky agreed, and then some. "Flood New York, give it back to actual people!" Ah yes, go tell Noah to spare two of every asshole.

But the Method kept all those hurtful words at bay. We were plugging into reality with ten thousands volts, interconnected beyond the homo sapien notions of experience. No time for festering exchanges on message boards, disappearing down rabbit holes of turgid hate. Only more and more stories of Radakovic, ever loftier tales of why and how we reached the full flowering of our potential. I did my best writing in the dead of night; more importantly, no one thought to question how it was that more and more morsels of wisdom were emerging from the ashes of Radakovic's home. "Allow your enemies their space to hate; they will destroy themselves in the process." See? Aphoristic gold.

Those on our side more attuned to the ongoing state of legal dismemberment questioned our tepid response. The lawyers who had taken it upon themselves to represent the Movement sought out Mora and her inner circle for counsel, but found their lack of response beyond negligent. The situation was becoming urgent, they argued, for outside forces now believed, perhaps falsely, that the Movement had muscle; a paramilitary outfit of professionally-trained ghosts, able to strike any target in the city at will.

I eventually discovered the backstory on that whole death squad thing.

A journalist, I forget if they were a skin or one of ours, had been working on a piece about the spate of targeted violence undertaken by unknown forces in those first chaotic days following the Transformation. They'd gathered intel on a few hits, Feng's and Janet's Dominican case among them, and asked a leading question at a press conference: Do you think these emergent death squads are tied to this growing movement?

For the mayor, keen to impress the powers above and stir the hornet's nest, making the connection was a no-brainer.

"I have no doubt in my mind that those with the means to profligate violence would find solace in the arms of an invisible terrorist mastermind, and rest assured, we will make sure these individuals are brought to justice."

Bracken tasked FBI headquarters with profiling these various death squads, and determining which acts of violence were carried out by them during a time where just shy of four hundred criminals were slain across Manhattan. Internally, a few too many former agents' names were connected to these homicides for management's comfort and their records were to be cleansed. Our good friend Sanders was among them, as was I. In fact, I was the only one implicated still manning their desk. The department's eventual conclusion was that I was an unwitting participant who had clearly restated his loyalties. My records were then cleansed for posterity too. Sanders, however, was a different story.

Halifax was incredulous. There was no way Sanders would dare align himself with a monster like Radakovic, irrespective of the fact he'd been AWOL and diligently ducking Halifax's calls ever since the Transformation. Janet and I were ordered to ramp up our hunt for Sanders, the mission now one of compassion. Halifax would never have worked with a terrorist. Not a chance. Sanders' name had to be cleared for the good of the department and we would be the ones to do it!

Times like these I needed a Reuben. Thank God Eugene was a believer. I bumped into him, literally, on the sidewalk outside his old eatery, practicing the Method in public. This happened to be a personal bugbear of mine, as I believed the light within was better sought indoors and away from prying eyes, though I chose not to divulge this. I mentioned in passing that the leader of the Movement had particularly liked Reuben sandwiches. Eugene was beside himself at the news.

"For real, Lenny? Wow! What you FBI guys can't dig up. Come inside, man. Tell me more. Tell me everything—I mean, everything you're allowed to share."

He frantically ran toward his old station, apron at the ready, though his enthusiasm proved premature. Ingredients were slim, so, apologising profusely, he offered to scrounge up something decent through his suppliers as soon as possible, assuming they were still willing and able to ship to the city. He would do everything in his power to serve the Movement, he assured me, gripping my shoulder with manic intensity. I gave him my card and told him to call me as soon as he had a Reuben ready to deliver. Eugene lit up, his unseeable grin shining through the air. I left our chance encounter with the modest solace of knowing I'd made his day and that, more importantly, he'd soon be making my favourite sandwich once more, this time giving it the love it deserved.

REPATRIATION DAY

Repatriation Day. A propaganda coup of colossal proportions for us. Locate your heart strings, take a breath, and prepare to have them tenderly tugged.

A genial spring breeze blew through the avenues, infusing us with optimism, and the reunions brought excitement and teary-eyed smiles both seen and felt. Parents, siblings, compatriots, long-lost distant relatives. They had their photographs taken at the processing centre in Union City, filled out some paperwork, including a waiver stating they wouldn't enquire about the Method or engage in any Movement-related shenanigans on pain of imprisonment, then in turn received a day pass authoring travel across the Hudson to the stated address of their invisible friend or relative.

The well-to-do came to collect their artworks and other valuables, only to find more often than not that a new breed of inhabitants had appropriated their lofts. Deals for family heirlooms and the like could be struck, if the occupants happened to be feeling a generous enough portion of the spirit of Radakovic. Sometimes these cosmopolitan socialites sought help from the military down on the street in disbanding these squatters, but seldom did the soldiers or police intervene. Orders were to protect the peace, not retrieve the family Rembrandt.

For the majority however, the experience of reconnecting with loved ones, touching them all over in wonder, sadness and relieving familiarity imbued a flood of compassion and tenderness, all talk of war and vitriol momentarily forgotten. They prioritised the sharing of old pictures over the taking of new ones, for obvious reasons. Suitcases and duffel bags filled with requested trinkets, photo albums, sentimental objects and favourite foods. The (mostly one-sided) exchanging of gifts. The mother of one Movement member with young children had brought a selection of hand-knitted sweaters, swept up by stories of rampant nudity and fears of her grandchildren catching cold, despite the indications a sweltering summer would soon be upon us.

Another mother of a kid who had recently become a daily visitor of the Rec Centre scolded Sasha when she found out that the children did not sleep within its safe walls and were left to fend for themselves at night. Sasha said she was getting cots from the barracks sent across, a lie that MacCready supported wholeheartedly when he fortuitously came by to check in.

In the same way that visitors were fascinated to learn first-hand of our experience as ghosts, tales of life outside the barricade piqued my interest. Many were clearing out of Brooklyn, the comings and goings of the military proving too much for that borough. Reassuring to hear the horror recounted first hand and confirm that what we were seeing in the media was true. Helped to solidify the existential dread.

Yolanda's parents, I'm told, did not let go of her the whole day.

I spent the morning coordinating and sabotaging a takedown of Sanders. Halifax had repeatedly pushed for Sanders' wife, Christine, to attempt contact. She'd finally agreed on the proviso of reducing his troubles further down the line, based on the nightmarish future Halifax had painted for her fugitive husband. She needed to talk sense into him, Halifax demanded, his breath a heavy steam of unrelenting coercion. When Sanders questioned me on the matter I provided the rundown; where Christine would be, the route we'd ensure she took. Sanders did not show, though he waited all day to catch a glimpse of her from the third floor fire escape of an alleyway as she walked down Park Avenue, over to their favourite street corner where good news had spurned a proposal. A brief ray of sunshine peeking through the clouds.

Sanders thanked me later, as Halifax's frustration escalated to new heights and the case became more and more of a prickly prospect.

I can tell you of countless little victories that occurred on this warm spring day. I'm sure the ghosts, wherever they are now, will attest to them.

THE FALSE MESSIAH

When a power vacuum opens, opposing ideologies are bound to clash. With the Movement now recognised as a decentralised phenomenon, seemingly devoid of public leadership, the CIA looked to occupy the empty throne with one of their puppets. CAUGHT! read the headlines all across the country. They'd nabbed Radakovic hiding like a dog on a private homestead in rural Pennsylvania. Information spread about his rambling manifesto, a carefully concocted exercise in discreditation—See, this is the evil monster you've been blindly following! Now will you finally repent?

I received an urgent message from the supposedly non-existent leaders, requesting my presence at a meeting to discuss the alleged capture. We gathered discreetly behind the lanes of a bowling alley in East Harlem. Disillusionment aside, I always wondered what kind of mechanical marvel allowed the pins to find their place once more, and sought to peep behind the curtain of the other hidden cogs that made this island run. But to the matter at hand: the party of ten, the reclusive inner circle, fearful of their progress and momentum running dry and leaving them consigned to the mire of irrelevancy. They spoke in alternately hushed tones and raised voices. Yvonne asked for my thoughts as to the credibility of the story, as best as I could discern. It was an imposter, surely? A hoax, a ruse, planted to destabilise and discredit the Movement?

So I shared with this willing audience my tale of a blatant CIA disinformation campaign, which may or may not have been a fabrication cobbled together from drops of watercooler hearsay.

Mora remained quiet and the rest eventually simmered down too. She said it was time to go public, and that she would reveal herself in exchange for proof, the only proof acceptable in her mind. If this individual was indeed Radakovic, then he would find no issue replicating the Transformation. Mora suggested the lawyers act as mediators, to the unanimous approval of the inner circle, barring myself. I did my best to quell this path, citing the clear security risks apparent: the government was simply drawing Mora and her inner circle out of hiding in some sort of sting operation.

But Mora was undeterred. "You said it yourself, he's a fraud who must be exposed."

She'd been quiet for long enough, itching to speak freely while the celebrities and influencers spoke on the Movement's behalf, soaking up the spotlight, pushing the Movement in directions further from her reach. Rightly or wrongly, the truth of this Radakovic claim must come to light, she justified.

Don't think of me a disgruntled disciple, but, I mean, c'mon. I'd steered them safely with secrecy this past month, and coloured in the blanks surrounding our divine inspiration. So by all means, discard the principles that built your empire. Let the well-equipped hounds pinpoint you and your associates.

But I wasn't mad.

The lawyers (positively giddy that they now had a legitimate line to the inner circle) fronted the media on the steps of City Hall and posed their challenge.

Radakovic must perform the Transformation on a willing participant on the Island, for all to see.

As suspected, there were many issues with this. The US government couldn't allow a captured terrorist to conduct said experiment in public. You wouldn't ask Bin Laden to recreate 9/11 to prove it was him. They were the one's calling the shots here, dammit. And all this rueful "Radakovic" wanted to say, without coercion, was that his vision, a mistake he now deeply regrets, has been corrupted wholesale by the Movement. All he wanted was to become invisible himself for his own shameful desires, as backed up by the initial character assessments of his former colleagues. To see the devastation he'd wrought broke him. It was his duty now to accept his punishment, beg for forgiveness and await the reversal of his creation by the hard-working, honest minds of the government.

The media ate this up. Tumbled over themselves to condemn the ludicrous demands of the Movement. A brutal return serve, and the world awaited the Movement's reply. I walked the streets around Fed Plaza, conducting anecdotal polling to see which way the wind was blowing. Most citizens felt deflated; the demands of proof would never be met, and Radakovic's confessions of this all being one colossal accident, engendered no fans given their newfound sense of purpose in the method.

In the ensuing wait for a response, the government rolled out further incontrovertible proof they had our leader in custody. His former colleagues signed off acknowledgment on recognising his voice in the confession tapes released. A dye cast of his face was recreated. Fingerprints a supposed 'one hundred' percent match too.

Finally, the Movement responded. In fact, it was Mora herself who spoke in a recorded audio the lawyers presented to the public.

You have provided all the proof, except the one that matters most. The individual you have captured is clearly not Emile Radakovic. Please continue your search. And inform us when you find the real one.

Simple. Elegant. Exactly what we wanted to hear. Who in their right mind would argue with that? An unforgettable hair-raising moment for those who'd never had the fortune of meeting her. We were forever indebted to such courage.

A brilliant ploy! Here was a ream of carefully vetted lies, trumpeted by no lesser a figure than General Bracken himself, met with a simple counter by Mora. And this was good enough for the rest of the Movement, no matter the amount of supposed evidence and witness testimonies splashed across the front pages of every newspaper.

Our course trajectory restored, we were free again to forge ahead with purpose.

Standing in line at the food trucks collecting our MREs and our food stamps for corporate fast food giants as a little weekend treat, we'd greet one another cheerfully, each introducing ourselves as the real Radakovic. Made a big show of it. And when we reached the front of the queue, we never forgot to remind the soldiers to praise the all-knowing one for bringing us all together.

FACT CHECK: The US Government maintains the Emile Radakovic captured in Pennsylvania is real and insists the Transformation on May 18th was nothing more than an accident. The US government supports Emile Radakovic's calls for the disbandment of the Movement, and its ongoing compliance with all demands made by authorities.

CONEY ISLAND KID

Juggling the demands of 'catching' Sanders and relaying uncovered truths to the Movement's inner circle was affecting the feel and efficacy of my practice of the Method, so I decided to take a week off, enjoy the warmer weather and wander. Perhaps I'd been too judgemental and would benefit from an al fresco setting like Eugene, or the many countless younger ones whose insecurity of not knowing who they were had dissipated immediately upon their first experience with going native, the exhilaration of unashamed nakedness, the casting off of all former shackles.

Case in point for my needing a holiday: feeling nostalgic for former times, I'd taken the subway to work. After Canal Street we'd ground to a sudden halt in the darkness of the dimly lit tunnel, still several hundred feet shy of the next station. A jumper had been picked up by the thermals. I was reading about Juan Ruiz, injured New York Yankee and one of the only starters stranded in Manhattan. He'd undergone an excruciating, all-encompassing body tattoo in the hopes of getting an exemption from the quarantine. This marked the first time someone had sought a face tattoo to improve their employability. Lawyers on both sides amassed to discuss the legalese, while I'm sure the Yankees and the Commission debated the merits of having an eyeless freakshow touring the country. Knowing how the little slugger with an explosive anger ended up, I wonder if the words of Radakovic had been insufficient in reminding Juan it was unwise to taunt the Itch.

Halifax was deeply troubled by my decision to take a week's unplanned leave, and words were uttered of a vociferous nature, but I knew I had him when he began to bargain. "Just make it three days instead, OK? I really need you. Please."

"Well, if you really need me..."

I wandered all over uptown, talking to strangers, listening to stories of the first days of their physical reordering and what made the Method work for them. The Humans of New York guy must've been kicking himself; he'd been out of town at the time of the quarantine and subsequently barred from returning, perhaps for fear of his humanising ways. Ousmane Ndiaye had only been in the US as a tourist from Senegal. Now he was here, possibly forever. A dream holiday turned into a surrealistic nightmare. "I've seen all of Manhattan, every nook and cranny, everything I wanted to see from when I first saw *The Avengers*. Now I will never see my family or even myself again. Still, praise Radakovic."

Chinese tourists left stranded pleaded with their government to flex some diplomatic muscle and wrangle them a flight home, but the US, fearing the CCP would discover the secret of Transformation and use it to create a generation of Communist infiltrators invisible to the naked eye, politely declined under the auspices of national security.

But no matter where they came from, and regardless of their personal circumstances, they universally relished the Method, clinging to this silver lining like it was the only thing keeping them together, even though the entire process was one of letting go.

Sasha informed me she had a date the following evening and asked if I could host a slumber party at the Rec Centre. Apparently, Devon had requested to get away for a while, and Sasha, like Halifax, knew she had to bargain and cut him a little slack.

I asked who the date was with.

"Macklin."

"Good for you, Sash. You guys make a cute couple." I said, a little agitated that I'd been kept out of the loop on this. "So, you two gonna get married, move out to Philly and raise some kids of your own?" I pulled a face whilst making the obligatory 'smoochy smoochy' kissing sounds.

Sasha punched me hard in the shoulder, terrific aim for something she couldn't see. "It's not that," she said. "He's nice. Got a big heart. Kind eyes."

"Nice he's got eyes at all. You be back by ten now, you hear. And no hanky panky."

"You can fuck right off."

***

The kids wormed around in their sleeping bags, spares issued by Macklin's company. Torches were passed around. I was patient at first, the cool uncle, but soon wished I'd brought my 9mm. Took me hours to get them settled into those damn sleeping bags, my wits worn paper thin.

They'd asked for ghost stories, tales to send shivers and chills down the spine. Some had enquired, doubtless wide-eyed, if I'd ever been in shootouts or raids while in the FBI. I affected a thousand-yard stare and pretended like it was all too much to remember. The truth was I'd stayed in the van most of the time, or helped coordinate things back at HQ. Then I remembered my thousand-yard stare was lost on them.

"You ever see anyone get their brains blown out?" asked one little chap.

"Yeah. You, if you don't get inside that sleeping bag."

Once I had gotten the younger children to stop crying and assured them that no one was getting their brains blown out, this was the ghost story I settled on. The Ghost of Coney Island. The younger children, like Yolanda, begged me to stop, retreating into their sleeping bags, but I sensed them peeking every so often.

I knew the hypocrisy of what I was doing, but I had to do something to restore order. Do as I say, not as I do. Some of the older ones called bullshit but otherwise kept quiet until the very end.

Then there was one who gleaned a different meaning, took this mischievous vagrant as a fine example of how one ought to be. I did not intend for this to happen, I assure you, but these are the facts and this is how it went down.

The Ghost of Coney Island was a dear friend of Emilio Radakovic. His bulging eyes were the first features to greet you, running circles on you like the teacups on the boardwalk when you first entered. Some say he was born on the Thunderbolt, popped right out of his mother's womb as the ride plunged. He had a cleft lip and burn marks across the right of his scalp. A weird character before the Transformation, and this did not abate thereafter. His favourite thing to do was waiting for naughty kids to misbehave, to stray from their groups.

Recently he's been taking kids' clothes, kids who foolishly took them off. With no clothes, kids go missing real easy. They get lost, never to be found again.

I felt bad for the kid, this Albert. The weirdest of the weird, he'd taken the story as gospel, the Ghost of Coney Island quickly becoming his new hero. Forget Batman, the Avengers, here was a champion of the disenfranchised, the oddballs and outcasts. He begged me to take him to Coney Island, or at least get him as close to there as possible. Whereas the adults of quarantined Manhattan could retreat into the Method, no lasting effect was experienced by children, their youthfulness and hyperactivity counteracting the transcendence felt by adult practitioners. There was no need for them to retreat inward. Not just yet, anyway. I stopped short of telling Albert I'd made it all up. Instead I said they were probably going to open up a new Coney Island in Central Park soon. And that the ghost may even visit this new park in his search for new victims. Albert ate this up. I didn't see the harm at the time. Maybe I should have just told him they closed the park. Perhaps that would have changed things. Too late now.

Unfortunately, our inspired little Albert decided to sneak into the James Earl High barracks and steal a pair of thermal goggles, in tribute to his new vagrant hero. A soldier spotted the goggles floating away, put two and two together, and chased him down, whacking the back of Albert's fat little head with the butt of his rifle. The Guardsman didn't stop there. An anger had built and had to be quenched. The rest of his squadron had to pull him off the boy. X-rays later showed Albert had sustained several broken ribs, a fractured forearm and skull.

Sasha was beside herself. The parents, skins living in Brooklyn, demanded the soldier in question be arrested and tried for assault. Macklin had military police carry out the arrest. Questions circulated as to why the Guard member had utilised no other means of restraint. The man's history of domestic violence was brought to the attention of the media, and regurgitated with acidic judgement on the streets. Talk of retaliation tagged along for the ride too.

I asked the inner circle for their opinions on the matter. Peter and Yvonne, ascendant power couple of the inner circle and Mora's most trusted confidants, agreed to a discreet walk in Central Park to discuss their thoughts. I must say, to be entrusted with propelling our new religion forward and handle it as well as they did with their limited experience, kudos to them.

After some deliberation, they suggested the man be stripped naked and forced to walk in shackles through the once-peaceful neighbourhood of his jurisdiction, subject to the whims of the people he'd failed to protect from himself.

I fed this to Sasha, she fed it to the parents, and the parents served it to one and all.

> FACT CHECK: False. Peter and Yvonne claim that you, Leonard Walcott, first suggested this punitive measure, citing discussion with Albert's parents and TBS afflicted uncle, along with interpretations of justice taken from the notes of Radakovic.

Everyone on the Island weighed in. There was a widespread sense that the investigation into the incident being conducted by the very institution that had caused said incident would, to put it mildly, skewer the course of justice. Numerous historical precedents were cited as evidence. Black Lives Matter coordinated their groundswell, asking the Movement to anoint their crusade.

"They treated him like they've always treated us black people, don't matter if they can't see his skin," Albert's mother cried out in anguish to the wall of microphones encircling her. Authorities dismissed this forced march as a potential punishment, but even in their denouncement they gave it credence. Bracken went on the record saying that the rule of law, the rule of America yada yada still applied to the residents of Manhattan, be they skin or ghost.

Macklin found himself in a bind. While many in his company agreed their fellow soldier had gone too far, the fact that Macklin had even considered the claims of that 'Rec Centre bitch' proved his sympathies were a decided liability.

Macklin relayed his grievances to me, adding an awkward apology for not mentioning he'd gone out on a date with Sasha. He was jittery, sweaty. He asked that I try to talk to my people, talk to Sasha, de-escalate things, like I'd done before. I coolly promised him I'd call off the death squads, then as soon as I'd left the room made a call to Sanders to see if this was possible.

***

The death squads shaved their hair. To let it grow long was for the hippies, those unwilling to prepare for the turbulence on the horizon. And if they were to form an army, it was best to dress the part. Besides, the shit made us itchy when we weren't in the Method. The Movement would soon adopt the death squads' close-cropped style. Like Neanderthals shedding body hair, the next logical step in our evolution. Chemo Chic. There was talk of weaponising our shorn locks, a silent noodled mass for stuffing down an enemy's throat and choking them out.

What we were alleged to have done with bone was sinister. Femurs taken from the corpses of exhumed ghosts. Carved, sharpened to a point. An invisible dagger for the discerning assassin. Rumour and hearsay, I swore at first. Propaganda against the death squads, as if the name wasn't bad enough.

I asked Sanders once, early on, if it were true what the media were speculating. "Do you honestly think we'd try sharpened bones against assault rifles? A little impractical, but not a terrible idea. In fact, it may be useful for some Ops. Thanks for the tip."

And so the Hair and Bone myth began to circulate. An essential accessory for the discerning invisible dissident. News reports eager to stoke fear suggested both were being sourced at an alarming rate, readying for vengeance, and the National Guard were dispatched to patrol the fresh cemeteries in Central Park.

THE NEXT STAGE

'I am the Naked Truth.
There is no progress further than I.
Won't you Join me?'
— Emile Radakovic

The Method. Like the soak of a hot shower on a winter's day, the raw and stark reentry into the reality of objects and cold impermanence was inevitable. The transitory nature of the process could not sustain the Movement forever, and so a more enduring solution was required. The pressure was on to delve deeper than Mora's neat trick allowed, to discover the purpose of our circumstances and 'ascend' like all those New Age hacks claimed was possible. It was heavily inferred from the stories of Radakovic that there was more to the Method than feeling the universe fall still when one indulged (what he called absorbing). A next step into the sky, an expansion of stillness into something more. "Touch the God light, and experience your own miracle," as our Saviour suggested. Redacted evidence I'd been privy to sealed the deal. Traces of Radakovic's Holy DNA discovered on skin samples taken throughout the Island all but confirmed his ongoing reach from dimensions beyond.

The responsibility of instituting this vision fell to Mora. To navigate our transition to the Next Stage and permanently raise us all up to a higher vibration. Find it, Mora. Find a way! Ignore the noise of the authorities squeezing in, and lead us to the holy land. Mustn't disappoint.

Reports circulated that the Guard member who brutalised Albert the Weird was only looking at a minimum sentence. Pressure mounted for serious jail time from the family, who, with the help of humanitarian lawyers inside and outside the quarantine, were making an extraordinary plea for the boy to be returned to his parents outside the zone in Brooklyn, on compassionate grounds. The government, having for the past two months held staunchly to the position that the American public wasn't ready to accept these freakish individuals no matter the circumstances, politely declined this request and put the blame back on the Movement and their alleged insistence of nudity delaying a return to integration with the rest of the country and a whole sense of normality.

Knowing full well there was no chance of a permanent repatriation for little Albert the Weird, and that the parents felt they couldn't join their son in the zone (they had other kids to take care of) I made a bold play on behalf of the family. I made contact with the Movement and emphasised little Albert's Make-a-Wish request was to be allowed to play around in Coney Island while he recovered from his injuries. A long shot, but it was my moral imperative to condemn the actions of the Guardsman whilst minimising and to a larger extent hiding my involvement in the boy's thought process. I felt somewhat responsible for the boy's condition, though I'd never admit to it and would deny it vehemently if accused. Lawyers were briefed on this small reprieve, little Albert expressed his happiness and backdoor negotiations with the government began in good faith, intended to bring a little joy to a wounded boy. Little Albert the Weird, given free reign over the whole of Coney Island, a ghost town closed for maintenance, running wild, stealing the clothes of imaginary folk and getting sick from the fairy floss served by unimpressed National Guard members in carnival attire.

And yes, it amounted to nothing in the end, but I gave it a shot. Hey, I'm not a goddamn miracle worker. At least Albert made a complete recovery. The wonders of youth.

> FACT CHECK: There is no record of any discussions regarding Albert Green's 'Make-a-Wish' request. The boy is also listed as having been discharged from hospital only two days prior to the Night of the Long Dark, after enduring ongoing complications from an infection. The identity of the mystery visitor alleged to have intimidated the boy into silence remains unsolved.

Devon, angered at the injustice, bristling with fervent masculine rage, cornered me, asking if the death squads needed any help with their work. I'm not sure what a crack team of former SWAT members could use a hot head like him for, but I made a few calls and sent Devon on his way. No good deed goes unpunished however and Sasha blew her lid at me for letting him go. So I chirped back and suggested she ask her new boyfriend for assistance in covering Devon's shifts.

A tough few days, but to soften the hardship, Eugene delivered me two Reubens, one for myself, as a faithful customer, and another for our glorious leader, Mora Kelly, presumably as a token of carb-laden gratitude designed to help Mora ascend upward to the Next Stage in our evolution. Oh, what a glorious lunch that was! So it wasn't all bad.

On June 4th, Mora made the announcement on social media. She'd done it. Pushed through the light and extracted even more of its magical rays. The sun and moon and stars had spoken to her, each in turn. All thanks to Radakovic. The details were sketchy, instructions as yet non-existent, but all would be revealed two weeks from Sunday in Central Park. On June 19th, everything would change.

Leaders of Black Lives Matter, orchestrating protests across the US, fighting the police brutality stemming from economic unrest in the other 49 states as well as ours, voiced their displeasure at the timing of the announcement, arguing it detracted from the fight for little Albert and other black youths doing it tough across the nation. The big reveal also clashed with Juneteenth. They didn't take kindly to a supposed ally wresting the spotlight from them, much to the delight of far right commentators. Black Lives Matter Fought for ALL WHO WERE OPPRESSED, as they continually reminded the Movement.

Now I never was part of the roundtable discussions on this one, but I suspect Mora's reasoning was plain for all to see: little Albert was not black anymore. He was a ghost, like the rest of us. Nevertheless, an apology was issued and the date dutifully pushed back, though I'm not sure if the rescheduled date was intended to make any friends. July the 4th. A new Independence Day. Inner rumblings from the inner circle suggested Mora had overruled their misgivings and was intent on ruffling the feathers of not only BLM but pretty much every American, progressive and conservative alike.

The hatred swelled, as you can imagine. The usual vitriol and then some, with many progressives calling it a misstep and demanding the date be pushed back again. I confess my disappointment too. Who wanted to wait that long for the secrets to the entire universe?

The day after the announcement I was summoned to one of the inner circle's meetings. A small pokey apartment on the Upper East side owned by an elderly true believer, Yvonne's aunt, I'm told, who served us all hot green tea while we marvelled politely at her antique furnishings. Mora's studio had finally been raided; fortunately her yoga mats and Bose sound system had been the only casualties.

I recognised the voices of Douglas, Wendy, Peter and Yvonne of the inner circle. The team of lawyers were there too. The head lawyer, the one who appeared on CNN, spoke first, making a case.

"We need to change the date, preferably bring it forward. Putting it on the July 4th Holiday, America's birthday, is a tactical error of the highest order. People want some respite from the troubles, a day to reset, watch fireworks, have barbecues etc. Even the BLM protestors will be taking a break. That's what polling suggests anyway. I understand you want to make a grand statement on a day of symbolic importance, but it may ultimately prove too divisive."

Mora remained silent, either deep in thought or completely overwhelmed.

"And just what is the secret, anyway?" one of the junior lawyers blurted out.

Yvonne was quick to shut this down, despite the mystery of it shrouding the musty room, colouring our every thought. "All will be revealed in due time. Our conduit, the first discoverer of the Method following His invention of invisibility, has decided the truth will be revealed on this date. She has spoken."

"But you already changed the date once to accommodate Juneteenth!" one of the lawyers objected.

The head lawyer returned with courage. "We're sticking our necks out here for you, Mora. We just want to know what the plan is. A little information, for Radakovic's sake!"

The room searched for Mora, who finally spoke. "Where the little and big travellers eventually meet, you can slip inside; a needle through thread. A tiny dot, then ash."

The inner circle and the lawyers stared in perturbed fashion, left to ponder this riddle and pretend they understood while in reality desperately awaited elaboration.

"Everyone needs to learn the truth at the same time," Mora reassured. "Don't worry, they'll all watch us, no fireworks nor barbecues will diminish their curiosity. They will watch us leave our physical vessels behind. They will feel us drift beyond this island, wherever our whims take us, and it will be magnificent. Radakovic has given us the tools to be our own gods, over watchers on a different plane. Just ask our federal representative, Mr Leonard Walcott." All eyes shifted and turned to me, with a little help. "No, not me, it's him. Over there."

I did not falter in my big moment. "We have classified evidence from Radakovic's surviving possessions alluding to another state of existence. Radakovic theorised it, has clearly experienced it, but no specific instructions were left behind. Thankfully, it sounds as if Mora has corrected this."

"The government hasn't figured it out yet? Even with their illegal experiments over on Rikers?" said Peter, Yvonne's husband.

"Not to my knowledge."

Knowing when they were beaten, the lawyers feigned satisfaction and moved the agenda onto the more mundane matters of logistics and permits.

I caught up with Yvonne and Peter after the meeting. "Has she told you anything?" I asked.

"We know as much as you. I think she's playing it close to her chest because she fears for her life."

"Have you seen her do it? Ascend to the Next Stage?"

They deliberated a moment before answering. "No. Not yet."

Janet sent me a text asking for intel on the Next Stage. So did Eugene, and MacCready and Sanders and anyone with an inkling I might be in the know. News of the Next Stage was on everyone's lips and many doubled down on their efforts to break through in their practise of the Method, to be the first to unlock Mora's discovery. An op-ed piece on the Movement finishing up once the cool winds of Autumn hit (forcing the nudists to concede) were met with claims that the Next Stage would fix these earthly restrictions, citing a short YouTube video where a man was able to control his body temperature and run about shirtless in the snow.

The only person who didn't seem to care was Sasha. "She says we're going somewhere else. I don't fucking buy it. These kids aren't going anywhere. Don't see them sitting cross-legged doing meditation, so who do you think's going to feed them when you yeet yourselves over to the other side?"

"That's not what Mora says will happen."

"Do you know what will happen?"

"No. Not yet."

"Exactly. Bullshit."

They'll tell you I saw Mora one final time before the rally, before the great unveiling. They will claim we sat together on a park bench bathed in sunlight. That I faced North and, due to the way benches work, so did she. They will say things like verbatim, questions of credibility, accusations of lies.

To paraphrase: What did you really ever know about Radakovic?

FACT CHECK: Written notes recovered from Yvonne reveal Mora came to you with serious doubts, and you continued to reassure her all the same.

THE BIG REVEAL

Now you know why the riddles that arose in the aftermath induced a swarm of internet sleuths to decipher them. If these keyboard warriors followed the clues they'd solve the mystery for their side, an irresistible global call to arms.

Of course, it was all nonsense, half of the wisdoms originating from bouts of inane late-night inspiration. Or when I was at work while Halifax paced his office, scratching away (the prescribed creams ineffectual), discolouring the walls and ceiling with his two packs a day habit. My level of alertness peaked every once in a while when he'd burst in with a new wacky plot to retrieve Sanders, and convince him of the error of his ways.

I wrote Radakovic's many snippets of wisdom, each and every one. Mora replicated them word for word. There, you've got me. Whatever else you found in her riddles, are merely the insecure ramblings and philosophical calculations of a yoga instructor with the weight of the Island on her shoulders.

***

I'll tell you about the last time I saw her. The honest truth. Sheep Meadow in Central Park, July 4th, 2027. Another sunny Tuesday. Memorable to most. We've skipped the part about the furore which emanated from the East, West, North and South of the country. The rest of the mainland, in other words. We skipped the building of a large stage, open to all the cameras, drones, choppers—enough to block out the sun, feeding hungry eyeballs all across the planet. In far-off locales, in every time zone, they tuned in, bleary-eyed in the dead of night or on the only TV in the village, as if the aliens had finally landed and promised everyone considerable bundles of cash.

Three million of our people peppered with roving swarms of yours, covering every square inch of available viewing space. We all came fully clothed, a necessity for logistical purposes, all hopeful that the itch of excitement would keep the regular Itch at bay. We marched in orderly fashion from all our homes and shelters, scores of American flags waving through the air but a few translucent flags too, made of clear acrylic sheeting, also being determinedly bandied about. The Central Park Brass tooted their instruments, while celebrities of the old world ushered in the new: De Niro, A$AP Rocky, Rihanna, Seinfeld and even my main man, Denzel Washington, gave rousing warm-up speeches on their spiritual transformation under the guidance of the great Radakovic and his inestimable gift. No better role than where they stood. To close, they'd undress to deafening cheers and wolf whistles. Guard Soldiers held firm lines along the edges of the crowd.

Did you know Yankee Stadium's ownership lobbied for their home turf to be the site of the big reveal, as if they could somehow buy their way out of quarantine? Insured to the eyeballs if anything went boom, blinded by the untold fortune and historic significance of hosting the most intriguing event of the 21st century. The hottest little pocket of earth for a fleeting moment at 15:00 GMT.

I didn't exactly get the best view, being about five hundred feet from the monolithic stage. Speaker stacks, scaffolding, viewing towers with sniper nests, camera cranes and wire bridges obscured the sight of many, but the vibe reached all. For me, it was just nice to feel the green green grass of home on my bare feet, our largest garden, our closest connection to the earth. I was there with Janet, the two of us meant to be another dutiful set of eyes and ears for the government, Halifax thankfully having declined our invitation. Sasha and the kids watched on TV back at the Rec Centre, with Sasha no doubt doing her best to downplay the historic occasion.

In the idle hours leading up to the event, we speculated with our surrounding believers. It was heartening to hear some of the spurious rumours and hearsay I'd concocted dutifully echoed as little tidbits of gospel truths:

"They're putting radiation poisoning in the food to reduce our multitude of special abilities other than being invisible: Flight and laser shooting eyes—and cause impotence," according to this one heavy breather.

"The Next Stage will allow us to abide in the Method permanently. Our bodies will no longer emit any heat,

making thermal detection impossible. We'll be able to walk through walls and float wherever we want. Chafing will also be resolved."

"The Itch dissipates with salt water and a spray of bleach."

Here my dear friends heralded the true arrival of American exceptionalism. But we were humble. We would not demand worship, despite millions across the globe recognising our unrivalled divinity.

Protests against the big reveal were ongoing nationwide. Skins demanded the military break the event up, preferably incarcerating us innocent ghosts in the process, while the White House and Bracken no doubt flapped their lips about some 11th Hour rule of law. Declare martial law? It's already been declared. Well then, declare a state of war! The show must not go on. Many memes circulated from alleged patriots about lighting up Central Park like the 4th of July because... you get the point.

This is when the blastwave theory truly came to the fore. As with Y2K and the Hadron Collider before it, there remained an inescapable dread that a calamity of some kind was imminent. They feared she was a nuclear event. The Method was merely a small unfurling, like someone turning on a lamp in a small room. But whenever she did whatever it was she was going to do—results could only be catastrophic! She'd scatter herself and her heretical teachings far and wide. There would be Mora in Pennsylvania, Brooklyn, perhaps even as far as Canada. An organic AI capable of God knows what—and unchecked too!

Where was the government's response, these once-polite citizens raged. What's the point of having all those weapons if you can't even use them? What are we to do, just roll up the shutters, stay indoors and hide from this invasion of the unknown? A fleck of Mora in your coffee, influencing it on a molecular level, turning cappuccino to a weak flat white? Who knew the depths of the depravity! The spawning of spiders from a split reality crawling in. Would the bug spray still work? your households debated.

Invisible fallout and what it could know, if it were sentient. The scientists, with the military breathing down their necks, were forced to prepare a suite of countermeasures. The AI teams, perhaps unsurprisingly, believed the best weapon lay in AI, but Skynet diehards advised this unwise.

What about like a gigantic metal dome, lowered over the entirety of Manhattan, like an overturned cup upon a saucer? Too costly, humanitarian issues notwithstanding.

Some kind of 5G force field which could hold the impending blastwave at bay? Again, there were objections from niche interest groups and cold hard facts of implausibility.

And when Mora spread the gift of such knowledge to her devoted legion, then more would detonate like mini self-contained Hiroshima blasts in a chain reaction, going the way of the original Transformation and taking the entire Eastern Seaboard with it, releasing each skin from their prison.

Expecting the worst, the army prepared lines of retreat. Those in New Jersey and the surrounding boroughs hastened to seal up their homes against the expected noxious miasmic current, this unstoppable atomic wind of self-awareness. Along corridors of all hallways, creaking in every place, no modern space spared. Each house, home, domicile, haunted. The Invisible Yorkers read these fears and played along in counter-gospel. If Radakovic was the first to ascend, then Mora was an expansion, blending into the fabric of reality.

And before any of these 'doomsday' scenarios could come to fruition, someone found an easy fix with a well-considered vantage point and a pulled trigger.

But it was the timing that counted most.

You talked to people afterwards, and they all gave their crystallised opinion. They were there on the grassy knoll, surrounded by an abundance of people, yada yada. Truthful, as you know I always am, I wasn't looking when it happened. My eyes had drifted lazily away, fresh off the Method. Trying to latch onto her Method. Then came the crack in the sky. And like that, gone. Like Barb. Or was she? Depends who you ask on your wanderings and their propensity for true believin'. The cameras clicked away. Captured every minute detail, yet somehow nothing was remotely conclusive.

Mora graced the stage. Upon her head, the liberty crown, amazed by all her people watching her for the first time. She choked on her words at first, eliciting a nervous laugh as encouragement. For the nineteenth time, asked those of us still clothed to undress and engage in a preliminary Method with her, a precursor to the big reveal. It was a quiet Method, a 'last sleep before Christmas' kind of Method. Relaxed. And then we opened our eyes after drifting effortlessly in the wind, our molecules bouncing softly off one another. We clapped and roared, a boundless energy of hysterical anticipation, edging us toward the cliff and into flight, the time finally upon us.

'Friends, fellow travellers, sojourners on this precious earth, rejoice! Let the people of every nation rejoice and be glad! The moment of ascension is finally upon us, the gift our precious leader bestowed will finally bear its priceless fruit. This time, none will be left behind. Concepts like 'us' and 'them' will cease to have any meaning. Today, all of us will weave ourselves a new reality, together."

Rapturous applause followed, the cheers deafening.

"That's right. That's right, my friends, my beloved children. Radakovic's children. Finally and truly together. No longer imprisoned by flesh. A new world, devoid of pain and fear. From now on, there will be only joy, and light! The light beckons!

"To those who fear our light. Fear the unknown—well, Fear not! For when you shall see as we do, you will know everything for what it is, and there is nothing hidden that will not be revealed.

"Our enemies are trapped in their old notions of materialism, they are not in tune with the world around them. When we enact the Method, we are one with our environment, we feel its everlasting presence and we accept its grace fully. We must strip them of their chains and show them true freedom!"

Cue the tightening grip on weapons, the clutching of pearls in every living room across the nation.

"Those who wish us ill, will never fully comprehend the truth we see. For though they may believe otherwise, it is US who truly sees through them!

"Death will not be our end. First I will demonstrate, and then I will instruct..."

She removed her shawl, the Liberty crown brushed from her head. A hush drew over the crowd, the suddenness leaving us holding our breath as to not miss a thing. The microphones buzzed, feedback reverberating throughout Sheep Meadow, wider Manhattan, the rest of the world. The air tasted metallic, much like when I'd awoken with my cheek on the sidewalk way back at the beginning of all this. Purple and green lights panned slowly across the stage, but I suspect this was a creative touch from AV rather than the manifestation of otherworldly energies.

Many were there who claimed they felt something. Placebo or not, I stand by that metallic taste. The rest I cannot explain. Others, like Janet, said she saw the air move on stage, like a large pocket of gas pooling outward. Tiffany, my bar conquest from before, who had snagged a spot only thirty feet from the stage and, like many, owed her appreciation of this new life to Mora and the teachings of Radakovic, felt a surge of electricity in the air. All had our hairs standing up, no doubt about that.

Then 15 seconds into whatever Mora was conjuring, that's

when your boy snapped one off. Loud crack in the sky. For a split second I thought it was her. Wouldn't that have been nice? A human's soul shooting off in all directions before everything pulled back to the source, a tsunami returning to the ocean. An explosion of feeling, pure and beautiful. But no, just a simple bullet whizzing through the air to end Mora, end the Movement, end our hope—or at least an attempt.

You asked for the truth. Here, then, are the many versions I heard.

The official government account: Victor Rodriguez, proud member of the New York National Guard, trained marksman, a hundred feet away in an erected watchtower. A history of aggravated assault on a group of ghosts gone native and, most importantly for the occasion, a clear line of sight, goes rogue and decides to solve the mess himself. The beginning of the East Village 2nd Battalion's starring role.

The alternative, more conspiratorial account, also courtesy of the government: Mora Kelly, unable to reach the promised and much-vaunted Next Stage, decides to become a martyr and pays Victor Rodriguez, a sympathiser, to kill her in order to sow resistance against the government.

The media felt comfortable running both narratives.

Peter's version: He was first onto the stage. I recognised his voice as he scrambled with a microphone. No one knew him by name but they understood by his proximity to Mora that he must've been inner circle. Thermal recordings will say he stood in shock and consoled the deceased. We could hear the weeping, felt the tears trickling down, and did likewise. Janet gripped my hand.

"How could they... how could they..." Peter mumbled over the speakers. This moment of shock from the former professor was later revealed as doctored footage and audio.

FACT CHECK: Not doctored. Witnessed by over three million eyewitnesses. Captured by seven hundred and eight professional cameras.

Peter did his best to collect himself. Something had happened, whether Mora had completed it was anyone's guess. "It is done," he announced. "Mora has become the change, the wind, the blood of life... She will communicate with us shortly from beyond. We, uh, will be making a formal statement shortly and will disseminate the final instructions online. Uh, let's perform one last Method together to celebrate Mora's ascension and we'll, uh, conclude things from there..."

Often during an assassination there is chaos and disorder, but to our credit, in total shock, the people obeyed, though I know that at least for me there was no levity in my soul, but a heaviness keeping me firmly stuck on this sorry sodden earth, chained to the undergrowth of reality. Rage built within. I could not sit idly by in my memory of playing with checkers pieces as a child in Barb's living room, the colour of the carpet reminding me of blood, how it used to look when someone kills another in cold blood.

When I opened my eyes, I was not alone in my fury and sadness.

"Thank you," said Peter. "Now, go home in peace, and await further instructions. We will all reach this Next Stage soon. Go, please... and, uh, thank you all for coming."

And as you may have seen, from countless camera angles, the majority filed out peaceably enough, the lines of Guard members trembling, tightly-wound, as droves of the invisible passed by, their clothes having been left where they stood, heat steaming off their barely-restrained selves. A miracle that no one attempted retaliation then and there, among the other miracles, of course, with Mora ascending.

We didn't move with the crowd; like some others, we edged closer, bumping into those that remained. A line of Guard soldiers stood by at the base of the black monolithic stage. I walked along their ranks, asking them if they saw the shooter. One trying to appease said he caught a muzzle flash but couldn't pinpoint the location; another looking down the line spat, "Don't tell these ghosts shit."

Others repeated they didn't see anything, until I reached an impasse.

We went around the back and found ambulance workers arguing with burly security ghosts dressed in black. The paramedics, ghosts themselves, pleaded that Mora had clearly been shot, but the security kept them at bay, advising everything was under control. I told the security who I was, and they let me through. I found Peter pacing in a room underneath the stage. Yvonne was there too.

"Where is she?" I asked.

"She's ascended," Peter reiterated. Whispered, in fact, causing me to lower my voice.

"Where's the body?"

Peter felt around for my arm. "There is no body. She left it."

"Who's with you?" Yvonne questioned.

"Her name is Janet. It's OK, she works with me. Where is the body?"

"I told you. Mora's not there anymore. She ascended. She left, she must've..."

I did my best to remain calm and not slap some sense into the befuddled mess that was now evidently in charge of the Movement.

"Yes, she ascended, you said it loud and clear to the entire world, but maybe she left her body behind since she doesn't need it anymore. So I ask again, for all our sakes. Where is her body?"

"That. Yes. We haven't moved it. We're still figuring out what to do."

"Sanders' men want to take it away." Yvonne stepped in.

"Good. Let them. Quickly, before the authorities intercept," I said, though saying it hurt my heart. Sank me further down into the grime of this horrible new reality. "There's going to be a murder investigation. No doubt there's already footage of her body dropping to the floor. For Mora's sake, we don't want them to parade her about as some kind of evidence she didn't ascend."

"Of course we don't," Peter concurred loudly, returning from his shock. "Because she *did* ascend. Or, she would have if they hadn't killed her."

"What if we state it's simply a body? A shell. Who's to say it isn't true? Rile up support for the Movement?" said Wendy, Mora's friend for over fifteen years, who had joined us.

"Because she *did* ascend!" said Peter, finally convincing himself, much to my relief.

"What about us?" Janet interrupted, her voice raised. "When do we get to ascend? When are you going to release the instructions?"

"We're working on it," said Yvonne.

"You do have the instructions, don't you?"

Yvonne and Peter stayed quiet, overwhelmed, so I answered for them. "Mora often spoke in riddles. We're trying to simplify the instructions, so no one gets it wrong. We don't want any frustrations to boil over..."

HALIFAX'S RECKONING

I left them with my suggestion and parted ways with Janet, undecided on how she was going to react to my first name basis with the inner circle. The inner circle butted heads with the lawyers long into the night about releasing Mora's reams of private notes and scribblings to the public, much of it containing my impromptu recollections of what Radakovic was up to. I wasn't far off about the riddles, as all saw the next morning—and all I was going off was the wafty wisdom she spun that last meeting of ours. "Where the little and big travellers eventually meet, you can slip inside; a needle through a thread. A tiny dot, then ash."

If I had to take a stab, and it seemed like the most logical theory encircling the thoughts of an unstable woman, Mora believed that during the repeated process of simultaneously expanding your presence and making yourself infinitesimal, this created a Venn diagram of opposing forces, in the intersection point of which your soul found passage to slip inside. And so you'd pass through to another dimension where snipers and emptiness meant nothing because you were elsewhere and everywhere.

Poor girl never saw it coming when that played out. Not my fault either. I told her she didn't have to go through with it. I did all in my power, to no avail.

Many outside the Island questioned the riddles of Mora; she had no idea what she was doing, and they were proof of a desperate individual thrown into the pressure cooker of leading her people out of an environmental catastrophe. If she really knew how to ascend, then why not just show people how to do it? Why not prove it for all to see, like how God sent Jesus down from heaven, killed him then resurrected him? Perhaps we'd have to wait three days, those same folk snarked.

On every corner beyond Central Park the National Guard and the police reiterated from megaphones that martial law remained in effect. Sasha and MacCready both reached out via text, asking for help I had no way of providing. Sasha required a barrage of emotional support; the older kids, grasping the brazen display of power by the military and its self-appointed spokesperson, Victor Rodriguez, were crying hard into their elbows. Devon had not returned from Central Park either. As for MacCready, well, he had tried to comfort Sasha but the mere sight of his military fatigues repulsed the teens at the centre. So he wanted to make sure I kept her safe and the kids accountable while his hands were full coordinating the sweeping of the streets.

The streets were not yet aflame as I trudged over to the Rec Centre. The expected knee-jerk reaction was to riot and destroy, but a debilitating sorrow suffocated the air. I heard sobbing all around from unseen folk, splayed on the road where they fell in despair, exhausted by the events of the day, the buildup and subsequent unravelling. If there was no salvation, if they weren't destined for something more spectacular than this, then to hell with it all. I wondered how long the lie could be maintained, how long faith in a better tomorrow could stretch. The government had been so focused on the Next Stage, strategising a hypothetical war against ghosts to be waged on every corner of the planet, so paralysed by fear of this Next Stage, they hadn't considered the fallout if Mora failed; what those once-hopeful citizens would do when the last light of hope flickered before death.

I'd heard nothing from work, or Sanders, and a cruel current of revenge rolled through me like a violent storm. Retaliation was expected, so the only way to ensure peace and order had to be pre-emptive cruelty and oppression. The time was coming to pick a side, the outcome ugly no matter what.

The National Guard took the shooter Victor Rodriguez into custody and kept tight-lipped about his whereabouts. Murder charges were expected to be laid, but in what must have been some nuanced political reframing, the Movement's lawyers publicly hoped to reduce the charges to attempted murder. For Mora was indeed alive in another dimension. The hashtags #SheLives and #MoraMoreThanMatter circulated, crashing against the doubters and disillusioned who demanded further instructions on the Next Stage.

Throughout the night the media played footage of the assassination over and over, like Zapruder's tape; pundits vying to discredit with angles, thermals and an array of overwhelming evidence that the Movement's leader did not ascend, never mind the fact she was slain in front of the world. No viewer discretion was advised, and condemnation of the shooting remained a secondary notion, "I'm disgusted by the act of the shooter, but you'll clearly see here when we pull it up in thermal..."

"He was just trying to defend himself—our way of life— you heard her inflammatory speech! Manslaughter at worst, not attempted murder."

And on it went.

★★★

Not quite ready to deal with the adolescent pinballs ricocheting off the walls as they grasped their first live assassination, I diverted course, texting Sasha I'd stop by the apartment first to pick up some comforts, but I never reached my front door. A hooded ghost in dark attire called out my name. Halifax. He was not alone. A clothed Janet tagged behind, agitated, itching away. To my surprise, they were not necessarily here for me.

"We need to find Sanders." said Halifax.

I sighed in frustration, ready to tell Halifax it wasn't a good time, but he cut me off with a dormant primal rage neither Janet nor myself had witnessed in a very long time.

"No! You will not brush me off this time! I know you're in league with Sanders and we are going to meet him right now!" He then flashed his handgun. "If we don't talk some sense into him, then he'll retaliate for what happened today. He could spark a war!"

"I thought you said he wasn't a terrorist."

Halifax's hand shook as he pointed at me like a frail

man. "You think I'm a fool. I know you've been talking to him. Keeping in contact. If we don't talk him out of doing something stupid, then we will have to take him out."

Guard soldiers stopped us on almost every corner. Halifax grew more and more frustrated explaining to the skins they were on official FBI business, his badge-waving flippant and unprofessional. "I'm trying to help you, for Christ's sake!" he'd explain, but they simply wouldn't believe it. Some skins refused entry point blank; they wouldn't detain us, but neither would they have us as guests in their neighbourhood. Said it wasn't their problem. Because of this, our short distance to the Hudson Yards took an hour longer than necessary. The plan, according to our fearless and deranged leader, was to meet this rogue operative, this head of a death squad militia and arrest him—Halifax had handcuffs apparently—a great start. The sun cast its last glimmer across the Hudson and not a moment sooner had the July 4th fireworks opened up a sparkling sea of red, white and blue; of crackles and booms across the Island and beyond. You got the sense these were not fired in celebration, but released in a spirit of vengeance and emptiness, the wilful desire to watch something explode, all directed at the Guard and police, skins or not, who had failed to protect their saviour. I'm impressed my fellow Americans had waited until sundown to express their rage.

A few bottle rockets popped away along the Hudson and we heard the louder reply of returning fire from the Guard. No time for the paintballs they usually resorted to when it came to crowd control.

"Is this the war you're speaking of?" I asked Halifax.

"No, I'm talking about assassinations. I'm talking about soldiers dying."

Another volley of M16s crackled in the air.

"Seems like they're well-equipped to deal with any threats."

Halifax halted our advance. "Sanders abandoned us! He has betrayed the Bureau and his country. I will not let him wage war on our troops and you shouldn't either. Don't you know what happens when you fuck with America? Do you think once you kill American troops they'll just let you all run around with your clothes off, waxing lyrical about your 'chosen' status?" He was holding his gun out now, and Janet had instinctively done the same, yet Halifax hadn't noticed she'd raised it cautiously in his direction.

I tried to calm him. "Look, I don't want things to escalate either. We're almost there, you can state your case in person."

"And you'll back me up if I need to take him down?"

"Of course," I supported, despite having neither a weapon nor intention.

The meeting point was an old, creaky maintenance garage next to the train yard, small and derelict enough that the National Guard left it unused, though judging from the gunfire they weren't too far away. Janet recognised the place and said she remembered there were entry points at the front and rear. Halifax said he and Janet would go through the back while I waited for Sanders at the main, which was evidently ajar. "We just want to talk, remember, Halifax said unconvincingly, "I don't want to resort to action."

Perhaps it was a stupid plan to begin with, because I spilled the beans to Sanders the moment I entered the garage, with the caveat that Halifax and Janet were not to be harmed.

But Sanders had already taken care of the cheque. "Janet gave us the head's up. He'll be dealt with shortly."

"What are you going to do with him?"

"What I've been putting off for months. He's been messaging constantly on my old phone. Tried to track it and execute a warrant." He sighed. "Had to be this night, my God. That's what happens when you allow things to fester. Timing's impeccable, at least it'll be one less distraction now."

"You're not going to kill him, are you?"

"Not if it can be helped. We'll re-educate him with the Method. Had trackers on him for a while. The man wears the same clothes and drinks the old Kool-Aid. He's blind to what he is now. We will open his eyes."

"And if he still refuses to see?"

"Then he can't be helped."

"They'll come looking for him. They'll suspect me if he told anyone about this mission."

Sanders was unphased. "Do what you always do. Talk yourself out of it."

"Fine. OK. I guess. So, what's the next step? Retaliation?"

"Not yet, we're still drawing resources. I will require your assistance once you're in the clear for Halifax's disappearance."

This was when he first brought up the Chinese nationals and the promise of favours for their safe passage off the Island and return to the CCP. I don't think I have to tell you that people smuggling is exponentially harder in a militarised zone with thermals, guards and dogs watching the land, sea, and sky, but I would also presume that money still had a knack for making folk look the other way.

We didn't have time to elaborate as Janet reminded us when she walked in, sans Halifax, that Hudson Yards was crawling with soldiers and immediate dispersion would be wise. Sanders said he'd be in touch and I shuddered to think what awaited me tomorrow.

***

You understandably may place higher value on what happened next and prefer I spill in exact detail each step to make my conviction smoother. But frankly, it's a side note to me how two Chinese nationals made it home to Beijing. We set them up as spies, with the requisite accompanying documents and backstory. Then it was a case of presenting them to the CIA, who arranged for them to leave Manhattan covertly. It didn't take long for the CIA to realise these nationals were unwitting participants, but a Russian mole within the CIA looking to sow discord launched a carefully timed raid, culminating in their abscondment into waiting cars. Reports stated that, tragically, three agents were killed in the raid and they discovered the mole but by that time, the two terrified Chinese nationals were repatriated and presumably experimented on until death. I would like to note my objections to this depressing outcome, and I informed Sanders as much, though I went along with it all the same, fearing his wrath if I refused.

All I did was arrange the forgeries required to pass these students off as 'reds under the bed' with prior connections to the late Human Trafficker Feng—a clever touch, you must admit. And I did this all from the comfy confines of Halifax's office, having been promoted after a brief search for the missing Halifax was called off. (A mental episode being the presumed cause.) He was smelling up the place, I'd been told bluntly by investigators.

I had many misgivings about taking the promotion and I assure you I still hoped that Halifax would come to his senses and be able to leave Sander's care a changed man— all forgiven too. Naïve, yes, but I'd like this optimistic outlook to be formally noted.

Before we departed that night and I never saw Halifax again, I asked Sanders what he thought of Mora's ascension.

"I saw a woman die and be reborn. Saw the world change. What we make of it is up to us."

***

The release of Mora's diaries coincided with a renewed period of vigour in the dreams of the Movement. A frenzy of theories spun in all directions, people poring over her words, searching for clues and answers that remained tantalisingly elusive. Mora was added to the wind and whispers down all the avenues. There would be another like Mora, it was rumoured, and then further claimed that Mora herself would guide them with the help of Radakovic. I don't know who started it, but suddenly all good fortune, every sunny day, every well-cooked meal, refreshing gulp of water and welcome snippet of small talk—all mentioned the hand of Mora in one way or another. Sticklers, such as myself, would remind folk to give thanks to Radakovic too and it was no trouble at all to apologise and oblige.

Once their military intelligence deduced that concrete existence of a Next Stage was unlikely to be conclusively demonstrated, the government, realising the endless slew of riddles kept the masses occupied and distracted, felt no harm in perpetuating such hope. They hired crisis actors to spread claims of breakthroughs and encourage others to do the same. It was a better way to expend mental energy than outright rebellion and rioting in the streets.

> FACT CHECK: The US government has consistently refuted the existence of the Next Stage. No policy to encourage its proliferation exists.

Macklin accosted me the morning after the big reveal. Eyes bloodshot from little sleep, guttural rage in his voice, he gripped my collar, aggrieved I hadn't made it to the Rec Centre the previous night, as promised. His barracks had sustained a heavy shelling of cherry bombs, black cats, M-80s and Roman candles, following which he ordered his soldiers to abstain from returning fire or partake in crowd control, which they took as tantamount to lying down and getting fucked. So in retaliation his soldiers failed to intervene when the police subsequently found the suspected fireworks agitators and engaged in a bout of extemporaneous Whack-a-Mole.

Conversely, I hear Victor Rodriguez was not manhandled; the National Guard did not beat him to a pulp when they arrested him.

Macklin needed to know why I didn't have Sasha's back, or his own, why I went AWOL while their little neighbourhood endured a miniature Shock and Awe. Mac could not keep Sasha safe, and this was somehow my fault. Thankfully, Sasha appeared and Macklin released me, his whole demeanour shifting to that of a remorseful puppy as Sasha marched him to the dog house. I felt no pleasure in demanding an apology, to which he sheepishly obliged before making a hasty exit.

Sasha seemed to be the only one unaffected by the shooting and the puzzles and the mythology waiting to absorb her. What was affecting her was simply lack of sleep; the colourful freedom rockets went off long into the night and it wasn't just the soldiers who had endured a barrage. "Salvation? In those ramblings? Please. Tell me to read the Bible, why don't you? It'd do about as much good."

I offered to take care of the kids for the day, mostly to keep a low profile, and also to take my mind off what had happened to Mora and Halifax. The kids moved Sasha's cot to the admin office, and she crashed there.

We herded the children into the main hall for hoops while

I fielded phone calls from their parents on Sasha's phone. I could tell a few were on the fence about repatriation, a fine line to toe—if the situation got any worse they'd feel compelled to be there for their children. But there also wasn't any sense having the whole family stranded and endangered. Knowing though that fewer kids in Sasha's care would do wonders for her psyche, I turned the screws and subtly reiterated the duty of a parent, that familial bond which must be upheld till the last breath.

As a peace offering, Mac sent a few soldiers over with MREs for distribution. They remained guarded and on edge, with a few pointed questions about whether the Rec Centre had been used to launch fireworks. I told them no, and one gave me some sage advice: "You're all so fucking ungrateful. You know that? We're here trying to restore order and normalcy to this place and you people would rather see it burn. Stay away from the barracks, unless you want trouble. Captain MacCready doesn't need Sasha." So I played kind and grateful and remorseful for the depravity of my people and sent them on their way, making a mental note of their names.

THE VOTE

The skins wanted New York back. Mora's disappearance
had quelled their fears of this whole 'ascension' business
posing a legitimate threat and renewed their appetite to
conquer and restore their rattled exceptionalism. Out with
the new and in with the old.

In our favour, and buying us a little time, was the
president's abrupt reticence to invoke his executive powers
to relocate us, a change of pace for him stretching back
well before our creation. For this next act, he would seek
the approval of Congress before proceeding with our forced
eviction. Panicked teenagers making a pact after a drunken
hit-and-run. All branches must be complicit. And thus
the real reason for these consultations, where to place the
displaced? Who would draw the short straw? Not in my
backyard! Over our dead bodies! We heard in unison. So they
put it to an urgent vote. Lightning quick. An emergency
hearing in Congress, scheduled a mere three weeks from
Mora's assassination. A vote to go to war, expel us from our
city. Relocation followed by reclamation.

Camps fell into two categories: The Republicans suggested
Guantanamo or FEMA tent cities. Democrats suggested
something fancy up in the Catskills, or some other far-flung,
sparsely populated locale. Montana, perhaps. A top-notch

containment reservation to allay the guilt of undertaking forcible relocation in this most modern of lands. That and dump a potentially supportive demographic into red territory. (Of which Republican uproar about voting rights threatened to overshadow the more pressing issue, only to be quelled at the 11th hour once assured gerrymandering neutralised any real impact.) Either way, private prison contractors readied their competitive bids.

The media asked the Movement for comment. Peter and Yvonne, the next in line, suggested a vote of their own, scheduled a day before the vote in Congress. Fabulous idea. A vote between staying put in NYC, or moving to a specially built development reflective of our utopic ambitions. FEMA camps would not do, even temporarily.

In those early days of the Movement, the inner circle had discussed with blue sky optimism the possibility of a new home, something akin to a sprawling commune replete with food security, an agreeable climate, and verdant serenity. Utopia, paradise, bliss; far enough away from the perennial threat posed by the skins, yet contained in a way that subdued their prickly anxieties. The group was divided. The more sceptical members (Parvin, Bella, Lorne) did not think such autonomy possible and feared being trapped wherever they eventually dumped us. They argued it was safer to stand our ground, declare our intentions to make New York our home no matter what. As you know, Peter and Yvonne believed relocation was inevitable (which I guess proved true enough in the end) so the practical path was to focus on securing the best terms possible. Mora?

Never engaged in these talks. Radakovic would lead the way, soon enough, she had said.

In light of this impending vote, I was happy to lend Radakovic's wisdom wherever the Movement preferred. If they wanted to stay, then of course it made sense. Radakovic had granted us this holy metropolis—chosen this land to plant his seed. He'd claimed it for us! One must not stray from their birthright. We must hold firm and defend it till the last.

But if Radakovic thought the purpose-built idyll, with all necessities accounted for, raised up and blended perfectly with nature in a sustainable workers paradise was the way to go, then I'm certain I'd find words of his conveniently supporting that thesis as well.

Me personally? Oh, shucks. I simply wanted peace between us. The opportunity for both to exist in harmony. I will say this though: things can get a lot worse behind closed doors. At least in New York City, the cameras relayed everything.

TIFFANY'S FRIEND

The East Village disappearances. That's what we're up to. A welcome distraction for myself, affording me the chance to order my thoughts and appear suitably busy in my new role as acting Group Supervisor. What Chinese Nationals? Gerrard who? Haven't you heard—they're snatching women in the night!

Four days had passed since Mora's big reveal. A memorial service, a conciliatory act courtesy of the government, played out in the meadow where she allegedly shuffled off this mortal coil. Only the media showed up, both sides still clinging to their version of events for the time being. Convenient timing for a hundred hazmats gathering Ground Zero materials, combing for any evidence of spiritual chain reactions...

Tiffany, my one-afternoon stand from the early days of our transformation, fired off a couple of texts at me, looking for an inside scoop on Mora's riddles; to see if the FBI or the government at large had cracked the case of page three, or the haiku of page eight. It had been almost two sexless months since our brief liaison at that hedonistic bar, and this may have been the reason I indulged her on the haiku. I certainly had nothing else to offer.

While I was wracking my brain trying to figure it out

(haikus were never really my thing), Tiffany sent another message that sent the conversation in another, more disturbing direction.

A friend in her Method group, the equivalent of a Radakovic bible study with sexcapade intermissions, had stopped replying to her texts and quit showing up to their meetings. Her friend wasn't suicidal, was deeply invested in solving the riddles and ascending, but she had brazenly live-streamed the mistreatment of a fireworks distributor ally at the hands of soldiers during the aftermath of Mora's ascension. This video, taken in the East Village near Tomkins Square, was her last known whereabouts. I asked to meet with Tiffany, to obtain further info on her missing friend and, of course, to comfort her if need be.

I visited the East Village barracks on the way home from the Rec Centre. The colonel who ran things there had been reported in the media for returning considerable gunfire on the 4th and coordinating with the police in a manner that made the search and destroy missions in Vietnam seem tame by comparison. So yes, Tiffany's friend Laura sharing damning footage of their exploits did not bode well.

Speaking of Vietnam and other comprehensive victories: peace talks. A de-escalation of recent troubles post-Mora. A plan to leave the place like Saigon, Baghdad, Kabul, tidied up and in good nick. Moving forward. Onwards and upwards. These peace talks were a way for the government to finally sit down with the inner circle and get the rules straight on how they'd like their abandoned citizens to be governed, regardless of the location. I sent Peter a text asking if we'd get Brooklyn and Long Island, allowing me to become a warlord in the Hamptons. I was only half-joking.

Finding a missing person was not too dissimilar from my work in trafficking. Follow the breadcrumbs of their routine, and rack your brain with the limitless possibilities. I wasn't doing the Method with obsessive regularity anymore. Still felt a little guilty about Halifax. Perhaps also fearful I might get caught. I was on edge, wide-eyed and harried as I carried out my investigation. The Guard soldiers proved unhelpful with my questioning; they hadn't seen her, or anyone, referring me in distinctly impolite terms to the local precinct, who likewise rebuffed me immediately. They didn't have anyone detained, but would be damned if I could inspect their cells.

A week passed, a long hot week of heated discourse on our uncertain future and enduring concerns the skins were going to fuck us, sans Vaseline, no matter our wishes. Tiffany still hadn't heard from her friend, but Janet received a tip about another person going missing within the East Village. A map drawn up of missing people would find the area a Bermuda Triangle of missing protestors, mostly women. Cops had nothing to report and without their help our leads were cut thin. We went door to door, fielded a litany of complaints about Guard soldiers impressing gun barrels on foreheads in their spate of warrantless searches, as well as the subsequent inaction from the cops when reports of this mistreatment were made, but nothing about any women gone missing. (Cops must have been busy licking military boots.) This was unfortunate, as missing person cases almost always went cold in the absence of such information. I gallantly tried to reassure Tiffany as best I could over the phone.

"Don't worry. If we can find her in 72 hours or less, there's a good chance of her still being alive. A real good chance."

"But it's already been way more than 72 hours! Oh my God! Is she... is she dead, Leonard? She's dead, isn't she? Oh my God!"

"Did I say 72 hours? I meant days. 72 days."

"But I think I've heard that before. It was on an episode of NCIS. And you just said—"

I hung up, deciding the best thing I could do for Tiffany for the time being was to put my phone on silent, ignore her calls and texts, be more careful with my wording in the future, and only reply in the event I had good news.

Unsure if it would help, I explained the situation to MacCready. He was still pissed at me for not being there for Sasha on the day of the big reveal, but he owed me one after setting the cops in his area straight, along with my incalculable damage control when that little psycho Albert was beaten to a pulp by one of his men (he disputed my success in the latter, and we debated the point for some time). Nevertheless, MacCready drove down to the barracks erected at Tomkin's Square Park and met with the Lieutenant Colonel and they made small talk until questions about missing women surfaced. The Colonel's demeanour abruptly changed, and he was quick to point out that this was the local PD's jurisdiction and that MacCready had some nerve accusing his units of nefarious deeds when child beatings in MacCready's slice of town had almost plunged the city into widespread riots.

"But a few invisible women go missing in a city of millions, while those ghosts take potshots at us from every vantage. Sure, I'll get my top guys on it."

MacCready grunted at me to get more evidence before pushing the issue again.

By the end of this hot and sticky week, each day threatening with an 80% chance of war, I decided to get my hands dirty and asked Janet if she wanted to stake out some suspect areas within the neighbourhood or attempt the impossible task of getting a warrant for bugging the police station. Janet had a better idea. She suggested we contact Sanders.

The unyielding Sanders was more than happy to assist with gathering intelligence, more so than sharing updates on how Halifax's treatment was coming along. In fact, Sanders already had an entire network devoted to keeping tabs on this bothersome Colonel as he went about tightening his reins in the East Village. It soon became clear, from listening to conversations recorded by Sanders' wires inside the barracks, that something off the books was going down in a barricaded townhouse on E. 12th Street. Something about 'what to do with them,' an ambiguous refrain with seemingly no concrete answer. The phrase 'settling the score' was also repeated several times, which seemed less ambiguous.

We staked out the townhouse and observed a group of five guard soldiers entering the building under cover of darkness. We counted five individuals, and took pictures of their entry and exit, a couple of hours elapsing between each, as evidence. If one of those being held captive inside was Tiffany's friend, she was likely still alive. I asked Sanders to hold off on rescuing the hapless invisible detainees and that I'd handle it from here. Sanders' deference was succinct and dripping with textbook savvy: the longer the captors held onto their secret prisoners, the more likely they'd panic and do something stupid.

With all this in mind I went through the proper channels ASAP the next morning. The judge who'd granted the warrant for the redundant Feng raid argued that the evidence gathered was too flimsy and illegal. He didn't want to touch it unless someone above me in the Bureau guaranteed it. Not even my elated position in Halifax's absence moved his will.

I hear you loud and clear. You're implying I gave the go-ahead to Sanders to undertake the rescue mission, rather than taking the bureaucratic route. But I'm telling you he just went for it. Broke them free when he hadn't heard from me in a timeframe to his liking. The renegade! The hothead! Still, you had to respect his knack for getting results. Six women found gagged and chained to beds in squalid rooms of darkness. Sanders personally untied them, escorted them to safety, then had his team wait silently for the predators to return. Five Guard members did not report for duty the next morning, and the military briefed the media the following night. *A detachment of five Guard soldiers, faithfully delivering supplies to needy invisibles, reported missing in action. A callous ambush by a cell of murderous ghost operatives suspected. We are hoping for their survival, but the terrorists in question are yet to release a list of demands.*

None of this was a particularly good look for Janet or myself. Our official request for a warrant had been knocked back, and vigilante justice promptly enacted in its place. Oh, the hammer would slam down hard on my fingers in some hellish underground cell.

The Colonel yelled at Mac down the line and Mac passed the summation of there being 'hell to pay' my way. The Colonel's troops commenced search and destroy missions in conjunction with their regular activities, which were also search and destroy missions, working in tandem with the lapdog local PD. A digital army, monitoring CCTV footage and drone recordings, analysing an endless onslaught of tortured confessions, tapped conversations and surveillance data, offered almost omniscient eyes and ears. Going door to door, they broke down each in turn, violating every conceivable refuge and Miranda right of the inner-city maze. Detained and questioned each 'non visible person of interest', throwing in a few decent kicks for good measure. No one had any information to give and most drifted off expeditiously into the Method as a form of silent protest.

Condemnation flooded the airwaves, permeating the hearts and minds of the wider world. Those filthy ungrateful ghosts. How dare they—those soldiers were national heroes! They selflessly gave up their time to support these heathens, provided them with food and a semblance of dignity.

Reminded them of their duty to society. To America. And this was how they were repaid?

Bracken and the White House press secretary, ever the unashamed opportunists, placed accountability squarely on the inner circle, imploring them to not only condemn the actions of 'their' death squads but dismantle them entirely. We can't just leave you alone if this is the kind of law enforcement you will dish out.

Sanders' men were already at my apartment by the time the shit was hitting the fan.

"Bring nothing. No more phones. Here are our safe houses. Memorise their locations then burn after reading. Do you know where the judge lives?"

"In a high-rise here in Chelsea."

"Mm. If you can get to him in time, then maybe they won't make the connection. Otherwise, stay out of trouble."

I asked for permission to make one last call to Sasha. Sasha asked me what the hell was going on. What the fuck had I done this time.

"Those missing soldiers, they will link them to me," I explained. And I envisioned a cold, cold time on the run, living as a fugitive, sleeping in gutters, stealing MREs and clothes like a scraggly old Coney Island vagrant. Sanders' solution was ludicrous, I hadn't killed anyone before, never mind a judge. I told Sasha I'd have to disappear for a while, but that I'd try to get messages to her somehow. Sasha protested. She needed me. I should just cooperate and clear the air, otherwise I was just as bad as Devon running off to chase his anger.

FUGITIVE

You've made many claims against me in my stint as a fugitive. That I was here, there, everywhere—which I was... But these violent acts—goodness no! Innocent on all accounts. I would never hurt anyone. True, as I wandered the avenues, I felt I had finally become a legend, in the manner of Mora and the great Radakovic himself. Even the Ghost of Coney Island was left impressed by my feats of survival and evading capture. But orchestrating rebellion? Running and gunning with Sanders, Molotov in hand? Oh, dear no. Where on earth did you get that impression?

I did my best to maintain a low profile. I wandered aimlessly around town the first day, a day of rain showers and a muggy afternoon. Felt fresh in the rain and indulged in the Method. How long could one stay in it? Avoid the cruel mechanisms of reality. I assumed this was the goal of ascending. What were the side-effects of doing so with blunt repetitiveness, little and big, small molecule, large memory. Open eyes, watch the naval boats roll lazily across the Hudson. Close eyes. Feel the sun shine bright on my face, filling my cheeks with warmth. Rinse. Repeat.

In a throwback to the era of flower power, the streets were once again flooded with hallucinogens of every kind. Acid heads, certain their truth-seeking psychedelic missiles held the key to Mora's riddle, ensured its easy access on the streets of Manhattan. I took a dose from an unmolested LSD stand far away from the troubles of the East Village and wandered back to the bar I met Tiffany in. The place had shut up shop, trashed beyond repair, but a single couch, partially burnt along the edges, still maintained some semblance of comfort and suddenly I had a bed for the night, allowing me to sink deep into the Method, the mind-altering chemicals rappelling me further down into the depths of my subconscious. Total dissociation. Turn in, tune in, drop out.

At some point I changed the scenery inherent to my Method. The point of the Method was absorbing the Now in all its bothersome splendour, taking it all in. But on this night, head full of acid, daydreams of old crisscrossed in, and suddenly there I was, mind, body and soul in a tropical island cove. Crystal clear waters as warm and inviting as bathwater, tropical fish gliding past in mute recognition, and a stunning backdrop of palm trees and lush foliage. Everything where it needed to be. Perhaps these were not in line with the visions of Radakovic, too far from the holy land he'd chosen here in Manhattan, but I think you could relate to wanting to watch TV on a flat screen in a penthouse rather than a crackly old black & white box in a warzone. If the Next Stage was about being everywhere, then I could definitely be everywhere in this tropical haven.

★★★

The judge who had knocked back my warrant before Sanders' intervention had not snitched, as it were. A change of heart, either based on the horrific things those soldiers did to the girls, or a modicum of self-preservation after seeing what befell opposers of the Movement. Suffice to say, he would not be a problem. The determined companies of the East Village 2nd Battalion, and the local lap dog PD Janet and I had officially visited—well, they were another story. Each day, more and more citizens were taken away, collateral victims in a hunt for revenge, for Sanders, for me.

You want me to feel bad. To feel never-ending guilt in knowing that I could make it all stop, if only I turned myself in. Sure, it'd stop the guilt, but the detainments? The ever-dripping trickle toward irreversible war? You know this would not end with me. They could just as easily catch me and declare I was still at large. The search could continue forever, ad nauseam.

Excuses, excuses I hear you say.

***

Finally, the government laid down their ultimatum. Enough was enough. Unless, at a minimum, the hostages were freed and the death squads disbanded, all Invisible Yorkers would henceforth be required to be micro-chipped. The President spoke as if these missing soldiers were the last straw, not an opportune excuse to introduce what had been mass produced in secret earlier.

The blessed time had come when the patriots fearful

of tyranny now demanded we do the right thing by our country and receive our tracking chips.

Then as quickly as they announced, their micro-chipping agenda was derailed by the government cheese revelation. Let us not forget about the government cheese, nor ever forgive. A survival ration stockpiled since the 80s, it had flooded the streets as comfort and nutrition, an accompanying snack for each MRE supplied. Since the very beginning of our occupation.

I confess, I had nothing to do with this scandal.

But it was a welcome distraction watching the outcry unfold.

Private sector research into the effects of invisibility on childbirth had been rebuffed in the interest of national security. So when health conglomerate Purdue Pharma was discovered by a competitor conducting illegal studies on the ground in Manhattan and accessing buried government figures behind the mountain of red tape, the ensuing news story raised alarm bells for our people. While the competitor cried foul to the regulators and the media regarding Purdue's backdoor manoeuvring, many on the Island found the public omission of findings the most troubling.

A malicious notion formed in our thinking. What were they hiding? Why was this research conducted then subsequently quashed? In a time of information warfare, it was always preferable to blame first and concoct evidence later. The government was looking to sterilise us, in short. And suddenly we were well-versed historians, noting multiple precedents of these kinds of social engineering treachery! The Tuskegee experiment, the Uighur cultural assimilation extravaganza and the Nazi's eugenics program, to name but a few.

In the absence of concrete evidence, for instance a convenient mass vaccination program, our anxious citizens duly sought another culprit. And so we landed on the food, namely the government cheese that many swore had tasted different when they were kids.

FACT CHECK: The CDC has concluded that there was no contamination of nationalised dairy products resulting in sterilisation. Hospitals in Manhattan recorded over one thousand IBS afflicted child births post Transformation, as well as over 841 confirmed instances of pregnancy related health checks for TBS mothers. Government research into the health impacts of TBS on child birth was conducted with no ulterior motive. The CDC acknowledges a generalised mistrust generated by the hysteria significantly reduced the number of participants for future study.

The effects of this brazen attempt of genocide were manyfold. Pro-lifers on the mainland fell over themselves to congratulate God for severing our unnatural bloodlines. For those at the adult table, talk of micro-chipping, barcoding our wrists, was shelved from the upcoming bill, at least until a brief investigation into the allegations of mass sterilisation had been conducted and the government cleared of any wrongdoing.

And so the paranoia began. All food intended for Invisible Yorkers was treated with suspicion. Some did not care and carried on as normal. Others coordinated protests in front of barracks, demanding the Guard soldiers give up their unsullied food. Unopened MREs were hurled at windows.

Corporate franchises, those brave few greasy staples still standing, saw an uptick in violence. Pizza parlours had their basements invaded by enraged ghosts looking for evidence of conveniently labelled sterilisation chemicals. I watched on from the other side of the street as a McDonald's employee fended off a counter jumper demanding the truth, followed by fists when no answers materialised. No, I do not want fries with your lies! Cops swarmed in and arrested the aggressor, but a mob of natives surrounded the cops, demanding solutions. Where are we supposed to eat? What have they not tainted?

***

As each citizen revelled in some form of civil disobedience and took a liking to the fight, Sanders' death squads found no shortage of volunteers, as they swelled to the size of a small army.

Talk of a telepathic connection made its way around the Island, similar to how twins have an extra sense of each other (besides their immutable creepiness). But in truth, organisation of a naked invisible army is a complicated business.

They'd communicate with sign posts and graffiti

markers spaced throughout the city, and in-person using a silent language of touch the thermals could detect but not interpret with accuracy. The death squads left letters containing their demands on the steps of police precincts across Manhattan.

We will not release the National Guard hostages until Victor Rodriguez is transported back to the Island to face our justice.

In response, General Bracken and the POTUS trotted out an old favourite: We will not negotiate with terrorists.

The streets grew clogged with protest. Thousands were beaten and detained with a side of questioning. I say again, where did you plan to put us all?

A losing battle. A rear guard action. Guerrilla warfare at its best. Roman candles to Molotov cocktails, an explosive evolution. Each dawn awoke with civil disobedience. These pleasant tidings drew in the cops. A fight over food, say. And the death squads would watch from the shadows, select their targets, wait until detainment occurred then disarm and kill as they pleased. A fitting way to demilitarise the NYPD and add to the arsenal. Pop goes the po-po.

The NYPD sided with the army, at first. Bootlicking was the only way to keep their guns, keep them clinging atop their invisible brethren on the bottom rung. As a former upstanding upholder of the law, I sympathised with their quandary. To take away a cop's gun was to take away their sole tool, the blunt instrument of first and last resort. Faced with such tyranny (from the people they were sworn to protect) how could they relinquish their dearly beloved? No. This would not stand. If they had to live in fear and watch their back every time they suited up in their Itch-inducing uniforms, then so be it. By the holy powers granted in the Second Amendment, till death do us part!

And so it would be. Relations predictably soured when a platoon of Guard soldiers, having superior blunt instruments, mistook a police squad for insurgents and opened fire.

To drive this wedge beyond repair, the death squads began to masquerade as police with stolen uniforms and identify themselves to soldiers as such before taking their shot. So began Sanders' blood-soaked ultimatum New York's finest (all 25 thousand of them). From the rookie cadets to the Commissioner herself; each was given the opportunity to gaze at the horizon and see which way the wind was blowing. Every mistrustful glance, raised weapon and friendly fire tragedy by a jaded occupier, bringing civilians and cops closer together in their suffering.

"He was behaving strangely," a Guard soldier would recall to his superiors, and that was all the justification necessary; fuelling indignation within the local PD, who were encouraged to 'tread lightly' as a solution.

A sinister campaign of intimidation far more persuasive than leaflets or protests. Not the approach I would have taken, but we aren't all skilled operators in coercion. If the Method had not swayed them, then so be it (I'm sure Sanders argued).

The outside world accordingly chimed in with their condemnation. Headlines and bylines alternately screeched and cajoled. Comments sections collected the enraged. Why are they turning their homes into a war zone, when all we want is the bad guys to face justice? They are doing their cause no favours. Sickening. They're gon' lose, so why fight to the death now? Just surrender already. You have nothing to be scared about—the microchips won't hurt. At least not that much. A slight sting, a mosquito bite. That baseball player who tattooed his own body and went crazy from the Itch—he was already loco. Don't worry, they'll come up with a fix for the Itch. Don't worry about a thing, hun, let us slip this chip into your hand—doesn't even have to be your dominant hand. Look, see? Don't bite the hand that feeds you—just let us inject a chip into yours.

Gunfire clattered, echoed; ricocheting off buildings day and night. I'd do my best to avoid confrontation, but sometimes you found yourself in the wrong place at the wrong time; swallowed by a heaving march of natives, identified by their waving articles of clothing and their sonic wall of war cries, and you turned the corner and found yourself caught in the crossfire between a mob and a trigger-happy outpost. Often I fled, hair raised all over my body, exposed to the elements.

The Guard did not bother with identifying our fallen comrades. So, when the crematoriums, working around the clock, failed to keep up with demand, the Guard found more public means of disposal. In Central Park on the Great Lawn and even in Sheep Meadow, they dug mass graves for the dead and then set the bodies alight, before burial. It was decreed that no ghost body was to leave the Island.

Whether these cruel policies and procedures were the result of superstition, national security or a demoralising, big fuck you, I am unsure, but the smell of burning flesh, visible or not, filled our city for weeks.

***

Now our side was saying the sterilisation chemicals acted as suppressors for ascension. Hungry for something more substantial than hearsay, I went and found Eugene, my Reuben man. It was too late for me to have kids, but a well-made Reuben wasn't too paltry a substitute in filling the existential void. Eugene tearfully informed me of a rumour going around about the TRUE hidden motive in sterilising us. He blamed himself—the sandwiches he'd gifted to Mora had used the government cheese. Here I had the opportunity to correct him and admit freely these delicious relics did not reach their target, but I did him one better. Hugged my downtrodden comrade and told him Mora loved those Reubens, and if it was going to be her last meal then at least it had been a good one. Sensing him unmoved by my reassurance, I corrected myself and reminded him that Mora was still very much alive and watching over us, that this madness with the sterilisation and brutal trampling of our rights would surely dissipate in time. And because I was starving, I asked him for an old favourite, if it wasn't too much to ask. Nothing on me in way of recompense, but there was that old elbow ribber: for old times' sake.

He agreed but then said in a low, broken voice, "Don't

think I'll be open much longer, down to the last of my imports..."

I didn't think much of it at the time, so engorged was I with my Reuben hitting the damn spot. But as I later found out he was good to his word, filling the kitchen with gas and tossing a cigarette from the sidewalk. Took out his building and the one next to him, and his detainment and statement involving Mora and myself would eventually lead you to me.

Still, how can I stay mad at the guy? Those sandwiches made my life worth living.

***

Home had been desecrated. The FBI turned it inside out. Drawers emptied, books shaken for notes, cabinets dissected for clues and all laptops scanned and confiscated for forensic inspection. Sasha oversaw these extractions in seething silence. In my mind's eye I could hear her roar of objection in her curt replies. No, he hasn't contacted me. He shouldn't have done whatever it is he did and neither should you do what you're doing to us.

To take apart the history of a place—only relevant information considered—well isn't it all? To speak of me was to speak of my history, my mother, the socially conscientious nurturer who reached between the class divide and lifted me into her world.

They only took what they considered of potential importance but they didn't realise the whole place was important to me. It was where Barb had raised me, the carpet was my carpet, the feel of on my bare feet was mine alone, it was where I had refined my practise of the Method, and now it had been walked all over, trampled upon, tainted in anger and disrespect.

Now I've got all the time in the world and it's squeezing me out like I never thought possible. Idle hands crave peace and war at the same time. Before, when I wandered, before I became an exile in my own land, there was a home to find sanctuary in. Obvious but it bears noting: wandering sure changes when survival becomes the focus.

Barb survived the cancer for a long while. She demanded to be allowed to pass in her home and I did my best to accommodate. I remember her wasting away in her bed, next to the sun-lit window, repelling the dark force inside the room, hanging heavy on each picture frame, each reflection of a life lived. "Take care of Sasha. Take care of yourself." Instructions or choices, Barb? I held those frail hands many nights. Stroked them softly, waiting for the heaviness to leave and the relief to begin, both hers and mine.

An unburdening of the soul. That's what it felt like in the Method now, the lightness a stark contrast to those days of grief and torment. I was getting closer, Barb. The end of the road was nigh.

Growing up, Barb used to tell me all about the Warsaw Uprising of 1943. Freddie had an uncle who had fought in the resistance to the bitter end, she said. They had a smattering of Molotovs, a few hand grenades and the odd pilfered Luger. Meagre means, but they had the will to die with honour on their own terms, rather than being shipped off to Treblinka without a whimper. The Germans smoked them out of basements and sewers, burned down the ghetto that sheltered them, house by house with incendiaries and flamethrowers. I didn't want to believe our military would take inspiration from the SS but with the sterilisation investigation uncovering more damning evidence and enraging the populace to the brink, I knew that escalation of war would force Bracken's hand. Once again, the armchair experts of the world wide web declared our destruction a foregone conclusion. They wept with crocodile tears the regrettable yet unavoidable path the army would have to take to break our resolve; nothing short of levelling the city, and bravely rebuilding it anew. Times Square, Wall Street, the Rockefeller Centre. Restored to their glory in a boon of construction, the likes of which the economy desperately needed.

I wondered what Barb would make of all this. Whether Freddie would've found all the panic and shuffle amusing, or simply pathetic. What they'd have made of the streets being dug up for bricks, protestors twirling their clothes around in provocative dance? Go get 'em boys. Or would she retreat into the old squabble of her peers, saying this one isn't my fight, my fighting is done. Let the injustices of the world happen only in broadcasts to folk unrelated. What would she make of the outside world looking in, and us the most scrutinised group on the planet, raised to mythical status as all-powerful despite our greatest exhibit bearing us totally vulnerable?

I bid farewell to my home once more. The next few days were a blur. I kept myself out of the loop, focusing on scavenging for food, searching for places to squat, to survive. One night an explosion rocked the derelict Soho basement bar I and a couple of other vagrants were sharing. We peeked above the surface to find a riot van on fire. Rolling up behind it, illuminated by large searchlights, an Armoured Personnel Carrier angling its turret in revenge. We returned downstairs, I crawled into a booth and waited for the distant screams to die down.

★★★

Another day, another regrettable slew of dead NYPD officers. "If they aren't with us now, then they will pay the price when the army leaves," a passing citizen informed me as we watched some ghost cops violently clash with a cluster of nudists demonstrators on Canal Street. Sanders' police uniform deception had gotten a lot of good cops killed, the Police Commissioner stated factually, as if all wasn't fair in love and war. But her voice sounded unassured, over-the-top to us. You can't serve two masters. Us or them. And we'll be around for far longer, I can assure you of that.

The death toll rose on both sides, though the lopsided figures favoured the boys in blue and combat fatigues. Voices for annihilation repeated their doom-laden mantras. Replace the Guard with the Marines, they said. Time to cede the city to the sinful invisibles and then annex it straight back from America's new violent neighbour, transforming us from citizens into the more palatable-sounding enemy combatants.

And who should turn up in the nick of time, emerging from the forgotten depths to bravely stand between us and the skins? None other than the False Messiah, that captured "Radakovic". Wheeled out by the government once more to urge calm in the calamity. Submission to our inevitable fate. Embarrassingly championed by the inner circle as a means of support for their Utopia vote.

Well, Peter and Yvonne, if you say so, I wholly trust your judgement...

★★

East Village 9th Precinct bombing. Don't know how I'd been so foolish to have ended up here in my aimless meanderings. I should have been uptown, where the chances of protests and the wanton destruction were comparatively slim. Instead, I found myself in this gentrified territory of hip tiki bars, vintage record stores, and trendy minimalist fashion fronts—a mutually agreed-upon battleground where the aesthetic backdrop and its subsequent destruction carried more weight in the collective imagination.

There I was in East Village, deep within the heart of the infidels, dreaming of bygone walks with Barb along extinct streets of wonder, awaiting my inescapable fate as the world collapsed around me. The soldiers of the East Village 2nd Battalion had regressed into tweaked-out wasteland savages; twitchy, quick to anger, first to kill.

Reports of overmedicating on pep pills came as no surprise. Such was their stained reputation, replacements from the North Carolina National Guard were being fast tracked. But until then, the Colonel's crusade had become a shared obsession with his men, and together, they had adopted it with considerable gusto, firepower, and rampant unlawful engagement.

The cops of the East Village, having stepped aside from the very beginning and allowed these Search and Destroy operations to continue unabated, finally felt the personal fury of Sanders. Their allegiance to these barbaric soldiers had up until this point kept them safe, and harder to reach. But a message needed to be sent: with the power of Radakovic, Sanders could strike anywhere.

So one fine morning a stolen SWAT van loaded with a bespoke mix of homemade and military explosives is returned to the first floor of the 9th Precinct at speed. A load-bearing wall collapses and a handful of hapless administrative staff on the second-floor tumble to the blazing rubble below. The assailants are spoilt for choice in terms of getaway: run away, pose as casualties in the chaos, or leisurely strip and join the growing swarm of dismayed native onlookers.

"Why are you fighting us? We're not the ones doing this. It's the skins!" the local NYPD captain pleaded on the street to the faceless masses who refused to disperse; even with a platoon from the East Village 2nd Battalion surrounding us, threatening slaughter once the media crews stopped filming.

"Prove it. Fight with us. Fight back," The crowd demanded.

Watching the aftermath of the station bombing, one could not help but feel the immense power of Radakovic's gift, drawn to the promise of innate supremacy, of immortality, of defying the very laws of nature herself. Of becoming something more than human.

Or so I would imagine some of the zealots must have felt.

★★★

Well, well, well. How quickly the tide can turn! The media was now reporting that Invisible Yorkers could conceal their thermal identities. Undeniable proof of the impending Next Stage. Your local commentators may have downplayed its significance and joked it wasn't as grandiose a reveal as Mora had intended, and I might have agreed with them, if it weren't for the clear tinge of anxiety coursing through each soundbite and article.

A few folks claimed it was some new form of technology, either an ingested chemical or a thin mesh sheeting which camouflaged the user into the background, thus disguising their thermal emission.

"Like the cloak of invisibility in Harry Potter?" I enquired of one such informant.

"Uh, yeah, sort of."

"Genius."

I tried the safe houses Sanders' men had me memorise during my first night on the run. I felt a compulsion to learn the truth of what was going on. Guess I was a little desperate for some sliver of hope to cling to; something that would turn the tide our way—my way, if I was being perfectly honest. But most of the safe houses were abandoned and the occupants of those still inhabited doubted my connection to Sanders, having cycled through many generations of replacements, and sent me packing. I didn't know the secret code, they said. It had only been a week and a half and I was already out of the loop.

Righteous indignation. You best believe I wrote one safe house a strongly worded letter on respecting one's motherfucking founding fathers, adding a few choice opinions on what Radakovic would do if he discovered they had rebuffed me.

FACT CHECK: A series of letters recovered from a safe house in the garment district partially matched this description, signed by 'the real Radakovic'. The letters included advice from 'the real Radakovic' relating to Vote preferencing, arguing Manhattan was a holy ground that must not be ceded by any means. The same letter claimed the Utopian city will be engineered with a kill switch to extinguish the population once it is safe to do so. Each letter is supplemented with vitriolic condemnation of all skins and a call to arms in the name of justice for little Albert, Mora, and the women of the East Village, with specific instructions from 'the real Radakovic' to never give up any prisoners held, and to destroy without mercy all members of law enforcement who refused to bow to the gift of the Method.

> Seemingly no effort was made to conceal the handwriting style; all seven letters matched and were congruent with forensic analysis of Leonard Walcott's style.

***

We are all drawn to the past, my wanderings were no different. The spot where they took Halifax, the place in Sheep Meadow where they silenced Mora. Eugene's. Home.

The Rec Centre.

I was careful. Or tried to be, at least. I asked to borrow the ID of a brother heading for a protest downtown. He told me he was already borrowing it from someone else. Nevermind. I scoped out the Rec Centre. Waited a long time at the stoop of a basement entrance. The nearby intersection was devoid of citizens, inhabited only by Guard soldiers, discarded clothes of vibrant fast-fashion rolling like tumbleweeds across the avenue on hot gusts of wind. Commotion, a distraction of any magnitude, was all that was needed. As night approached, I smashed a window, scavenged. Some tiny hovel, abandoned, dust filled. A cat had lived here. I found a summer dress and a middle-aged ladies' library card. Bailey Cartwright, 40 years old. Only a year younger than me. Workable for an afternoon saunter.

My sandals clicked across the street as I approached the Rec Centre's paint-peeled door, which turned out to be locked. The sound of approaching boots left me frozen. I turned, my summer dress swinging gaily. There was no cover to run to and the confidence in my disguise withered instantly. There was still time however to rip the dress and sandals off and back up into the corner wall framing the entrance before standing completely still, which is what I did.

Mac smelled me first, regarded the sad yellow blouse where it lay scrunched and discarded by my feet. He stared for a little while then banged on the door. "Sasha, open up."

After all this time I had never really used my 'gift' in the ways that many comics and workers of fiction believed it was ideally to be used—to function as a fly on the wall, a voyeur, an unseen witness to all the madness and lusts of the world. An undetected force of near-limitless stealth and deviancy. Of course, this didn't come naturally to me, but I did my best to get my head around it.

When I heard my sister's name, the cogs inside my brain came grinding to a halt. A bead of sweat broke from my rigid frame and fell in slow motion to the ground with a faint splat. Mac's head drooped against the door in anguish.

"Sasha, I just want to talk. Want to make sure you're OK. I didn't mean for any of this to go down this way. I don't know how to make this right. Just promise me you'll be all right. Please. I need to see you."

Tears streamed from his face. I was no more than a few feet away and my shallow breath did not match the needs of my racing heart. He reached for his phone, tried to call, left a message, another pleading mess.

Mac retreated backwards, gazed up into the old windows

above, some of which had been shattered. I took this time to release some tension from my chest. Sadly, more sound came out than intended, as my back and feet scraped against the wall in shuffle. Mac's attention shifted to the summer dress, which he thought moved out the corner of his eye. Must've moved it with my feet. His eyes narrowed and he drew closer. "Sasha?" he called out, a noticeable tremble in his voice. I returned to frozen. A few more feet and I'd be closed in. What would the harm be in saying hello? He was a kind man, an understanding man, though a front row seat to his slow unravelling made me reconsider. I sized up his threat. He had a holstered 9mm—and we both wanted to speak to Sasha. So, I said his name, calmly.

First the shock, then the recognition.

Anger.

Understandable, but not worth the risk to engage further. I split, bolted back onto the street without looking back. Mac called after me, said he just wanted to talk, but I had momentum and let it guide me, my calloused feet pounding on the bitumen with a heavy, rhythmic thud-thud-thud, bruised heels and shin splints be damned. If I'd stayed, listened to what Mac had to say, who knows? Maybe things could've been different for both of us.

If I'd stayed, I would've learnt that Mac had come to Sasha's apologising on behalf of the barracks for a recent defensive response to hundreds of Invisible Yorkers throwing Molotovs and attempting to ram a Chevy SUV full of ammonium nitrate through the front door of the former school. The assault was a complete failure; the

Guardsmen neutralised the Chevy and killed over thirty of the assailants. Their actions were completely reasonable under the circumstances, but Devon had not made it back to the safe house and he had listed Sasha as his emergency contact.

Well, if nothing else I guess it explained why the barracks looked a little worse for wear.

Once clear, I broke into another basement apartment. This one was actually being lived in—the occupants may have been off fighting the good fight at the time of my arrival. But they'd taken their ID with them. I took a Home Knicks jersey, a baggy maroon hoodie, some weathered sweatpants. No shoes fit however. Damn.

The next place, I climbed the fire stairs around the back, window shopping, with my primary criteria being 1) unoccupied, and 2) tasteful décor, in that order. I found my match on the fourth floor. There wasn't much in the fridge and only a quarter-full box of cornflakes and a can of spaghettiOs in their pantry. Barely enough for them, let alone me. I still planned on finishing both, however.

Before, you could bet on a neighbour calling the cops at the first sound of a break in, but of course now the cops were too busy shooting people to bother with such trifles as home invasion. I found two photo IDs. A choice between Dominic Ramirez, 27 and male, or Casey Donovan, 24, female. Still, no shoes that fit. I ate their food and waited by the fire exit next to the bedroom window in case they returned. Hours passed and nobody returned for curfew at eight. Perhaps they had been detained, or better yet killed.

I kept the light off as the sun finally set and returned to my old home by way of the Method.

My gracious hosts did not return that night, and so I spent a passably peaceful evening in their bed, waking every so often to the sound of distant rockets pockmarking tenements and high rises.

The next morning, I relaxed properly into their tiny one-bedroom abode. I was on the couch, licking away at dry cornflakes crumbs when I heard footsteps in the hallway. I rose. A key jangled in the doorway. A muffled sobbing and the weight of a body thudding against the door. I scrambled for the fire escape as a voice screamed. It was not one of fear or terror, but anguish. A woman, must've been Casey. "I don't care!" was all I could make out as I crawled out the window. "I don't fucking care anymore!"

Plan was to head uptown instead this time, hoping for Washington Heights. I'd assumed from prior FBI intelligence that these parts of New York, had been relatively unscathed by the visceral troubles downtown, given that early into our quarantine, a great number of residents had upgraded their digs to abandoned penthouses in the Upper East Side.

But there were checkpoints now every two streets and at each avenue. A cop approached and asked for my ID.

"What year were you born? What's your star sign?" the portly cop said.

"Is this a club, sir? Are you trying to pick me up?"

"Where are your shoes?"

"I like the feel of the ground beneath my feet," I said.

"Where are you going?"

"Just going for a stroll. Inspecting the boundaries of my prison."

"You're going to go for a walk without shoes?"

"That's my choice, yes."

"Listen... Dominic, go home and get some shoes."

"It itches—my feet, they get the Itch real bad."

On cue the cop scratched rigorously against his uniform. "Hey, you think I don't got it the exact same way?"

"Then why are we wearing anything at all?"

This set the cop off. Fired him up. Still scratching, he said, "Either you go put some shoes on or I take this further."

So I eased off and turned back.

The Rec Centre was within the designated confines of said checkpoint block. They had emptied the MRE trucks of their supplies for the morning and folks were heading home to chow down, undress and, in most cases, prepare for daily protest. I tried to lose myself in the crowds of people, using them as a cover for passing the barracks to the Rec Centre.

Two guards with thermals stood by the front entrance. The door was open, and I spotted Sasha with her lime green work shirt out the front corralling her kids in. I thought about trying to pass as one of her charges, but she was inside before I could subtly make my move. The guards locked the door behind her and I kept walking until I found some protester's discarded shoes that finally fit.

SURRENDER

August 1st.

Peter and Yvonne announce the results of our internal vote. An overwhelming majority (92%) have voted to remain in Manhattan, likely attributed to mistrust of the sterilisation report, the threat of micro-chipping, or the accompanying 'kill switch' revelation, which had recently gained prominence.

August 2nd.

Despite the above, Congress passes the Translucent Re-homing Act with unanimous approval. A stretch of Nevada desert, once home to atomic explosions, is earmarked for construction of our new, state-of-the-art home. A welcoming climate for nudity, rumination and dehydration. Relocation to temporary FEMA camps to be fast-tracked. Microchip technology to be trialled with option of permanency depending on the results of the trial. (By what metric would they possibly consider the trial a failure?) Estimated completion of our new, supposedly self-sustaining home: four to ten years.

August 30th.

Scheduled Moving Day. Relocation of an estimated 3.8 million Invisible Yorkers. Four weeks' notice.

FACT CHECK: Leonard Walcott has admitted previously the kill switch rumour was something he was toying with.

While the outcome of their informal vote opposed Congress' Translucent Re-homing Act, the White House had the smarts to formally recognise the remains of the inner circle, specifically Peter and Yvonne, as the sensible new representatives of the invisible diaspora, and our new society in transition. Peter and Yvonne's precarious appointment rested on ensuring a cessation of hostilities until Moving Day. This involved the immediate dissolution of the death squads, an end to all domestic terrorism and antagonising (protests) and a general cease-fire, with the understanding that those detained from our side would be let go in exchange for those five missing soldiers, assuming they were still alive. A slight impediment to success was that nobody had run the prospect of surrender by Sanders. And despite intense aerial surveillance, search warrants being enacted in every building, over 100,000 troops and cops actively looking, phone taps and every available satellite network keyed into an area of only 23 square miles, they could not find either Sanders or their missing heroes.

And as I've said before, the Invisible Yorkers were ok with that. They didn't want the death squads to give these vile skins up. Even though the path to peace was clear, everyone knew what those sick soldiers had done. And given all the talk about how Victor Rodriguez was set to get off light for his crimes, the general assumption was that those men would too, were they to be released.

This was the death squads' counter offer: they'd release the soldiers once the ongoing investigation into potential sterilisation was complete (with a public admission of any cover up) and Victor Rodriguez returned to the city to face justice.

The government, and by proxy the inner circle of the Movement, rejected this outright. No mass sterilisation campaign had occurred, and they had the crisis actors (pregnant ladies/CGI babies) to prove it. The investigation, they argued further, was fast approaching the same conclusion. Clearly, the government remained hopeful that scientists could prove that the lack of new pregnancies in Manhattan were because of unknown physiological factors; some mysterious side effect of going invisible, as opposed to intentionally contaminated cheese.

> FACT CHECK: The pregnant women and babies alluded to by the government in their response were not crisis actors, nor CGI.

The inner circle made one more public plea to the death squads to respect the principles underlying the Method and hold out some hope for the truth of Mora's ascension, using the rumours of thermal evasion as proof they were getting somewhere with it all.

Sasha's Rec Centre remained tightly guarded. Movement between city blocks relied on mass protests breaking out into an uncontainable swell of bodies. I tried to stay close to the Rec Centre. Squatted wherever I could. Sometimes I'd sleep outside, reeking of piss and shit, and get moved along by the cops, never suspecting me of being one of the FBI's most wanted fugitives, the brilliant Leonard James Walcott.

I would catch glimpses of Sasha and the kids returning with their MREs. She never went to the MRE trucks herself and I didn't see Devon either. At first I thought this was because she didn't want to see Mac. I did not know both were already dead by this point. From afar, judging by her posture she looked sad, tired. Weren't we all?

When I passed a Subway eatery that remained defiantly open, it reminded me of the comfort that Eugene's Reubens once gave. It'd been almost two weeks since our last encounter and I wondered if he'd finally gone and shut up shop. Late that afternoon a march downtown picked up steam. I hitched a ride and peeled off halfway along when they deployed the tear gas, Dominic's ID getting me through a checkpoint. I decided after Eugene's I'd try to pass home on my way back uptown, even though I knew it was risky.

As I reached Eugene's, I was certain the coast would be clear. All I had to do was wait for the right protest/skirmish to draw attention and I could take a look myself. Strangely, we were unhappy about being forced into refugee camps in the desert, so there was bound to be some distraction. Everybody had bigger fish to fry than yours truly.

And that's when you finally caught me.

THE CIA

Eugene's was burned out. What I learned later was that Eugene had been muttering about his connections with Mora and an FBI agent when the cops came to detain him for setting fire to his own store and the laundromat next door. One could easily pass this off as the insane chattering of a disgruntled arsonist, but for no good reason at all, someone decided to do their job well and put two and two together.

Why had you staked out the deli? Why not my apartment, or the Rec Centre? Perhaps you'd waited too long at my home with nothing to show for it. Or you'd listened to poor, raving-mad Eugene, about how his divine sandwiches always drew me irresistibly back, over and over, the familiar taste and the nostalgia, a bait I simply could not overcome.

Eugene Harris lived upstairs, above the shop. Or at least he did until he blew it up. Here's more about Eugene, my weak link: he makes a great Reuben. Did I mention that already? There are other facts about Eugene I gathered in the small talk one exchanges about the weather, the Knicks, the Mets, and so on, but all these boiled down into insignificance compared to the fact that he made great sandwiches and I couldn't help myself. I knew it was inevitable, but of all the crimes and evidence that could have resulted in my capture... the fact that my yearning hunger for a toasted corned beef and sauerkraut sandwich proved to be my undoing made for extra embarrassment.

You waited. Watched me linger awhile at the charred remains. Saw me wiping the tears from the eyes. Any other fool would simply shake their head and move on. But I matched the height and when your point man approached from an adjoining street and called my name, you had your confirmation. In hindsight, I should have said no when asked if I was Leonard Walcott, but you caught me in a moment of emotional fragility.

Were you expecting a fight? What was I supposed to do? Go native, go post-thermal?

The rest of you swarmed the street. Hooded me. Bundled me into a van. You don't have to know much of the law to know we'd forsaken due process. Ten minutes. Several checkpoints. No answers to any of my questions because I didn't ask any. I'm not ashamed to say I teared up again in the darkness, and this time it wasn't over sandwiches. I thought of family. Barb, Freddie, but mostly Sasha. How she didn't deserve her lot. How her kindness and attachment to that Rec Centre was a testament to her character and a weakness that would get her in the end. I never told her that, and now it might be too late.

Our interview. Another dingy, dank basement, the smell of paint chemicals hanging thick in the air.

You said your name.

"My name is Franklin Pell. I'm with the CIA. As you can see, I am what you would call a skin." (I would also add he resembled a young Paul Giamatti.)

"Franklin, I'm Leonard Walcott, former FBI investigator. Human Trafficking. Currently homeless. Hungry."

Here was the rundown. You were impressed with how I had ingratiated myself with the inner circle and the death squads, and equally dumbfounded that no one else had picked up on this. Let's attribute this to a chaotic environment, sure. You were willing to give people the benefit of the doubt; not just myself, but Sanders too.

"So, it's Sanders you want," I intuited.

You smiled. I hadn't seen a smile in quite a while. A cowboy grin invigorated by the Wild West we'd cultivated here on the Island. "You're catching on quick. We understand there's been some bad blood between Sanders and the United States Government. A messiness in this once beautiful city that foreign players have tried to capitalise on. I'm here to try and make something of this situation for us. Plain speaking, we'd like to bring Sanders and his little army into our fold. And we'd like to do it before Sanders crosses the line on a scale that will tarnish him as a workable asset. Some members of my organisation believe they'd already gone too far with the Xi raid (Chinese nationals extraction). But lucky for you, I'm an optimist! I believe the window for cooperation is still open."

"And you'd like me to convince him before he does something violent and irrevocable with those missing soldiers."

"It's in no one's interest to escalate an unnecessary war."

"Why don't you ask him yourself?"

You chuckled. I laughed too.

"Why me?" I asked. "Why not ask, say, the inner circle?"

Franklin rolled his eyes in a chummy, friendly way. If only. "They're on limited speaking terms, I'm told. Besides, we don't want the inner circle to get their hands dirty. If they can guarantee peace and order then they'll have our support. But frankly, I don't care too much about that. Not my department. What my superiors want are the capabilities Sanders offers. There's no harm in changing the direction of your enemy's wrath. You, you're being hunted. Maybe he still trusts you."

"Maybe I don't want to be of assistance. What then?"

Mr. CIA man, you scratched your beard, coughed. "We hand you over to Colonel Ford of the East Village 2nd Battalion for torture. See how long you last."

I thought for a microsecond. "OK, I'll do it."

"Fantastic. Easier than expected."

"What support will I have?"

You grinned. "Absolutely none. We'll track your position, but you'll mostly be on your own."

"So, I give Sanders one of your business cards...?"

"Phone number and this location: Hudson Star yacht charters, at the Chelsea Piers and we'll take it from there. You get him to turn, you end this war before it really kicks off. You're a national hero—off the books."

It was always important when discussing a job to understand remuneration. I decided to high ball for a feeler. "What if I want off the Island—and not to one of your FEMA hellholes?"

You smirked. *Really?* you said with your eyes. "Where? Do you not know what they think of you and your kind? Where will you go that will accept you?"

"Not for me," I corrected, shifting selfish to selfless, "for my sister—and my former boss."

"You know where Gerrard Halifax is?"

"Yes, Sanders is holding him for reeducation. He's lost his mind. Awful business. Wish I could have stopped it. But mostly I want freedom for my sister. I want her to go somewhere safe. She's dating a Guardsman, a captain. They're having troubles, but maybe there's a future there. They still have a chance, anyway. Of finding some peace, far away from here. I know the government has land holdings in all kinds of private, tucked away places..."

You grinned, shook your head in disbelief. "A noble dream. A little far-fetched, perhaps. But if you can get it done, who knows? I'll pass your request along."

I asked how they thought I could get Sanders on board. What enticements I could offer? Taking my lead, you suggested I paint Sanders a selfless future. "He has a wife and a baby. His work can set them up for a brighter future, and little Sanders can grow up knowing their daddy is an American hero, instead of a war criminal."

And after a few more shocking revelations, you let me go. A last mission of redemption. Though I'm sure you had your doubts redemption was the primary driver. You handed me a phony CIA ID and the means of a ride for safe passage through the checkpoints to get me started.

"If Sanders is interested, get him to call this number and

we'll organise extraction from the Chelsea Piers. We'll take thirty of his best to begin with and see if further investment is warranted."

As for the revelations: talk of thermal evasion had been a false plant on the CIA's behalf. A way of raising perceived threat levels among the public to a useful level. Not out of the realm of impossibility, you noted, but thankfully a far-cry from the wild speculations during Mora's rise and fall. I can only assume that you'd want me to pass this onto the Movement, to either discourage or embolden the belief in thermal evasion to our detriment, a far-fetched hope we chased to our doom. Masterful if I may say so.

"We must've had you worried for a minute there," I said.

"Quivering in our boots," you joked.

Time was ticking away. With our relocation approaching, the window of opportunity to attack skins on the ground was closing fast. The stringing up of the missing five or one last hurrah of vengeance. "We understand the pressure of the situation, but I don't believe the government will want to work with Sanders if he can't overcome his current grievances and see the forest through the trees."

What about the other thing? The sterilisation.

You tensed, shifted uneasily. Eyes all over the place. *Ask anything but that*, I felt. "Let's say it was true. Would you believe it was the independent work of a nationalist group, saboteurs of the cheese supply, operating entirely unbeknownst to us?"

"No."

"Can't blame you," you shrugged, absolving yourself of

complicity and all future crimes committed henceforth, "but that's what they will conclude in the investigation. Eventually."

I could hardly believe my ears. "That's fucking monstrous!" I couldn't help blurting out. "Even with everything that's gone on, I still didn't think the government would stoop to intentionally sterilising its own citizens."

A terrible tragedy, you sympathised, but again, not your department. "We're not evil, Leonard. We simply want to make sure we come out on top when all's said and done. I'm sure you can understand that."

And even if I couldn't accomplish what you asked, there was the prototype tracker you had your men inject into my abdomen, with no thought for pain killers. You knew one thing about the tracker: "For some reason it makes it harder to engage in and enjoy the Method; whether it's psychological, or the body rejecting a foreign object I'm not entirely sure. Call it a happy accident. We want you focused, after all." Removal was theoretically possible, providing I knew a good enough surgeon, otherwise I had three days before the CIA cut their losses and settled for my recapture.

"I'd best get moving then."

"Excellent idea."

FACT CHECK: Franklin Pell denies the many damning claims made in the Walcott 'revelations'. Pell's operations reflected those of the wider CIA: Sanders' elimination, not recruitment, was the top priority. No such offer was ever made.

The inference the government investigation intended to blame a nationalist group for contamination of the Manhattan cheese supply with infertility-causing chemicals, is completely without merit. The government reiterates no record of sterilisation or lowered fertility rates exist.

No method-inhibiting effects were claimed by Franklin Pell or reported in testing of the tracking prototype. Leonard Walcott's inability to practice the Method is likely psychosomatic, the result of drinking too much of his own kool-aid.

REFUGEES

"When one sees the light, one must not shy from its truth."
Early Radakovic. Wise. Hopeful. "If a chance arises to play
the CIA for fools, one must not waste the opportunity."
Later Radakovic. Brooding. Pragmatic. Genius. Contextually
prescient.

My chauffeur was a stocky, silent skin. We drove straight
to the Rec Centre. It felt good to be free of the fear of
constant capture, if only for a moment. Also uplifting to
know I'd been promoted once more, if only for a moment,
and only under threat of torture. I was definitely making
up for lost time climbing the ladder, an enviable addition
to my CV in these final days.

The drive uptown through Chelsea was comparatively
uneventful. I hadn't been inside a car for what seemed
like months and marvelled at the leather seats and ease
of movement across the Island like I was some kind of
prehistoric cave dweller. I gazed eastward along the streets,
flashing lights of red and blue and tear gas billowing
upward in distant avenues. The driver noted the West Side
had been quiet, though only moments later we passed a
checkpoint cleaning up after some kind of incendiary attack
and only half a block later we heard the distinct chatter of
M16s warding off a sniper nested in an office block and the

accompanying scrambling comms to deal with it.

The setting sun shimmered across the tops of skyscrapers above and I stared in wonder at the view, transfixed by the calm normality of it, a moment of tranquillity before night descended and war began in earnest again. A difficult conversation lay ahead—but I had no idea how bad it would be.

I imagined selling Sasha on the promise of exile, not as some slow, lonely death in the parched expanses of a distant desert, but a space where she could actually live free. A little cabin out in foothills of Montana, perhaps, or the oft-preferred tropical island idyll of popular imagination. I'm sure Mac would have accepted either.

We pulled up at the Rec Centre. The two guards were gone. I tried opening the door. Locked. I knocked. A hard knock. Silence. I was about to leave, but the pitter-patter of small feet from inside glued me in place.

"Who is it?" A youthful voice. A little girl. Too young to be answering the front entrance, let alone defending it.

"Yolanda?" I asked. Silence. "I need to speak with Sasha. It's Leonard. You were living at my house, remember? I gave you food, shelter. Any of this ring a bell?"

The sound of heavier footsteps. "What are you doing there? Who is it, honey? Get away from the door. Who is this?"

I hadn't recognised her voice. Older lady. I repeated my request.

"I'll need to confirm this with Sasha," she said, shooing the girl away.

She returned and opened up, a pump-action shotgun at her side. Why, come on in. She introduced herself as Patty, a Midwestern transplant stranded in Manhattan, working at a daycare in Tribeca. "We brought the kids over here when Lower Manhattan got real bad, but I think we'll be on the move again soon. Government's set up shelters in Washington Heights. Away from the fighting. I'm trying to convince Sasha to leave tomorrow, but she's not in the right frame of mind."

"Why's that?"

Patty seemed to choke up at this and, unwilling to empathise with her due to time constraints, I cut her off, as tactfully as was possible under the circumstances. "Where can I find her?"

"The basketball court."

At the far end of the court, a ball was throwing itself mechanically, over and over, in the hoop's direction. Sasha had evidently gone native, something the other kids seemed uncomfortable with, given that Sasha had always remained clothed in their company. The kids, and there were a great deal more of the energetic sprites it appeared, kept to their side of the court. One of the bigger ones seemed to recognise my voice when I told off a wild little one for crashing into me, and shouted, "Yo, it's Special Agent Nigga."

A few of them crowded around, asking if I was coming to play ball, what it was like out there in the streets, but I told them I was here for Sasha. They said to be kind because she was 'going through some deep shit.' I said OK and shuffled on over.

"Sash..."

She tensed at my voice, nailed her shot and stood frozen as the ball bounced away.

"Your new friend Patty said something had happened. Didn't say what though. You alright?"

The ball returned to her foot. She picked it up and threw it hard against the backboard with a bang, the aggression stopping the game at the other end. Patty came in and ushered the kids out of the hall.

She whispered, her voice breaking. I almost didn't hear her. "Mac's dead. Devon too."

We hugged as the news hit me, swelled like a tidal wave breaching the sea wall. A violent maelstrom of raw emotion kept at bay, but only just.

I sat down, and Sasha followed. She told me what happened to Devon, how he was part of a failed attack on the barracks. Revenge for little Albert. How the soldiers stormed into the Rec Centre afterward looking for rebels, payback, screaming at the kids, putting gun barrels up to their heads. Striking Sasha across the face when she defended her flock.

Devon could drive Sasha up the wall but a huge chunk ripped from her soul when the news broke. Then, only a few days ago, Mac went too.

They shot him, right outside the front door. Ghost rebels, his soldiers claimed. And those motherfuckers blamed me. Said I was the one who messed with his head, blaming him for what happened with Devon. That I kept him coming around, every day, pouring his heart out through the door.

If only I'd let him in, they said, forgiven him, then he wouldn't have been there, an open target...

Bullshit! No one in our neighbourhood would've fucked with Mac, he was one of the good ones, even after Devon... Yeah I slapped him up when he shared the news, but you know me, my temper. I was just getting it out, I didn't want—I mean he was... kind, the kindest gentleman. His heart..." and then the sobbing began. I hugged her and waited for the storm to pass. She loved him. I hadn't fully realised how much.

"They're lying, Leonard. His own men did it. They were embarrassed by him. Because he fucking *cared* about what happened to us! And when I get the truth, I want you to make them pay."

My poor Sasha, crippled with grief, clutching at a grand conspiracy over the obvious truth. It was war, and no skin was off limits anymore. But at this point, why set her straight? Time was of the essence, and so I decided to use the tragedy as a selling point for a ticket out of this fragile place. "If I did that, went toe to toe with Mac's killers, you'd need to go away. Protect yourself. Avoid any backlash they'll undoubtedly want to visit on you..." Then I played my trump card. "Or, God forbid, the kids."

When I felt she'd regained her composure somewhat I gestured at her native state. "This is a new look."

A scoff. A smile, I could tell. "Ever since Mac, I tried—I've been doing the Method."

"Oh yeah? So, you finally see what all the fuss is about?"

"There's... something to it. Not sure what yet. Maybe

228

this Mora wasn't a complete charlatan after all... Say, did you come across that flower symbol in her diary? The same one that Yolanda kept drawing over and over? It can't all be a coincidence. Does that mean she was telling the truth, that the Next Stage actually exists? I can't help but feel there's something deeper going on here."

The symbol Sasha referred to was a Venn diagram flower of sorts, and I had indeed borrowed (for inspiration) from the drawing pad of Yolanda as she expressed the pain of being separated from her parents through the magic of sketching comforting shapes. It was not my place at that moment to reveal the inner workings of Mora's mind that Sasha alluded to, so Mora's 'muse' remained uncredited.

I deflected the Venn diagram business, and we talked a bit more about the Method, Devon, and how exactly it was that I was walking around free. She then abruptly changed back to her simmering, inconsolable rage about Mac. 'I know they're fucking lying, Leonard. I can fucking feel it. Promise you'll help me get revenge. Promise me!"

I promised. How could I not? I loved her. She was my only family. I then sprung my new mission on her. My plan to cooperate with the authorities and ensure lasting peace in the city upon Sanders' surrender. Technically, the exact opposite of what I'd just promised. But if successful, I could get us both out of our fate in the FEMA camps, swatting flies and wasting away in vain. I sold her the dream of Montana, the tropical cove of peaceful seclusion, now sans Mac, but enticing all the same.

"I'm not leaving," she said bluntly. "I'm not leaving them.

Not like mom left us. With the shit she left me in. You don't even remember her splitting. I was old enough to feel it suck the air from me till there was nothing left. If there's peace here, why not stay? The Movement is still appealing our relocation. This is our home. Where our people are. The only ones who will ever get us."

She couldn't understand why I wanted to get her out of Manhattan, away from our collective fate. I felt the reasons were obvious. Because we may not have another chance, because I had lost faith in the Movement and the ability of the hapless inner circle to lead. Because I might fail in my mission and Sanders, the loose cannon, would not go quietly. And when Sanders was finished, who would the skins punish for our little insurrection? Who would be among the first to get strung up?

"If you abandon us, I will never forgive you."

"Look, it's a just-in-case. I can't guarantee what happens if I fail, maybe there's no deal, but that means we're all shipped off to the desert. Maybe the CIA will kill me. But what's the alternative? You're about to become refugees from a goddamn Rec Centre! Are you going to barricade yourselves in here forever? You need to think about yourself for once, Sash."

"I don't want to be alone, Leonard. That's worse than death to me." Then she started crying again. Sheesh. What was it with all this crying? Why couldn't she just wall herself off emotionally, like I did?

Once the waterworks had finally stopped, I gave her time to think it over. Told her I'd look into Mac's fate, as promised, even though I had no time to waste, and finding his killers would bring her no peace.

> FACT CHECK: MPs uncovered no evidence suggesting National Guard misconduct in Captain MacCready's death. CCTV footage revealed MacCready struggled outside the Greens Athletic Youth Centre with an unidentified ghost assailant before the Captain's own weapon was used on himself.

Sasha countered, said she'd give me time to realise that being here together was better than being anywhere else apart.

"But I don't have time!" I snapped, before asking Sasha to tell me who gave her the news of Devon's death. She didn't have a name, said it was some kid who'd come through her doors whom she'd mistaken for seeking shelter. This kid had chatted to her older boys for a bit once he'd bluntly given her the news, then left. He hadn't been back since.

I asked around the Rec Centre, eventually obtaining a name. This street kid, Jamie, had offered most of the teens a role in the revolution. The once in a lifetime opportunity to become cannon-fodder like Devon. I assured them Special Agent Nigga had no interest in getting their new friend in trouble, I only wanted to speak to his higher ups. "Can you tell your friend I need to speak with Sanders, tell him it's Leonard and I've been recruited by the CIA." While there was no direct landline or fax, one kid who may have been able to reach this recruiter through a friend of a friend, wanted to break out and check on his girlfriend, so I cut him a deal. Who was I to get in the way of love?

I helped prepare tomorrow's evacuation to Washington Heights with Patty, while Sasha went back to her free throws and her thoughts. Sixty-five kids in total, twenty of them from Patty's daycare. We packed piles of MREs, board games, sporting equipment, and organised sleeping bags for the kids, drumming up excitement for our fun, little excursion uptown. An adventure. I hoped none of them would die along the way, a distinct possibility given the widespread lawlessness and chaos, but wisely kept my concerns to myself. I let my love-struck messenger out the padlocked front entrance, telling him to be as quick as he could. If Sasha knew I'd involved a child in all this, I assume she would have stopped with the free throws and started with the slapping, but alas, these were desperate times...

We all slept on the floor of the gym, except this time there were so many of us I had no sleeping bag. I tried to lose myself in the Method, to reach its plane of effortless, unparalleled calm, but Pell had not lied about the side effects of the stomach implant, so I was left to do a poor imitation. I conjured my island cove, home, penthouses on the East Side, queen beds, double beds—hell, my stiff cot at the academy—batting away thoughts of a future spent lying in makeshift tents while they built our supposed utopia; but all to no avail. I couldn't transcend, not for a single instant. Fucking CIA. If this method inhibitor technology was our dystopian future, and access to our inalienable sacrament based on some kind of 'good behaviour' submission, then may Radakovic suffocate the lungs of all living skins.

Roll call in the morning, and still no sign of the would-be messenger. My increasingly frantic messages and phone calls were going unanswered. Must've been deep in it. "Present," I said when his name was called, altering my voice slightly. It seemed to work well enough, for the time being.

Get back here immediately you randy little shit, I texted, then waited for a response. Nothing. "Teenagers," I sighed, hoping Sasha wouldn't notice his absence too quickly.

***

About the same time that morning, swimmers fleeing the National Guard's crackdown were fished out by patrol boats in the Hudson. Downtown, megaphones blaring out across the avenues instructed all invisible residents to pack their belongings; most pointedly, their identification, in readiness for relocation. Why wait the whole four weeks? Beat the rush. Come, huddle in the shelters for an exclusive preview of camp living. Prepare for the inevitable surrender. If you weren't willing to comply, you were no longer considered a civilian. They hit you with paintballs if you weren't wearing clothes. And if that did not move you, they presumed you were part of the death squads and treated you accordingly. A sieve to separate the wheat from the chaff. First stop, Washington Heights, next stop, mass exodus into the desert. Was it forty years, Moses? I doubted we would last that long. They would make sure of it.

My messenger had still not returned, and heavy action in

the East Village was once again being reported. A relentless bombardment on a suspected Death Squad stronghold. The blame as to who let the missing boy leave fell quickly at my feet. I told Sasha the boy had simply wanted to see his girlfriend but Sasha appeared well versed enough in the love life of this adolescent and my ulterior motives to call bullshit on that. Either that, or his friends had snitched on me.

"Find him. Bring him back. Or don't bother coming back yourself." She didn't mean it. I'm pretty sure she didn't mean it.

"You don't mean that."

"I do mean it, you fucking asshole! You sent one of my kids out into a fucking war zone!" She took a swing and just missed.

She meant it then. So, another improbable mission and I hadn't even had breakfast. Speaking of breakfast, the food trucks were late. I joined a growing mass of civilians queueing outside the barracks. Mac's killers spoke of an armed holdup, blaming the death squads. Angry shouts broke out, stirring all gun holders to an unwelcome state of agitation. The accusations flew freely. They're rounding us up like cattle! Next stop, Auschwitz! Thankfully, a true believer subdued the crowd, recalling Radakovic's vision of the ideal Invisible Yorker requiring nothing but the Method for sustenance. Despite a few errant groans from ungrateful heathens, the majority accepted this stoic call to a higher authority and dispersed peacefully, stomachs left bare. Walking back to the Rec Centre, I couldn't help but take pride in the power of my words, the satisfaction satiating me for the time being.

***

Four mindless trips later to an empty fridge, and my messenger had still not returned by midmorning. A military convoy had been organised to take us up to Washington Heights, trucks instead of cattle cars, where no doubt cramming the peaceful of us would produce nothing but good vibes. I'm told Sasha got in an argument with Patty about accepting transport directly from the barracks and soon the kids were slumped with backpacks double their size and told to walk.

Again, Sasha refused my plan of abandoning her charges and escaping while she still could, once more ordering me in no uncertain terms to find my missing messenger and get him to safety. Since I had no idea where he was, waiting around in the emptied Rec Centre in hopes he would return appeared my only option so I did exactly that, absentmindedly throwing a tennis ball against the wall in the empty gymnasium to pass the time. When that got boring, I climbed up to the roof and sought a better signal to read the news.

GUNFIGHT IN EAST VILLAGE: DEATH SQUAD STRONGHOLD DESTROYED. Precise number of casualties yet to be determined.

POLICE REAFFIRM COMMITMENT TO NATIONAL GUARD, DESPITE MISTAKEN SLAUGHTER. National

*Guard has the full backing of the police commissioner in
pursuing death squad militants until surrender.*

My messenger finally returned around midday with his
girl and another teenager. They had backpacks full of food
and clothes. I told them to head uptown to catch up with
Sasha and the others, providing them with the route she
and Patty had planned on taking. "They didn't leave that
long ago. They're going straight up Amsterdam. With all
those little pairs of legs, they can't have made it much
farther than Sherman Square."

The three of them agreed, hoisting their own backpacks
onto their shoulders. I asked my new friend to tell Sasha I
had loyally waited for him to return. "Make sure you use
the word loyal."

The other person with them continued to size me up
quietly throughout our encounter, only introducing himself
as they readied to depart. "Janet sent me. She wants you to
meet her across town in the Upper East Side, at some old
rug store you and her checked out one time." Unsure of the
specific address and finding this whole operation sketchy,
I demanded he take me there as reassurance, but the little
twerp declined. His orders were to go uptown, spying on the
migration. "Guard is moving the women and children out
before they close in," he said nonchalantly. "Is what it is."

I decided not to summon my CIA Uber, and instead
crossed through Central Park to Yorkville on a bicycle I
found. I weaved freely along 68th street, dodging the piles
of rubbish and clothing left discarded along the streets

and sidewalks. The riots had died down, and in their place slumped a mass of defeated citizens. Folk streamed uptown, carrying what they could, the consolation of food, the promise of an uneasy peace, shuffling them forward. Soldiers and cops let them pass, scanning their heat signatures, guns ready, profiling the full-grown males, the supposed threats, though they'd just as soon treat a child the same way if it made them feel safer.

I slowly recalled my way and dismounted near the shuttered rug store. Same one Janet and I had checked out before. I did a few circles to confirm the all clear. Nothing but invisible birds, gliding about, chirping. I knocked on the door and one of Janet's poss ushered me in at gunpoint.

I was led past the showroom through to the back office, where Janet awaited. "Great to see you," she said.

"Likewise. Good to see you've made a few friends since we last spoke," I motioned to the armed men in black fatigues, sizing me up.

"Time's like these, we need all the friends we can get."

We were both after Sanders, but Janet's agenda entailed more hoops. Let it be on the record, in Radakovic's endless grace, that I offered the CIA's assistance in reaching Sanders and eliminating these unnecessary detours numerous times, but Janet rebuffed me at every instance. Janet kept Sanders' whereabouts close to her chest, I presume, to avoid the CIA acting prematurely with drones were I to run off with such information. Come to think of it, that was exactly her reasoning. Safer to bring me to Sanders, directly in harm's way.

Janet's time as a fugitive appeared to have been spent rising the ranks of the death squads, judging by her amassed posse of eight fidgeting about the room, scanning the windows for the enemy. But as the army had ramped up its campaign and Janet's eyes bore witness to cruelties that made her time in human trafficking seem like a picnic, her appetite to defend New York had withered. Now all her breakaway posse sought was indemnity and personal assurances of safety, more than the flimsy public amnesty could provide. Only the inner circle could guarantee this, Janet insisted, and her posse's plan was to join them, expunging their history with the death squads.

This is where I came in. Janet believed I still had sway with Peter and Yvonne, a perception I was in no rush to correct. The inner circle wanted nothing to do with me. Janet would fare no better. But without Janet I had no idea where Sanders hid.

Of course, I had to consider the possibility that Janet and her posse were using me to draw out the inner circle and assassinate Peter and Yvonne in a final act of retribution for their public disownment of the death squads, but this was a risk I was willing to take.

Janet evinced indifference when I probed the likelihood of Sanders' accepting the CIAs offer, a perplexing attitude given both our dreams of salvation hinged on his decision. I was grateful however that we shared the same urgent desire to reach our militant commander. The latest attack in the East Village on a rebel stronghold had hit the rebels hard: if news reports were to be believed, a church turned munitions depot had been turned into rubble. Was Sanders inside? Unlikely, but it meant the rebellion was likely on its last legs and edging closer to fighting to the death rather than surrender (and with it my chances of sealing my deal—not that this was my chief concern).

We were at East 87th. Before they were to join us in our collective banishment, Peter and Yvonne were temporarily lodged in a heavily-guarded penthouse on East 65th. Sander's location, undisclosed, was much further south of this.

I felt like an exasperated video game character, running around at the behest of NPCs all over this god-forsaken grid. To pass this level you must collect all the coins and defeat the final boss: the US military. You have pulsating sepsis and zero health left.

There were many ways to reach Sanders. Unfortunately, they all entailed a nearly 100% probability of the trip being cut horribly short by capture or death. Underground, we could walk the unused subway tunnels, but even with thermal reflective blanket prototypes handy, all entry points would note the suspicious expensive ghost sheets and we'd be cornered and whacked wherever we popped up. Above ground was even riskier.

Getting past the military blockades was impossible without help. "But if we promise Sanders' surrender, then the inner circle will give us clearance," Janet declared and all her lemmings nodded.

So the inner circle it was.

"Maybe they know the secret to thermal evasion," one

of Janet's men remarked, and I elected not to enlighten him of the CIA's planted myth. Maybe we'd be able to take Peter and Yvonne hostage and take their place, fool our way past the countless blockades on some pretence of official business, I thought to myself, knowing full well this was, by far, our only course of action.

THE INNER CIRCLE

Peter and Yvonne made their choices and made them well. Their formal appointment as our submissive new leaders no doubt came with perks; the Upper East Side ivory tower views and a security detail while Sanders' rebellion was crushed being one such example of what playing by the rules could achieve. I don't know what concessions they'd receive upon their arrival in the desert, but I would be damned if Janet or myself would miss out.

The outgoing authority, Mayor O'Reilly, was charming and insisted on a smooth transition of power, graciously offering his expertise in an advisory capacity, a premium set of training wheels while they found their balance. A monumental task to rebuild from war, best not to cull those (himself) who could help.

Privately, I'm told that the mayor hated Peter and Yvonne with a fiery passion and loathed directives from Bracken and his superiors to play nice in the name of a tokenistic peace. Mayor O'Reilly intended to help in any way that backfired and made the power couple look like those drowning refugees in the Hudson. These odd academics and the other dithering heads of the inner circle wouldn't last a month in the desert, he believed, and rightly so. If anyone was to be the kingmaker of the rabble, the most prominent of sycophants, then he was the most qualified.

Janet's team scanned their comms for information regarding the itinerary of our fresh incumbents. Yvonne had posted a recent selfie down in City Hall with the mayor and Peter and their collection of Radakovic fanboy lawyers (as noted in the caption). Way downtown, past the fighting in the East Village and a plethora of Guard soldiers herding droves of asylum seekers uptown to Washington Heights. I suggested we wait until they returned to their primary residence on 65th, there being little point trying to reach them at City Hall, but Janet's crew rebuffed this. Time was of the essence. They couldn't afford to wait until nightfall. We had to go now.

If only you knew, I remember thinking at the time, that tracker beeping away inside me.

"Is that so? Well, why doesn't one of you just message Yvonne right now?" I asked, sneering at their resultant hesitation. "Go on. Organise a rendezvous. Actually, if it's that urgent, why don't I call my contact with the CIA? I've got one of their drivers at my beck and call. We can get a ride downtown and breeze past any checkpoints, all the way to Sanders. Don't need to bother the inner circle for a hall pass."

Unfortunately for me, for all of us, they declined the offer.

I sighed. "OK, I know another way."

The way, as all good ways do, relied primarily on blackmail. My time as New York's Most Wanted had lowered my stock with Peter and Yvonne, their cold rebuffs of my pleas for refuge while a fugitive hurting me when I needed help the most. They hadn't offered a single hot meal, or a consoling word, nor asked for my opinion as to what Radakovic might have to say about proceedings. I was beginning to feel better about my plan to take them hostage and assume their identities.

I took in the silence and relaxed my breathing, then dialled Peter's number. Crucial to my success would be my ability to threaten their credibility. The phone went unanswered and rung out so I left a message:

It's Leonard. We need to talk. I can end the war peacefully.

No response. I waited two minutes, then tried again.

We need to talk. Now. Or I go public with my last conversation with Mora. I'm sure you don't want certain details being leaked. Might prove lethal to your relevance. Nice photo, by the way. City Hall! You've come a long way. Would be dangerous to topple from such a height.

Hopefully this brought them to their senses. With Radakovic's great fortune hovering over me, the phone pinged.

End the war peacefully? You started the war! Mora was wrong to trust you. We won't be making the same mistake, went the message.

I just want to talk. Face to face.

We're done with your bullshit. Never contact us again.

The nerve! I panicked. We had to leave this place pronto. I declared it was time for Plan B. "We haven't discussed a Plan B," one of Janet's subordinates pointed out. And that's when I remembered the elderly lady who had hosted the inner circle in those simpler early days, while we'd debated the exact date when our promises and expectations would reach their high water mark, before the tide rolled its way inexorably back. A thoughtful hostess, a true believer and, most crucially in terms of leverage, a blood relation of Yvonne's, if memory served correctly. Conveniently, she lived only two blocks away.

We scrambled some clothes and IDs and made our way carefully to the old lady's house. I still don't remember her name. Lucky for us, unlucky for her, a persistent back problem had flared up and she'd delayed her evacuation. The antique door caved with ease after we kicked it repeatedly, and we stormed in with forthright purpose. The lady, like some kind of oracle, pointed directly at me. "You! I thought I told you to never come back here."

"Ma'am, I assure you, we come with the sole intention of bringing peace.

"You broke my door."

"Yes, well... we had to let you know how serious we were about peace."

"But you didn't even knock! You just broke it, then barged in."

She sure had gotten chatty in the intervening months. After I told her to pipe down and listen, Janet and I explained our noble intentions of brokering surrender and guaranteeing an end to hostilities, carefully omitting my plan to tie up Peter and Yvonne and leave them trussed up in a closet, should we need to take their places.

This time I sent Yvonne a picture of the old lady's cosy

dining room, along with the usual schtick of coming alone. I just want to talk. No one needs to get hurt. Their reply was quick and their objections reasonable: they were still in a meeting with the mayor and everywhere they went they were accounted for. But they had a driver.

You're visiting an old friend, I advised them. A family emergency. The old lady's had a heart attack. It doesn't matter. Get out of there ASAP. If you aren't here in 15 minutes, I'll smother this old bag. Real talk.

It'll take at least half an hour in this traffic, came the swift reply.

That also works, I replied.

"We'll take care of the driver," said Janet's right hand man. "Discreetly," he added, as though to reassure us we weren't the bad guys. He pulled out a metal pipe from the sports bag he was carrying.

***

Greetings were cordial enough. Much like the old lady, they disapproved of our busting down of the front door. We sat opposite one another at a cosy wooden dining table. The old lady relaxed on the couch with tea while from down below, the muffled sounds of the driver being discreetly bludgeoned to death wafted in through the window. I coughed to cover the noise, which soon enough went silent.

"So, the plan?" Yvonne asked.

I took the lead on this one. "Rather than this war where tens of thousands of rebels, our own people, are slaughtered unnecessarily, I have a solution. Peace." There was silence. I know. It was brilliant. I was shocked too when I thought of it.

"Sanders' arrest?"

"Not necessarily."

I told them the master plan, one which satisfied all agendas, secret or otherwise. The plan that required their assistance getting us past the stringent sweeps and thermals, to wherever it was that Sanders was holed up. The plan that guaranteed extra assurances for Janet and her posse by attaching them as support staff to the inner circle with new identities once we ended the war.

They did not accept this plan. "It won't work," Yvonne protested. "Assuming you make Sanders disappear, a huge IF, by the way, then it'll come back to us. Every soldier and cop in the city wants his head on a pike. Sure, no Sanders— an orderly eviction. But the cops are with us for good and it's our asses if they find out we let Sanders slip away. The cops will turn on the Movement and voila! Our new society crumbles just like that."

I have to say I'm proud of Janet. She could have switched allegiances and given up Sanders' location. But she didn't and so sank Janet's lifeboat, while mine remained afloat. I'm sure she would adapt well to the CIA.

Peter, also misreading the situation and his leverage therein, felt it necessary to play the blame game, rather than show gratitude for my solution. "You know if you people hadn't chased a pipedream of staying here in Manhattan and started an unwinnable war, we could've delayed what's happening right now! We would've had more time to negotiate a perfect new home, with minimal outside interference and state of the art facilit—"

"You are bargaining with an administration which has all but admitted to plotting to sterilise us," I reminded them.

Here they parroted the party line; proof of pregnant ghosts, baby bumps too early to show but all the necessary hormonal markers in place, how no one really knew the full effects of invisibility and its reproductive implications, and so on and so forth. I allowed them to blather on with their lies until they ran out of steam, then calmly introduced the notion of Janet and I temporarily replacing them in order to break through the sweeps and patrols in hopes of reaching Sanders. Peter and Yvonne would be safely released by tomorrow following an anonymous tip off, their roles forced instead of cooperative, sparing them from any implication. A fine deal, assuming they didn't mind spending fifteen or so hours tied up and gagged. I left this last part out.

"What's in it for you?" asked Yvonne. "Playing so many sides, I can't say with certainty that any assurance on our part will stop everyone who has you in their sights."

"No harm in reducing the list," I said, drifting briefly into the sparkling warm waters of my tropical island cove, Saroya, a name that came to me then and there, as if a gift from Radakovic himself, bringing it closer to tantalising reality.

"You're insane!" blurted Peter. "There's no way we'll go along with anything like that! Not in a million years."

But once the rest of Janet's crew returned to the

apartment, her right hand man carrying the bloodied clothes of their chauffeur, they came around to my way of thinking.

As we prepared our disguises against the wishes of the now-captive Peter and Yvonne, a brief opportunity for levity presented itself and we imitated with glee the spineless ways of the inner circle's power couple: 'The sacrifice of Mora must not return pointless bloodshed', 'Oh, we simply must find inner peace and learn to coexist with our human brethren', (though said couple did not join in the fun and may have found our revelry in poor taste).

One of the more curious, reverent members of Janet's posse asked the pair about thermal evasion. Do you know how to do it? he asked, a tad too eagerly. The room grew quiet. Perhaps they didn't want to help their captors. Fair enough. Or they wondered how much these people knew, and whether it was some kind of bait. Would they look stupid for not knowing?

"We personally haven't achieved it, but I think we're getting close!" they declared in unison, overly cheerful, the perennial optimists, keeping that motor running on the broken-down bus to an expired enlightenment.

INFILTRATION, OR JOYRIDE DOWNTOWN

We hobbled into Peter and Yvonne's designated ride with all the grace of stumbling imposters, Janet's command of Yvonne's slender heels found wanting.

We were a fifteen minute ride away from Sanders, supposedly. Straight down Lexington, across to Seventh, avoiding anything to do with the East Village, then down to a nondescript building just South of Canal Street in Tribeca.

The afternoon sun was in full glow and the streets were overrun with National Guard and police, the usual blend of trigger-happy authorities on every block. Our driver, Janet's right hand man with a gruff, no nonsense attitude, sported a Nike Skin to sell the illusion of obedient compliance. The papers we'd acquired allowed for safe conveyance to certain approved locations, such as City Hall and the couple's home on East 65th.

We were outside of our designated travel zone and the guard at the first checkpoint expressed as much. I let Janet do all the talking as it was publicly known that Peter was a Caucasian academic and my impression of a white person veered dangerously close to Dave Chappelle territory. We were just on our way to a business dinner in one of the cleared areas with some old friends, Janet insisted, and we'd most likely be spending the night. "It was all cleared with the mayor. We had to leave our meeting with him earlier than expected so we didn't have time to get our travel pass updated. Call his office and check if you like."

It was obvious the checkpoint Guardsman was dutifully imagining the 'business dinner' and 'overnight stay' as some kind of coded terminology for an upper-class orgy. Soon he was on his walkie talkie giving us the go-ahead and we'd cleared the first checkpoint.

As we made our way downtown, each successive checkpoint required further convincing; Janet often deflecting their concerns with doubts of our own. "Do you have control of this city or not?" Taken aback, the soldiers would reassure us this was the case, yet their skittish eyes suggested otherwise.

By the time we'd passed Greenwich Village, 'almost there' according to Janet, the penultimate checkpoint required a name drop of the mayor's political advisor, which we had extracted from Peter shortly before I'd knocked him unconscious. The utterance of our high connections along with 'Yvonne's' Karen-like insistence immediately eased the furrowed brows and allowed further passage...

We'd not rolled 30 feet before the car's radio transponder cracked to life. Target is in a black SUV travelling down Varick St. Plate number CES-5937. Awaiting confirmation to engage.

This gave us pause and Janet's driver shuddered to a stop, before Janet urged him on at a steady pace. "Keep your head. No need to panic just yet." We approached another intersection and the radio chatter continued. Clear to engage. That didn't sound too encouraging.

Outside we watched the skins scramble. All eyes on us. We braced for contact, confrontation, a last stand of some sort. Our driver, who'd been scratching away at his Nike Skin, stiffened. "This is it," he opined, and the three of us drew our guns. Jittery soldiers fanned out, surrounding us in every direction. One ran into the middle of the road and motioned frantically for us to divert into the adjacent street at the nearby intersection.

"No. Keep going forward," Janet pressed.

Our driver continued with some urgency and the soldier jerked back, his weapon drawn but his attention up in the canopy of buildings and windows and endless vantage points above. That's when we heard the yelling. Our driver instinctively sped up, and then came the blast.

The rocket hit the front passenger wheel. We flipped; a slow motion loss of equilibrium, a brief feeling of weightlessness, of dreamlike disorientation, then the SUV came back down with a sudden jarring thud of metal on pavement, grinding, scraping its way to a stop. Broken glass and shouting. A ringing in the ears, if those appendages still existed. Concussion. Dying? A game of pong played out between the two remaining pixels of consciousness. Dying? Time for the final Method.

When the dust settled, I was hanging from my seat belt, my neck contorted. Janet suspended motionless next to me.

I tried rousing her, but no response. Boots surrounded the

car. The sound of shouting. My seatbelt was unclipped and I was dragged from the wreckage. "My wife!" I screamed. As the soldiers turned their attention to the passengers still trapped in the car, I noticed a manhole cover blown clean off from the impact. Before anyone could wrap me up with a blanket for consoling, I moved toward the hole. Someone tried to grabbed me from behind but their attempts ceased when our friend with the rocket launcher piped up again. As an inordinate mass of military at the intersection fired upon this rooftop rebel, I crawled over to the manhole, peeked down into the darkness and then lowered myself into it.

The Moment. That's what they named it. When Mora went. Exactly where she went is up for debate, but that's what they were calling it anyhow.

My moment was currently inching forward into the dark, splashing my way through a morass of shit and sludge and other equally welcome niceties of the Island's bowels. Ever the good Radakovian, I rid myself of clothing, crawling through a tight sewer in what I prayed was a downtown direction, head pounding and nostrils clogged with odours better left undescribed.

Darkness, detritus bathing my many wounds. I had no choice but to abandon Janet. She would be in the best hands available, assuming she was still alive. Leave it all behind. Wasn't long before I realised I was completely lost. Which way was downtown? Disorientation and fatigue dictated rest, but the fear of capture spurred me onward. Each successive manhole shaft offered glimmers of light and hope, yet the animal grunts of the military—rolling their heavy tanks along, barking their orders of eradication, firing en mass at presumably outmatched rebels, kept me from rising to the surface.

After taking the first fork in the sewer offered and scrambling upward against a flowing water channel, my surroundings expanded into a sizeable drain alley, running across town (Canal street perhaps?) but most importantly a higher ceiling for me to luxuriously stretch out. I found a passably dry wall and slumped against it. I was ready to die. Nobody needed me up there. Nor down here, for that matter. Attempt the Method until I slipped away completely? What would Radakovic think? Call me a coward, a deserter. Accuse me of abandoning the principles I had so carefully instilled. But what difference did it make whether I died down here or up there? Sooner or later everything dies. Damn, these noxious sewer gases were making me morbid.

O great and mighty Radakovic, let me see my way clear of this cold, twisted fecal labyrinth! Or at the very least stop judging me for submitting to defeat inside it. A lot of folk considered the Method akin to a prayer, an act of communion in which one abandoned oneself to a Higher Source—the universe itself—gorged the self upon the inexpressible sense of Oneness. The Method was wholesome in a quite literal sense: we absorbed everything, reflecting light, taking it all back in again. An in-dwelling of pure spirit. Beseeching Radakovic for answers in the Method was, technically, a serious violation of this ideal, though as the rule was one I had invented I felt justified in making the exception.

A small band of rebels found me slumped there in the muck. Three of them. One identified me through goggles. I appeared disoriented, not to mention in need of a shower.

"You've got me. I give up, I surrender." Though these three were dressed as police officers, as I gradually discerned between the blinding beams of flashlights, they were ghosts; Sanders' boys and girls, youth in their voices, doubtless on their way to some kind of violent reckoning. "I need to speak to Sanders, you need to take me to him," I spluttered. I revealed who I was, and the lack of recognition stung a little, as did their hollow laughter when I insisted.

"Insist! That's a good one." The sarcasm was practically as thick as the toxic odours wafting up from the sludge beneath our feet. "Cool your jets, old timer." These damn impertinent millennials. They bickered among themselves as to what to do about me, the overall impression being that they were eager to ignore my orders and continue on. They finally agreed on assisting the bare minimum, offering vague directions to their rebel lair. "If you're not who you say you are, they'll chew you up quick," their leader flatly remarked. One drew the short straw to give up her light, for which she did not hand over graciously. I didn't accept it particularly graciously either, but that was because I was still smarting about their not recognising me. Sure I was naked and invisible and reeking of shit, but the chain of command either meant something or it didn't.

Before they departed, the impertinent hussy who had so begrudgingly surrendered her torch reached out a hand towards me, as though about to stroke my face. "Finally, the recognition I so richly deserve," I thought momentarily, then noticed she'd plucked something from behind my ear.

"You have a used condom stuck to the side of your head." She held it aloft, wiggling it in front of my face like a translucent sardine, and the trio once more contorted in peals of laughter before heading off on their merry, idiotic way. It really makes one weep for the future. I tried to think of a suitably witty comeback, but a combination of fatigue, mortification and sewer gases appeared to have momentarily dulled my usually razor-sharp perceptual processes.

Hobbling forward, I gave thanks to Radakovic for His timely nudge, when a good part of me had been resigned to the end.

SANDERS

After what felt like days I eventually stumbled bleary-eyed upon the cold steel of a ladder and meekly ascended its rusted rungs. Assuming Sanders' trio of imbeciles could be trusted, this was the exit I needed.

Guns and flashlights were thrust against my head the moment it bobbed up. I sensed there were many ghosts in this crowded maintenance room of concrete and pipes; ghosts weary and desperate, the dusty haze of their surroundings giving them shape in the dim amber glow of the light above. Spirits tiptoeing the line between life and death.

None recognised my name or former standing as essentially a founding member of their little army, but I graciously took this in my stride. Take me to your leader, you deranged fanatics.

They held me at gunpoint in silence until one of their runners returned with a confirmation of my credentials. I was then forced to crawl once more through a DIY tunnel that had recently been bored and thirty feet later emerged in another dark basement filled with roller cages covered in reflective foil and rebels filing through to a multitude of other tunnels, at least two others that I could tell. From here I was led upstairs in a more civilised form of travel (read: upright) till the warmth improved and I was sure we had returned to the surface. From the claustrophobic ordeal of before came light and space, the main hall of a brewery abuzz with activity. The walls and high ceiling lined with aluminium film. Thermal shields I suspected. Frantic troops, identifiable only by their slung rifles, bumping into one another, scurrying to and fro like worker ants, packing plastic milk crates overflowing with cables, laptops and other electronics into more of these strange foil cages on wheels. I was bumped into no less than fifteen times in a single minute, no time for apologies apparently.

They guided me to the 'war room' on the second floor and into the dark, twisted brain centre of public enemy number one. Sanders stood clothed in military fatigues over a pool table littered with maps, coordinating troop formations and Radakovic knows what else to a handful of deputies shuffling piles of papers scattered across the room. Synchronising times and places of destruction. A thick cloud of stress hanging over their heads; shortening the breath, loosening the screws within, suffocating any sense of restraint.

When he heard my voice, I could sense him grin. "Welcome to the Final Offensive."

He was insane to say the least. "Time is of the essence. They've killed Peter and Yvonne and blaming it on us. Moving day could be any day now. No time to lose, no time at all. Tonight is the night."

"Peter and Yvonne are not dead. Janet was in the car. Your people attacked us! It was Janet and me in the car."

Sanders dismissed this for all those present to hear. It couldn't have happened that way, and even if it did, the damage was already done. Now all the former powerbrokers, such as the mayor, would swoop in and fill the resultant power vacuum. Peter and Yvonne's fates sealed regardless.

Sanders then moved to ask why we didn't use the tunnels, but before I could shift the blame for this oversight on the other members of my now dispensed posse, another voice broke in the room, asking about Janet. I informed her Janet had been unconscious when I was forced to leave her and shimmy down into the New York sewer system.

"That explains the smell in here," piped up another voice, helpfully.

No need to fret, I reassured the first voice, No need to fret, they would have given her due care. Hopefully.

The person broke into an immediate sob. Sanders consoled her and suggested she excuse herself. No crying in the war room. I asked if we could speak privately about some new information that had come to light. He was dismissive at first, time being of the essence, if I recall his demented ramblings correctly. But he eventually relented and ushered me into a corner office.

"A friend of Janet's?" I asked.

"Her lover."

I smiled, recalling Janet's bout of loneliness in the middle of the road that now seemed so long ago. At least she'd had someone. In retrospect, this may have been her entire motivation for undertaking this mission—and another reason she hadn't divulged this precise location or what

Sanders was really up to. Can't say it didn't hurt, the lack of faith and trust. I dabbed at the tender spot in my abdomen where they'd inserted the tracker.

"So, this new information you mentioned?" Sanders pushed.

"Yes, surrender. A new job, a financial windfall for your family and all their descendants."

"Who got to you?"

"The CIA. They want to cut a deal. An immediate surrender. Immunity from prosecution. Something other than the FEMA camps. Picture this, an army of invisible spooks, under your command, restoring American superiority one black ops at a time."

"How many?"

"Thirty of your best, to begin with."

"And abandon the rest, to be carted off to some refugee camp, left to rot in the desert?"

"You can't save everyone. But if you go ahead with whatever it is you're going to do, it won't help anyone."

"And who are you saving, Leonard? Yourself, as always. It's just bait. A ruse. Relocation is one of their favourite lies. Don't trust them. They contaminate our food and they know we have to eat it or starve, but I will not go peacefully, Lenny. Have you ever seen displaced people thrive? There is no land more promised than that which is right here. New York is our birth right. Radakovic decreed it. It's ours. We won't leave it under any circumstances!" he slammed his fist down hard on the desk.

His brain rotted by propaganda, I had no choice but to

play my trump card. "Don't you want to see your family again?"

Sanders lowered his voice, and the air turned cold. "Don't you dare..."

There was a polite knock at the door and he yelled a forceful "Fuck off!" in response. Shook me. Dialled up the tension another notch. He then lowered his voice once more, in the manner of all good psychopaths.

"You know when I saw it all so clear? The very first day. After we parted ways I walked to the Queensboro Bridge and I watched those barricades rise up. No more than a few hours and I knew I was already too late. I was never going to see my wife and baby again. It made me furious, and I wanted to cause pain. Started with Feng and snowballed from there..."

An orgy of mayhem and violence, I believe the *New Yorker* termed it.

"You know I only spoke with them once since this all began. One time. My own family! While the world was busy being captivated by Mora, I called. Hearing my baby's cries broke me."

"You can still call them, speak to them. I know they miss you terribly. I'm certain the CIA will make arrangements..."

Sanders was disgusted at my blatant angling. But hopefully more disgusted with himself. "Christine know what I've done. I've already made my choices. There is no going back. It's just bait. Can't you see? The CIA doesn't need me for an army of ghosts. They'll figure out what Radakovic did to make us 'us' eventually—and replicate the transformation at will."

Technically, he had a point. And that point was clearly going to justify whatever awful act all these busy worker ants down below were preparing for. It would cut through all rhyme and reason like scissors through cloth. A suicide mission. The last hurrah. I understand you feel I should have done more persuading, perhaps even a bit of wheedling or cajoling. But I hadn't the faintest idea of what was to transpire.

"So, what's the plan then, boss?"

"Glad to hear you're finally on board."

"Not until I know what I'm joining."

Sanders paused, doing his calculations. "What did they say they'd give you if you brought me in?"

"A ticket off the island. Parcel of land somewhere. Best case scenario, something in the Caribbean or the Pacific Islands, but a little log cabin out in Montana will do fine too." And this goddamn tracker out of me.

"Always carving out your little slice... And if you don't bring me in?"

The truth was all I had. No sense in lying at this late juncture. "They'll kill Sasha if I don't. And if the kids are with her, we both know they won't leave any witnesses."

FACT CHECK: False. There is no evidence that Sasha was ever threatened.

Sanders laughed and a second knock on the door caused us both to tense. This time he simply ignored it. "Where's the proposed extraction point for me and my lucky thirty?"

I perked up, surprised by the effectiveness of my

persuasion. "Chelsea Piers. I have a phone number."

Sanders then retrieved a letter from a drawer of his desk. "When you report to your handlers, pass this letter along. You have about thirty minutes."

"You're going to let me go?"

"You can't stop what's about to happen. No one can. They're going to leave this island to us. No more bullshit pipedream utopias and no more occupiers. This will be ours alone."

I wondered how long it would take for the CIA to scramble units on my location, if they were keeping track at all. They had to assume this was Sanders' lair; so far down the Island, so long had I been stationary.

Sanders was admirably cryptic with his plans, the true sign of an inspired leader. "The skins are always debating what we invisibles can and can't do. So busy filling their heads with fantasy, they forget what their own kind are capable of..."

Sanders' weapon was not some freak theoretical explosion in a meadow. He was simply constructing an even playing field, if only for the night. (I pushed for clarity, but realised I should have pushed more when I eventually saw what transpired.)

"What's in the letter?"

"It's for Christine. An apology. Last words. Thought I'd missed my chance to get it to her, but now that you're here..."

"Sasha is in Washington Heights. Will she be safe from whatever it is you're planning?"

"Yes, she should be."

All I had to vouch for her safety was the word of a rebel commander whose mind had fused into a powder keg of bloodlust and uppers. But I was being let go, and I wasn't going to waste my luck. "I'm going to go then... My hand is out." Sanders sought it awkwardly and we shook.

"Get that letter to my wife... You know how to avoid thermal detection, right?"

The tone suggested I should have known how to achieve this impossible feat, so I didn't know whether to correct him or nod along at his knowing humour.

"Of course."

"Thank you, Leonard. I know I wasn't always the easiest partner before this, but it's been an honour to have worked with you."

"You too, take care." Best of luck with all your future endeavours.

***

Halifax? Oh, yes, I did ask him what happened with Halifax. One of the first things I asked Sanders, I forgot to mention. My main reason for being here, I assure you. To vanquish the guilt and redeem. And thanks to Radakovic and the patience of Sanders' re-educators, Halifax finally overcame his irrationality and became a genuine believer. Sanders offered to release him to the refugee migration to Washington Heights, but credit to Halifax, he decided to stay and fight. So, you can imagine my great relief, knowing it all worked out in the end for Gerrard Halifax.

***

Anyways, I was all set to be on my way, but a sudden commotion from the lower levels caused everyone in the war room to freeze. A rebel keeping lookout through a slit in the aluminium blinds, yelled out 'Bananas,' which I could only assume was a coded warning of some type, and the ants below broke into an even more frenetic pace. Sanders, who now stood firm atop the staircase overseeing his soldiers gave the order to fire but met panicked resistance from his fellow conspirators. Concerns about a retaliatory airstrike will do that.

How'd the skins find us? Could it somehow be related to this intruder who had swayed and courted the attention of our leader? That was the vibe I was getting, the tracker beneath my skin beating like a guilty heart for all to hear. His underlings landed on a similar theory. Before Sanders' deputies descended on me, I eyed off the exits, prepared to spin and juke my way out if necessary, eluding all bodies in a Benny Hill bonanza, a comedy of friendly fire whoopsies and "argh, almost swiped him."

But before any such need arose, Sanders halted their murderous advance.

"Radakovic spoke to me!" he announced. "He said my closest friend would betray me, someone who would send us to the brink—but whose betrayal would lead to our ultimate salvation!"

"How do you think us being surrounded helps our salvation?" his troops enquired, not unreasonably.

"Because, we now have them exactly where we want them. Send as many into the tunnels for the Canal St exit. Leave a small party here to defend the brewery and keep the skins at bay. Move as many cages into the basement as possible on your way down. Brothers and Sisters, the tide turns tonight. We will flay our enemies and reveal their insides—every single one of them!"

I held my breath, never having seen Sanders wax fanatical with such fervour. Fanaticism, it emerges, isn't so bad if you can work it to your favour.

Nevertheless, the predicament persisted about what to do to me.

"Radakovic said he will stay here and help us hold them off for his redemption. He knows how to handle himself."

This seemed to quell their misgivings as to their besiegement and, more importantly from my perspective, ended their menacing encircling. A flurry of floating rifles raced off downstairs, my skin saved once more.

That's the other, primary thing to be admired about the followers of fanatics—their relentless, commendable pursuit of orders to the death.

Sanders strong-armed me once the others had cleared.

"Guess I'm lucky Radakovic put in a good word for me," I smirked gratefully.

"I wasn't joking," he said. I still didn't know exactly what he believed; perhaps he didn't either. Like the afterlife, we can speculate all we wish, believe with unbreachable certainty there is nothing or everything waiting for us on the other side, but we'll never actually know until we cross that bridge.

He paused, waiting for me to say something. I remained silent.

"Go, you son of a bitch. Use the tunnel. That letter, make sure Christine gets it." A subordinate then interrupted our heartfelt goodbye, handing Sanders an AK47, which he raised in battle cry, a quasi-heroic freedom fighter leading his ragtag army of loyalists to do the only thing they believed they had left. Godspeed. I hoped his vague avowals of Sasha's safety weren't just empty words.

I made my way back to the tunnels, and it was only then, passing these strange cages, that it all clicked into place. Janet and her friends realised the expediency of finding Sanders, but they didn't trust me enough to divulge why. Oh, how I wish they'd told me what they knew. Because then I would have been more than just a transmission beacon, a sentient homing device. And I would have fought him tooth and nail, I promise you. But it was far too late for that.

At precisely eight o'clock, in a masterpiece of coordination, a dozen Chinese missiles acquired by Sanders were launched skyward. If there had been torrential rain, if the night had been blowing a fearsome gale, then it may have been a different story, a fizzle. But sometimes in life everything goes perfectly according to plan. Radakovic's divine schemes. Truly a glorious thing to behold—not that *I* wanted this at all.

An EMP is designed to destroy all electronics within a certain radius. Prior to this night, their effectiveness was largely theoretical. Not anymore. Delivery in this most non-theoretical of instances came in the form of foreign hardware, a Chinese-made prototype EMP rocket, detonated half a mile above the New York skyline, releasing particles that obstructed short wave signals and electronic devices, in some instances frying them outright.

I followed the other lemmings as far as the basement of an office building they'd burrowed through to. I blended in with mock fervour and words of encouragement. This is it, comrades! Our destiny! That sort of thing. And no sooner than I'd been handed the sharpened femur of a fallen comrade for use as a dagger, I'd slipped away. I'm astounded the AWOL rate of his militia wasn't higher, with lax security like that. Who would know? You really had to marvel at their blind dedication to Radakovic, Sanders, Mora and ultimately New York herself, the holy land of our newly minted people.

I'd made it outside. Sucked in air. Sweet relief. I figured it must have been showtime, the requisite doomsday countdown having begun in earnest. Times like these you think of your life, the little things that comprise the serenity within your Method; of living, your place in the world and the choices you made to get there. Couldn't say mine had amounted to all that much, when all was said and done.

This is the part where I seek forgiveness for my sins.

FACT CHECK: The timing does not add up. Peter and Yvonne's SUV was hit at approximately 4.05pm. Tracker signal was lost at Brewery at 5.12pm. Tracker signal recovered at 6.03pm and Mr Walcott headed up Greenwich St., crossing Little W 12th and entering the Highline, following it up to W17th and stopping at 7.15pm. No movement was recorded for over forty minutes until 7.55pm when Mr Walcott exited the Highline in the direction of the Chelsea piers. The coordinated EMP attack occurred at 8.03 pm across Manhattan and Leonard Walcott reached the boat by 8.10pm.

At no point from 6.03pm onwards did Leonard attempt to alert the authorities to the impending terror attack, leading to the catastrophic loss of life of over 1,242 National Guard and untold thousands of invisible militants and NYPD. Further investigation is warranted in determining Mr Walcott's prior knowledge of the onslaught.

TICKET STUB

A light fallout mist, electromagnetic pulses striking the ground one after the other after the other, distorting and dismantling the waves of communication we had heretofore taken for granted. Nothing like you've seen in the movies, more of a dull persistent thudding than the traditional boom of wars past; they just don't make explosions like they used to. But bad for Wi-Fi, you bet. Street lights surging brilliantly before burning into darkness. Then the gunfire increased. Rat-atat-tat. Screams. Confusion. Panicked chatter pervaded the entire island and spread from there. When those generals and admirals stationed outside the Manhattan radius discovered why their communiques and directives fell on deaf ears, who could blame the reinforcements for refusing to charge in? I sure as hell saw no air support courageously strafing the avenues; your pilots afraid of being plucked out of the sky like apples from a tree by the unseen fingers of the next EMP.

The Guard too were figuring out, astutely, that their radios were down. Their thermal vision goggles, once their eyes and safety net, malfunctioned. Suddenly the brain circuitry beneath each helmet clicked over. Every skin suddenly cut off, isolated. Changes the kind of conversations you have with the soldier beside you. Dulls your taste for holding the post. From every corner came visions of the invisible swarm, an ominous, all-seeing mob out for blood. All that talk, rumours of unknown origin, of the prisoner's revolt, unremittingly bloody threats of flaying soldiers and wearing the skin as some sort of trophy, filled those flustered heads of theirs.

If the ghosts could do this, if they could eviscerate the advantage of thermal imaging in one fell swoop, what else did they have in store...

It should come as no surprise that the Guard decided on a quick withdrawal. I watched as droves of Humvees stormed away, one-way signs and military etiquette be damned. But not every unit found an easy exit. Sanders' army had blockaded key vantage points, roads became cut off as nearby windows lit up with Molotovs ready to reign down. I even heard the rebels caved in the road at Canal Junction with subterranean detonations so assiduously that not even the all-terrain vehicles could manoeuvre through. The Guard spent their bullets wantonly, aimlessly, the enemy all around, unseen, the increasingly-erratic gunfire a symphony of anarchy. No shadow spared in the long dark night that ensued.

Only days ago, after Congress voted to exile us, there had been open discourse by the Feds on whether to banish the NYPD uptown to the top of the Island in order to reduce counter-insurgency shenanigans and clearly delineate for the Guard friend from foe; this being anyone invisible. Directives from the police union still awaited sign off and this delay would prove fatal and exacerbate the Night of the Long Dark. The Guard believed the cops were allies in Sanders' EMP assault and it only took a few pitched battles between the two parties to force this alliance in the chaos.

The East Village 2nd battalion and their Colonel Kurtz commander, three days into disobeying his orders to be relieved, saw this as a prime opportunity to run wild and abandon the few rules of engagement they had not already broken. They would not flee like the other battalions—Lord knows the nearby Williamsburg Bridge offered a safe exit—not when their enemy had so graciously come out of hiding. Practically foaming at the mouths, every soldier who participated in the resultant carnage did so both willingly and wilfully. I'm sure the battalion slaughtered many, piling the bodies of the oncoming swarm into an invisible wall, but they had to run out of ammunition eventually, and when they did, I can only assume the ghosts savoured their retribution.

FACT CHECK: All branches of government have roundly condemned the actions of the East Village 2nd Battalion. The air force maintains that the subsequent air strikes aimed to neutralise the rogue operators. Invisible militant casualties were regrettably accepted as unfortunate collateral damage.

The rest of the skins got out in a hurry—I know those convoys that made it past Sanders' barrage of rockets drove north and kept going over the Washington Bridge, abandoning their posts and dodging questions from the displaced in the camps as to whether they'd return. *What will happen to us?* What would happen indeed.

You left approximately three million displaced in Washington Heights. Figures before the vote estimated Sanders' army of Radakovic radicals at upwards of one hundred thousand; roughly ten thousand of those armed to the teeth and well versed in the dentistry of war.

Abandoning all those people, because of a few bad apples. And you call me the bad guy?

All this was fascinating, terrifying stuff, but anyway. I had a promise to keep and a letter to deliver. I suspected if the CIA did have people at the extraction point then they probably wouldn't be sticking around for long. Nobody seemed to care about little old me in all the excitement. I stepped to the side when convoys barrelled past, up avenues where Invisible Yorkers threw Molotovs and kitchen appliances and whatever else they had. I hurried by such scenes, taking no satisfaction in the Guard's decimation.

The piers were full of troops, cramming onto boats and speeding off. This did not bode well for me, considering the only reason for going to the meeting point was to deliver Sanders, and anyone surveying the engulfing firestorm with a keen eye would infer that he'd turned down the job offer. Nevertheless, I'd promised to deliver Sanders' letter to his family, so I pushed ahead, weaving my way between the shipping containers that littered the former driving range, not entirely certain which skittish skin to approach. I sought out the only few non-fatigue skins at the far end of the piers. Their inconspicuous nature suggested I was on the right track. If not CIA then some other agency I could readily surrender to. They waited by a small military jet boat halfway along a wooden jetty. I approached with caution and decided it best to announce my presence with a clear voice. One of them freaked out and aimed his handgun my way, popping off rounds and aiming for the letter, which slipped from my grasp and may well have done the same through the cracks of the wood.

I had nowhere to hide other than the dark water, so I remained still and tried again, hoping it wouldn't come to that. "My name is Leonard Walcott, and I helped you locate Sanders."

This did the trick and a customary back and forth of identification took place. I told them about the letter which had fallen from my grasp to the water below during their pot shots and they expressed regret. Several thunder clap explosions thumped from deep within the city, quickening the exodus of other military boats in the vicinity. Me being a known fugitive, these boat people decided I had intel pertinent to higher ups, Sanders or not. For a healthy cut, I presume.

Despite my desperate pleading to return to Sasha to keep her and the kids safe from the turbulent aftermath to come, they forced me aboard the boat at gunpoint. The city, my home, cut an ominous silhouette, as we waked away. The guilt was already setting in, taking hold. No one should walk away from a mess they make, but here I was. I could only hope what you had in store served as a fair punishment.

FACT CHECK: The two men on the boat offer a differing account in their testimonies. They were not CIA. They picked you up by chance, and have admitted to smuggling celebrities out of Manhattan. They handed you over after you provided your information, believing your capture would bring some financial reward. The two men were waiting for Denzel Washington, who had been stranded in Manhattan at the time of the Transformation. You begged them to take you, confessing to the following in order of claim made:

- working with the CIA
- wanted by the FBI
- Assassinated Sanders as you left
- high-ranking leader of the rebels with key knowledge on this latest attack
- looked like Denzel Washington

Investigators believe you knew about this group from Janet (from her time on the docks) and worked your way to a deal.

Psychologist has submitted their initial report below:

FBI profile notes no significant behavioural issues prior to TBS. Personality changes of megalomania, narcissism and cognitive dissonance not commonly attributed to "the Itch".

Patient takes full credit for creating the Radakovic narrative whilst absolving all responsibility for the repercussions of such promotion. Selective memory often presents itself when provided with contradictory evidence.

Patient's expression of remorse is negligible. While patient admits regret for leaving his half sister and his role in the disappearance of his former supervisor, Gerrard Halifax, patient takes no blame in influencing the child Albert Green, pushing Mora with ascension falsehood, or promotion of Radakovic myths; compelling sufferers of TBS to act out on rebellious fantasies.

Patient downplays his role in the Xi affair, where it is alleged the EMP prototypes were secured in exchange for the Chinese nationals. Timeline and involvement in the subsequent terror attack on August 6th also unclear. Repeated questioning is recommended to correct this, utilising admitted guilt felt by patient over leaving his half sister. These methods may also help determine the true fate of Group Supervisor Gerrard Halifax and secure admitting culpability for the murder of Captain Macklin McCready.

Patient is under the distinct impression he has secured his safety. He remains notably calm in his cell. Surveillance concurs with baseline mood detection. Patient's hunger strike motive not yet clear. Suicidal tendencies unlikely. His belief in "Ascension" to be probed. Patient shows good signs of providing requested intel, safe to continue information gathering with prescribed techniques. If the patient refuses to cooperate, reinsertion of tracking device recommended as punishment.

REFUGEE

My little parcel of land. An 8x10 cell. Glass walls, for your viewing pleasure. No direct sunlight, but I'm sure this can be rectified if I speak to the right person.

At least you surgically removed the tracker from me by day five or so, a concession to make me talk. And there is the flip-side to consider: leaving me stranded in an abandoned city, the power out and food low, tainted.

Now came time for the confessions. That which you have read until this point. Who knows if the truth, a slippery thing, found its way into these revelations. I can attest to most of it, from what I remember and chose to perceive. In any case, I'd expect a reasonable book deal.

Dreams. I often find myself in the fog of New York. Everybody is there, skinless, a mingling of voices at a summer social. Familiar voices filled with hope; I hear Janet's brief child-like levity as we play dress up Peter and Yvonne; Mora, as she guides us with the Method in that small yoga studio for the very first time. Mac, easing into his deck chair on the Rec Centre rooftop, a relief in his bones. Halifax too, his displeasure dissipating in his newfound peace. Even Peter and Yvonne, cheerful, riding the magical wave before it all came crashing down.

I see Sasha and we talk and all my apologies are accepted

and I'm forgiven; there is no petty payback of pickled overload or leaving me stranded on a sinking ship, for instance.

I've wondered what else you might like to know for a long while now. Months have passed since my first day here. Moving day, I forget the actual date, but I'm certain that this milestone came and went. You remained tight-lipped about the outside world until I neared completion of my confessions and equally valuable musings.

The day I finished and handed it in, I told you to marvel at my grand work.

A collection of tapes, writings, of a madman spared his end.

***

You granted me my first hour of internet access. I used that time to catch up on what happened, to connect the dots and to fill in my understanding of how the Night of the Long Dark played out. I'd asked your guards and interrogators about what happened but never felt like I got a straight answer. Google would swiftly rectify this.

I searched for news of my people. Some stories I've told you before.

Actual footage from drones was sparse owing to the EMP attacks. Civilian evacuations continued from beyond the barricades; Yonkers in the north and Queens in the east, Newark in Jersey and Staten Island emptied.

My people had not been removed. Yet.

Never ending news cycles filled with never ending opinions, guesses as to what exactly the natives were up to. Mass starvation perhaps? There was talk of brutal conditions, cannibalism, statistical analysis on slim survivability proffered—yet no mention of sending aid. Let's weaken them until they welcome us as saviours. Like old folk in a home, it was only a matter of waiting out the clock. No great loss if you waited too long.

Drones within striking distance had found themselves the target of pot shots at first, but even these had eventually quietened down. We wanted to be left alone in peace for the time being, it appeared, though the skins with their overarching need to know and control could not let this happen.

Tragically, the East Village 2nd Battalion were all but wiped out on that final night. Hollywood heroics awaited when focus groups gave the all clear on tastefulness.

The bad news kept coming; I was shocked to see Mac's former company also suffered heavily that night. Heartbreaking. I know we'd had our differences, what with their mistreatment of poor little Albert and killing Devon and then Mac himself, but they did not deserve the fate Sanders dished up.

The president had locked in a new moving day, a week before Thanksgiving, designed to put the nation at ease and really make the holiday true to its namesake. A November offensive with no surprises. Early on, a formal line of communication had been set up with leaders of the disenfranchised ghosts. Initially, it appeared the mayor had retained his position, after the untimely demise of Peter and Yvonne in that rocket attack. Subsequent media leaks however revealed these comms had abruptly ended and the authorities now spoke agreeably to no one on the other end.

I got a hold of the exact date, November 14th, two weeks from now. And then my connection to the world was once again cut. I marked the date on my cell wall, counting down the days with notches in a room with no sky, to the best of my abilities. Continued writing because that's what kept me sane, helped me understand the tale of myself.

I asked, begged for more information, but you have remained silent. "I've given you everything I know," I shouted, "please, just tell me when they're moved on safely."

***

A day before the 14th you drugged me. When I awoke in a daze and slowly recalibrated, I felt a pain in my abdomen. The tracker returned to its prudent place.

I did not ask questions so much as moan in agony. Practise of the Method did not lead me to my island cove, nor my childhood living room, feeling the fibres of the soft rug. It led me straight back to my 8x10 room. This time there was no breaking down the door within. Your rat in the cage emitting excellent data.

At your service.

With a clearer head as the days wore on, I realised this may mean transport, long-awaited repatriation with Sasha and the children. Family. But why not just cuffs? Why the need to drug me? And I noticed something else. The guards that gave me my food appeared edgier than usual. They were curt, avoidant.

Something had happened. Something which they did not like. I asked only one question at first. Am I being moved?

"No, not yet," said the guard, though studying his face, it was obvious he'd said too much already.

Answers would not be forthcoming even if I'd begged for them. I needed to regain some power. Difficult task as a naked prisoner, but not impossible.

The key, dear readers, was to pretend I knew exactly what had happened. I returned to practising the Method, pretending it worked like it once did. I refused their food. Called it tainted in the eyes of Radakovic. My mind weakened, wilted. Dizziness caused the room to spin. Sometimes I physically twirled around like a ballerina, a dangerous stunt for a man deep in the throes of starvation, but sooner or later they moved me, further down to what must have been the bottom floor, with walls so thick, the air stale, having never seen a hint of sky. They brought in the psychologist again—same deluded one as before, to probe me, examine this sudden turn in attitude. "What do you dream about? Do you speak to Sasha in your dreams when you undertake the Method? What do you talk about?"

I remained silent.

"You talked for hours before. Is this about the tracker? I believe it's part of your moving requirements, how do you think it will feel to join your loved ones? Reunite with your people?"

This morsel of hope felt like a fat, juicy steak to me, my insides screaming to indulge and devour. But I withstood.

I waited, and I waited, the pain and fatigue draining me, wringing out my soul, yet I remained perfectly still, knowing that they were watching, agonising. As I surmised later, my plan worked perfectly. They didn't want to tell me in case somehow, through Radakovic's mystical messages, I already knew. But my silence had driven them mad with insecurity, and the only way to know if I knew was to come clean and tell me everything.

My last great act.

This is what they revealed:

The food was buried, burned, tossed into the Hudson. The ghosts had turned to the metaphors of Radakovic's teachings and taken them literally. The consumption of food, tainted food, which HE knew from the beginning would happen, had to be forgone. Ascension demanded it.

Their last roll of the dice.

Most, if not all, starved to death, their choice of final resting place either in orderly masses of demise or tidied away in their homes for nostalgic comfort. Locating and removing these cold remnants would take many months, but the light at the end of the tunnel meant the city, the great Manhattan, would rise like a phoenix.

The psychologist was on hand to help me come to terms with this horrendous tragedy and assist with my transition to accepting food once more and continue with my reflection of events. They even apologised for not breaking the news to me earlier. My cooperation thus far, while not completely truthful or revelatory on the Chinese nationals' extraction, had yielded some interesting historical notes for posterity. In a few days' time, I was to be moved to a more suitable security facility for longer term assessment and care.

These were the lies they told, trying to pin it all on me! That I had supposedly pushed from the beginning some fanciful narrative of shedding our earthly needs in order to achieve enlightenment. That I had poisoned their minds with unfounded fears of sterilisation, of tainted food and unthinkable remedies to purify one's self!

I never mentioned any tainted cheese! Nor accused so blindly without evidence! Any dietary advice from Radakovic came directly from the twisted mind of Mora and those delusional leaders of the Movement.

You've got the wrong guy.

I was merely following orders. Style guides.

Sasha would never have let her children starve.

Ok, well, answer me this then: With all the lies I told, how could I honestly trust you? See. One had to read between the lines and find that small window Mora envisioned; beyond all the agendas and fears that keep us anchored in the mire of this world.

No. This was the cold, hard truth I'm sure you will come to accept, as have I:

There's no one left on the Island. This much of your fabrication is true. Your troops rolled in, drones and thermals scanning every inch, street by street. But nobody is home. No pitter patter in Grand Central Station. No strolls across the Great Lawn. No voices of resistance. Not

283

a trace of life. You searched for bodies, ready to stumble upon a mass suicide. Sure, you find scattered clusters of the dead, but these are mere fallen heroes of the Night of the Long Dark. The subways are still being explored, but you're yet to locate our missing citizens.

Millions of people, disappeared, gone into the ether.

You don't want to cause a panic, so you will be 'uncovering' more bodies in the tunnels and Central Park. This is what you must do to reassure your people. Life will return to normal and, like all past great societies, the ghosts will disappear headfirst into the vast membrane of history.

And so, you will ask me, point blank—no interpretation of dreams, or how I'm feeling—have I spoken to them? Have they made contact, these fourth dimensional astral beings? You will need to know, with my frontline reporting, how long it would be before those invisible scars healed and you could reclaim the city in earnest. No fear of reprisal. You attempt our extinction and hope to sweep in quick and easy, none the wiser.

So, we figured it out. And here I am. Left behind. For now.

I will laugh. For maniacal effect. The last laugh. You will not remove the tracker for any good reason and I suspect you may finish me soon if you get too spooked. But I shall refuse your food and my body will dissolve your tracker —AND I WILL ASCEND LIKE MY BROTHERS AND SISTERS.

Sister, we will meet again.

In the days that follow, you will leave me alone. The

facility kept on high alert to potential visitors. I'll lie in wait on the cold tiled floor. No chance of the rug or the warm cocoon of the Method. But no need. Because Sasha will return to me; a trail of guards left in her wake, their windpipes pulverised and crushed. And all around the world, our people will have spread, ready to expand themselves like my Radakovic and share our experience with all of you.

Radakovic's divine plans. Ain't they something.

Acknowledgements

I would like to thank my partner, Jess Perkins, for supporting my dreams and choosing me for life's adventures. May we continue to run through sprinklers. Love you Now, Forever, Always 107.8%

Huge thanks go to my friend, David Myrcott, who not only edited my first draft and fleshed it out, but also helped produce the digital Statue of Liberty image on the cover.

Further thanks go to my other friend, Craig Tuck, for reading over my second draft.

Many thanks to Lee Mawdsley, for designing the book cover.

To my Mum, who has always been there for me. And to Dad, who rudely didn't read this book, but is greatly missed nevertheless.

About the Author

Aden Simpson grew up in Sydney, Australia. He completed a degree in Commerce but then thought: Nuts to that, I want to be a successful writer. He is still working on the 'successful' part.

He now lives in Melbourne with his partner Jess, and dog, Goose.

Printed in the USA
CPSIA information can be obtained
at www.ICGtesting.com
LVHW040434271123
765005LV00026B/370

9 780995 352353